PARTICLE MAN

PARTICLE MAN

DERIC MCNISH

PyramusPress

East Lansing, MI

Text copyright © 2015 Deric McNish

Published by Pyramus Press, East Lansing

www.apub.com

Amazon and the Amazon logo are trademarks of Amazon.com, Inc., or its affiliates.

ISBN-13: 978-0-9966329-1-1
ISBN-10: 0996632913

Cover art and design by: Damonza

Produced in the United States of America

To my father, Rich.

ACKNOWLEDGEMENTS

Cheers to the generous people in my life. Here are some of them:

Christian Hecker, Joshua Corin, Jordan D. White, Cassandra McNish, Michael Kooman, Brian J. Soliwoda, Rob Roznowski, Kirk Domer, Christina Traister, Mark Colson, Alison Dobbins, Dave and Angie Wendelberger, Beth McGee, Dan Smith, Cecilia Pang, Tara Dairman, Nathan Stith, Danielle Sorken, Bud Coleman, Erica Peterson, Kevin Corlett, and Amanda Duffy.

PART I

CHAPTER 1

ONE DAY, MY big sister was nagging me from across the yard then suddenly she was nagging right behind me. The fact that she was nagging was hardly phenomenal. I was used to that.

She was on the porch and I was on the sidewalk. I was breaking the tails off bottle-rockets and sending them careening down the road to explode somewhere near the corner. I don't remember if she was irate because I was playing with fireworks or because I was using them in a way that wasn't described on the box or just because it was her time of the month. Well, it couldn't have been the latter because she was twelve. Unless that happens to girls of twelve? I really don't know. I'll file that bit of trivia under things I will never Google unless I have my own daughter someday.

That gave me chills. I can't fathom the ramifications of me reproducing. The responsibility of parenting aside, there's also the terrible uncertainty of whether she'd be normal, or whether she'd be like me.

So there she was, on the porch, shrieking about something or other. "Can't hear you," I called out to her, which was technically a lie, as I could hear perfectly well but I was definitely not listening. It was the sort of dismissal calculated to infuriate her even more. I had become quite the expert at angering her. I turned away, bent down, and opened my box of kitchen matches. They were the kind that you can strike on anything. My Uncle Jimmy could flick them against his thumbnail in one snappy motion that was pretty impressive but might be the reason his nails were thick and yellow. I turned away from her and in the blink of an eye... No, that's awful cliché, let me try that again... I turned away from her and before I could strike the match on my shoe she was right there behind me. I jumped and my entire box of matches scattered on the sidewalk.

"Can you hear me now, Squint?"

My name is not Squint. It's an unfortunate nickname and she was not using it affectionately. The tone of her voice was somewhere between a rusty chainsaw and a quarrelsome baboon. See, I've always had perfect vision in my left eye. Better than perfect. My right eye, however, is extremely nearsighted. That's the one where you can't see stuff that's far away, like the TV in a big living room or that pedestrian in the road in front of you. I had no desire to give bullies more fodder by wearing thick glasses or a monocle, and this was before contact lenses were a thing, so I just made do. Those of us that have one crappy eye and one decent eye know that your brain, unsure which is good and which is bad, splits the difference. So to this day I walk around all the time in a moderate haze, a sort of pleasant, fuzzy impressionistic imitation of the real world. I am perfectly content to just see the shape of that bluebird in the bush. Who needs to read the blackboard anyway?

Inevitably there comes a moment when, for example, you want to see precisely how low-cut Lori Nelson's dress is in the movie *Hot Rod Girl*, or whether that comic in the window across the street is *The Amazing Spider-Man* or lame-ass *Loma The Jungle Queen*. So I'd squint the bad eye and let the good eye do its thing. Suddenly, the world shifts into focus and I can see better than any bespectacled eleven-year-old. Shut one eye and bam: Hot Rod boobs are practically in my face. Bam: It's Loma, move on. Bam: That girl across the way is actually my pain in the ass sister, Joan.

"Squint!" Joan shrieked. "You lit a tree on fire last year. Did you forget that you are forbidden…"

"… you are forbidden to…" I decided that the best way to deal with her at that particular moment was to provide a little audio feedback. I started repeating her every word.

"Dad said that you aren't allowed…"

"… said you're not allowed…"

"Do you know what he'll do if you…"

"… he'll do if you…" I'd almost perfected the art. I could repeat her just a fraction of a second after she spoke. Since she was kind of predictable sometimes I could talk right along with her.

"Fine. He'll take off his belt and smack your ass…"

"…smack your ass… smack your ass… smack your ass…"

"…with it. Your problem." And she turned and walked away, leaving me to pick up a box of scattered matches.

She walked away. It took her maybe thirty seconds to reach the porch, an ordinary amount of time. If she ran, maybe it would've been eight seconds. Or three. Or two, perhaps. But I could have sworn that when she first joined me at the side-walk, it was… okay, fine… it was in the blink of an eye.

CHAPTER 2

I CAN'T DWELL FOR too long on the sepia-toned memories of my happy suburban childhood without feeling a little anxious. The weight of what I lost begins to sit on my chest. I've been through so much that now I have a much better sense of carpe diem. Seize the day, appreciate what you have, and other fortune cookie truisms become more meaningful when you look back on a childhood cut short and a happy life thrown into chaos.

Inevitably, I come across a memory that's wrapped in regret, like a doleful burrito. "If only I had…" "That moment will never come again…" "If I knew then what I know now…" For example, I certainly would've been more kind to my sister if I had known what was in store for her. There's no point to that kind of thinking, but it's always easier to daydream about a past that could have been than about a future you can still make happen.

Another example, I always wonder what would've happened if I had just told my classmate Julia that I loved her. I was fifteen at the time, four years after my bottle-rocket episode, and she was more fascinating and explosive than fireworks had ever been. She was all I could think about. Can a fifteen-year-old know what love is? What a cop-out. Of course he can. Nowadays, when I fall in love, it feels like the way it felt with Julia, with slightly less extremes of giddiness and devastation. I think I had convinced myself that I was too young, and that my hormones were keeping me from seeing things clearly. I never said the L-word to her and I always wonder what would've happened if I did. She and I were lab partners and while Mr. Pietrasanta, our Earth Science teacher, talked about igneous intrusions she used her hands to make her own intrusions into my pants pocket. It's amazing what a strategically placed jacket can conceal. The fact that we weren't supposed to be doing those things, being the good little Catholics we were with our rosary beads in our pockets and bibles by the bedside, made it difficult to talk about them. At parties we'd disappear together, locking ourselves in a bathroom and kissing, drunk on each other while everyone else had to content themselves with gin and whiskey skimmed from the tops of their parent's dusty bottles. The only thing we ever did that vaguely resembled an actual date was when we went to see a movie with a group of friends and ended up sitting next to each other. The movie was *Teenagers From Outer Space* and it was so ridiculously and self-consciously bad that we were embarrassed just to be there. It didn't help that the lights in the theatre that night never dimmed to comfortable anonymity, probably the movie theatre owners trying to keep their teenage audience from doing just what I had hoped we could do.

Things that are born as secrets tend to die in secret and she was the pain I carried around all through High School.

Yes, please, pass the Kleenex and start playing your violin. High School heartbreak. Everyone goes through it, and if they didn't then they missed out. All the same, it's still hard to think about, so I will drop the subject for now, give a little more background information, and then begin my spasmodic journey to the present.

Near present, I should say, as the meat of this story actually took place several weeks ago, when the world was about to end.

No, really, the world was about to end.

I'm not being hyperbolic. I don't mean the possibility that Donald Trump could have been elected president, or the kind of economic meltdown that seems to happen every couple of weeks, or global warming, or your favorite TV show getting cancelled.

This is just your good, old-fashioned non-financial, non-political, non-environmental world ending. You were blissfully unaware how close you came. The earth itself was moments from becoming, as a very brilliant man put it, "an inert hyper-dense sphere about one hundred meters across." That's what we're dealing with.

You're welcome.

CHAPTER 3

MY MOM WAS one of those British "gels" who fell for an American pilot during World War II. Dad brought her back with him, along with a glock, a Nazi armband, a taste for scones, and a medal for valor. It was crucial to her that my sister and I had dual citizenship. This turned out to be an enormous help later in life when it became unwise for me to stay in one place for too long. All this would seem to put me squarely in the boomer generation but I can assure you that I'm only twenty-seven. I don't just look twenty-seven, I am twenty-seven. As far as I can tell anyway. It's hard to keep track.

When my sister and I first went missing, my mom fell apart. After weeks of militantly rallying the neighborhood, the police, the Army, and anyone else who would listen, something unhinged and she was never really the same. Maybe if we had presented some rational explanation when we returned, maybe if we had some horrific tale of kidnap and ransom, then her mind could've accepted it and healed. We had nothing like that to give her. This is one of those moments that I look back on and wish I could have done differently. If only we had lied.

If only we had told her that we ran away or been kidnapped. Things might have been different.

Backtracking a bit, let me say grudgingly that my sister was right. Dad wasn't too happy that I was firing uncontrollable bottle rockets down the street. Since he didn't catch me in the act, it wasn't a big deal. The last time he caught me my ass was red for a week, although that particular incident involved an M-80 and a bucket of water, dear Liza, dear Liza. That beating was an investment on his part, because afterwards all he had to do was snap his belt with a loud "crack" and welts would rise in anticipatory fear. Though, in fairness, I think he was less upset about the fireworks than the fact that I was lighting the fuses with a cigarette.

So what if I was eleven and smoking? It was 1956. Smoking was like candy. Also, I'd filched the offending cigarette from my own dad's armoire. If it was good enough for him, surely it was good enough for me?

In the wake of that sisterly betrayal and the resulting fatherly scolding, I was determined to get her back. Revenge may be a dish best served cold, but I was an impatient little bastard, so I intended to dish some out that very night. Mom never threw anything away, so in a kitchen cabinet I found a splash or two of yellow dye left over from Easter. I diluted it in a cup of water and waited for my chance to strike. When my sister, Joan, walked to the bathroom in her nightgown to brush her teeth, I snuck into her room and emptied the cup of yellow liquid into her bed. I listened at my door, waiting for the delicious scream of fury when she climbed into bed and found that cold, damp mess. She couldn't tell on me, my eleven-year-old logic insisted, because then mom and dad would think she had peed in her bed. She'd have to suffer the embarrassment alone and miserable. I suspected she might cry all night long. That would leave her looking ugly the next day (well, ugli-er), which would destroy her social life as well, leaving her alone and miserable for all time. Not bad for an evening's prank.

I waited impatiently at the door. The water had stopped running in the bathroom. The hallway light had been turned off. She must have gone to bed. Five minutes. Ten minutes. How long would it take my insufferable sister to climb into her filthy yellow-stained bed? Still, nothing. I crept into the hallway and looked at her door. It was closed and the lights were out.

A wan glow crept up the stairs from around the corner where mom and dad were still awake in the kitchen. The deep bass of my father's voice reached me only as a rumbling vibration and my mother's was an accompanying pipe, flitting in to fill the gaps. I couldn't make out what they were saying, but from the music of it I could tell it was positive. Sometimes they fought and it was vicious and shook the house to its foundations. Other times they were disgustingly affectionate. On another night I might have crept down the stairs, careful to avoid the third, fifth and eleventh step, all of which were as loud as air-raid sirens, to eavesdrop. They never really talked about anything that was particularly interesting, but it was something to do. Once, I'd heard my mother use the word "uptight" to describe our neighbor's wife. That was kind of juicy. Another time, my father let on that he was about to fly to Micronesia. I spent the entire next month, a month when we were simply told, "Your father is away, working," imagining him hunting killer whales, riding dolphins, and firing his twin Browning machine guns into a herd of stampeding pelicans. I was terribly disappointed when the only thing he brought back was a dark tan.

I laid there, with my head hanging over the top step, waiting for the sisterly scream that never came. Finally, confused and disappointed, I crept back into my room. My teeth could be brushed the next day, but prayers couldn't wait. I knelt at the side of my bed, briefly wondering why a bed gets treated like a religious shrine when it comes to nightly prayers, and closed my eyes. "God bless mom and dad, and Joan, and Aunt Polly and Uncle Chris and Uncle Jimmy and Uncle Bert, and my cousins, and please help Grandma and Grandpa be healthy, and I would also like a decent prize from my next Cracker Jack box." I topped it off with an "Our Father," crossed myself, then peeled back the blanket and sheet and climbed into bed.

There's something about a young set of pipes that is enviably loud and resonant compared to us older folk. The sound that a wailing baby makes carries for miles and pierces to the marrow. An eleven-year-old, particularly one that was no stranger to cigarette smoke, has lost some of that potency, but can still be pretty damn loud. Especially when he climbs into what's supposed to be a warm, inviting bed at the end of a long, destructive day, and feels cold wetness seeping into his pajamas. My scream shook the house.

I jumped out of bed and turned on the light. My white sheets were stained yellow. My light blue pajamas were dark with wetness. The cold fabric against my skin made me shudder with disgust. Then I heard the heavy tread of parental feet marching up the stairs. Two sets of unhappy feet, each setting off the squeaky alarms of the third, fifth, and eleventh step. A door opened. The hallway light flicked on. Joan was up, too! My entire family would be at my door in a matter of seconds. Since it was a safe bet that I wouldn't survive the fall if I jumped out of my second story window and I wasn't quite ready for suicide at that point, I switched off the light and climbed back into bed. I pulled the covers up to my neck precisely at the moment that my door opened and my mom and dad marched in.

"What the hell is going on?" my father said without a lick of concern or compassion. He knew me too well to suspect that I was in any kind of danger. He assumed I was causing trouble. How unfair.

"Are you okay?" My mother's concern was seasoned with suspicion.

"Squint, are you okay?" That one was from my sister. Her tone of voice was loaded with innuendo. It was exaggerated concern, too much concern. It sounded saccharine and melodramatic. My sister would be a wretched actress. She knew something. I could hear it in her voice.

"It's nothing," I lied. "I thought I saw a big spider on my pillow but I think it turned out to be a shadow."

"A spider?" my sister oozed concern. "Oh, baby brother, let me make sure there's no spider."

She advanced towards my bed and grabbed a fist full of blanket, preparing to tug.

"No!" I cried, clutching at the covers with white knuckles. "It was a shadow, I'm fine. No spider. I'm tired."

My glorious father saved the day, dismissing my sister with, "Go to bed, Joan. Did you say your prayers?"

"I did, father," she replied, obsequiously, "but I'll say one more before bed. Dear lord, protect my half-blind brother from spiders." She skipped out of my room. Mom and dad each kissed my cheek and said goodnight. I didn't say anything, for fear their proximity to my open mouth and foul breath would betray my lack of respect for evening dental rituals. They turned off my light and shut the door. At eleven, getting tucked in was something I hadn't experienced for a while. Ordinarily, it might have been kind of nice. A kiss from the parents is a reassuring send-off into the uncertain world of sleep. Ordinarily. That night, though, I lied awake in the moistness, watching the shadows creep along the wall. Not until about 3AM, when every soul in our suburban town was comfortably vacationing in dreamland, did I peel back those disgusting sheets and stand shivering next to my bed.

Oddly, the first thing I needed to do was pee. The old hand-in-the-bowl-of-water trick apparently wasn't as effective as wrapping one's midsection in soaking wet sheets for a few hours, so I was near to bursting. I snuck to the bathroom in the darkness and carefully peed on the side of the bowl, rather than into the loud, echoing pool of water. While in the bathroom, I opened up the linen closet and pulled out a fresh set of sheets. Back in my bedroom, I first stripped down and tossed my wet pajamas to the floor. It had seeped into my underwear, too, so off they went. I put on a fresh pair of pajamas.

Thinking back, that was the first time in my life that I ever went commando. I didn't bother putting on new underwear that night and instead experienced for the first time since diapers the taboo sensation of abandoning my undies. It felt deviant, like a personal act of defiance, and therefore appealed to my mischievous side. And it was comfortable. That was something I'd come to enjoy and… I digress.

I threw off the sopping sheets and fitted the bed with new ones. That was where my eleven-year-old ingenuity ended. I had no idea how to clean the sheets. Or whether it was even possible. Did food dye come out? I still don't know. So, I balled up the pajamas and sheets and I stuffed them into my school bag. I'd have to dispose of them tomorrow.

I climbed into my fresh, dry bed and before I closed my eyes I had one last thought.

How the hell did my demon sister do it?

CHAPTER 4

I WAS BORN IN 1945, so this next sentence is going to sound a little cliché, but deal with it, whippersnappers. I had to walk to school, uphill, for three miles, in the cold. All of that is true. Let's focus on this particular day and construct something a little more uniquely my own. That morning I had to walk to school, uphill, for three miles, in the cold, not having slept, carrying a bag stuffed with soiled sheets and pajamas, with my sister. Also, I wasn't wearing any underwear.

At that time, High School wasn't quite the inevitability that it is today. It was perfectly respectable to go to a trade school instead, or join the military, or apprentice. Grades one through eight were sacrosanct, at least in our corner of suburban Illinois. All eight primary grades were housed together in a single four-story building that, in retrospect, looked an awful lot like an insane asylum. The dark gray stone reached into the gray sky and one expected to hear maniacal laughter coming from the barred windows. The colorful murals painted by school children only added to the psychotic atmosphere.

The uncomfortable reality of having eight grades under the same roof meant that bands of frightened little waist-high six-year-olds shared the hallways with hordes of towering thirteen-year-olds. It also meant that my older sister and I walked to school together every morning, so I had no opportunity to ditch the shameful contents of my knapsack before entering the building.

I sat behind Julia in English class. This was a few years before the Earth Science adventures began but there was nonetheless a precognizant attraction. Every day for an hour in that class I sat behind her and since the teacher was particularly boring I mostly stared at the back of her head. Her hair was pulled apart in two ponytails, leaving a parted line trailing from the nape of her neck up her skull. The line was a slightly different shape every day, and wisps of hair added variety. Earlier that year, operating out of impulses utterly beyond my comprehension, I took my pencil and pressed the eraser-head against her back, right between her shoulder blades where there would someday be a bra clasp. It was one of my more prescient moves, as if the pencil became a divining rod and pointed to something of future significance. Of course, she told me to stop, but she was quiet about it and she didn't tell on me. So the next day I did it again and again she said stop, quietly. On the third day, guess what? I did it again. But this time, when I did it, she didn't say anything. She just ignored it.

From that day on, while Ms. Franco droned on about whatever idiotic book we were supposed to have read, I explored Julia's back with my pencil. Every day I ventured farther from the starting point. One day I left her alone entirely and I swear she reached behind her to scratch her back and she looked at me as if to say, "Does my back bore you now? What the hell?"

I had carte blanche to explore, and my favorite part had

become that parted trail at the nape of her neck. The eraser was sufficient for the greater part of the back, but a finer instrument was required for this new region. For that I used the point of the pencil. It took only the lightest touch and goose bumps would rise on her neck and her entire body would give a quick shiver.

Later in life she would have a small star tattooed on that very spot. By then she was in her thirties and I was only seventeen. She didn't recognize me, not on a conscious level, anyway. We'll get to that. Please don't skip ahead to figure it out. That would be cheating.

"Open to Chapter Five and read the first paragraph aloud," said my teacher, fixing me in her gaze.

I grudgingly fished out my copy of *Around the World in Eighty Days*. "Phileas Fogg, in leaving London, doubtless did not suspect the great excitement which his departure was going to create."

"Then perhaps you can tell us a few examples of the excitement that Fogg's departure was going to create?" Her thin lips curled up into some horrifying yellow-toothed teacher version of a smile. Ms. Franco thought she had me. She was convinced I was illiterate or at the very least a terrible student who neglected all his assignments, but she had yet to really catch me in the act.

"Absolutely, Ms. Franco," I reflected that loaded smile right back at her smug face. "One example is that gamblers were betting on whether he would succeed."

I should be upfront with you, the reader, to whom I would never tell a lie. I admit that I never read a single word of that book. Well, except for that sentence that she made me recite. The United Artists movie version of *Around the World in Eighty Days* had been released a few weeks earlier. It would go on to win five Oscars and although not one of them was for acting, I had become a fanatical fan of David Niven, he of the British accent and pencil moustache. It was an epic movie and I'll sound my age when I say this but: They Don't Make Them Like That Any More. Nowadays, if they need more than a few hundred extras in a scene they just use computer animation. There were over ten thousand actors in that movie. I would have killed to be one of them.

"What is that?" Ms. Franco's voice ripped through my reverie.

"What's what?" I asked. She extended a bony finger and pointed to my book, so I said, "It's a book."

She stood at my desk, the dark flowery print of her thick, floor-length dress reaching like a thorny vine up to her scowling face. There was a musty smell. She picked up my book and turned it over.

"This, what is this?" Ah, it was a corner of the book, moist, curling, and yellow, another casualty of my stash of wet sheets.

"That's… umm… well," I stammered, unable to think of a logical thing to say.

"What did you do to this book, young man?" she said, sternly.

I decided to pass the book buck. "My cat peed on it."

Two things happened at once. First, the entire class erupted in laughter. I was grateful for that. There's something so rewarding about making people laugh. The second thing was that the book dropped with a bang and a clatter as Ms. Franco erupted in a torrent that included phrases such as "filthy," "disrespectful," "neglectful," "sinful," "turning over in his grave," and other things not fit for print. As a result, I spent the next hour sitting outside the principal's office waiting to be punished by a higher level of disciplinarian.

Class was over and the halls filled up with people of all sizes. To my surprise, one that was approximately my size but with pigtails, approached me.

"Do you have a cat?" asked Julia, who stood before me.

Julia's dress shimmered prettily as the rush of students caused it to flutter where it fell loosely to her knees. She smelled altogether clean and pleasant, like soap and flowers.

"Yes, I have a cat." I had no cat. "His name is Nivens." My non-cat suddenly had a name.

"That's a cute name," she said. She hesitated a moment, then stepped away. She was immediately carried away in the current of moving children as I sat there, immobile, contemplating why I had lied to her. For the next three years she would ask me about my cat and I invented stories about all the cute and clever things Nivens did before I invented his tragic death in 1959. He was a good kitty, even if he never existed. Nivens gave me a reason to talk to her. She'd ask about the cat and I could direct the conversation to other things. I learned about her. I learned that she loved dancing, and took lessons outside of school on evenings and weekends.

The principal raised his voice, branded me disrespectful, and sent me home that day with a note for my parents. Luckily, I was able to dart away from that forbidding building before my sister spied me. Along the way home, I passed our church, St. Anthony's. I took the trail behind the rectory and emerged in the parking lot out front. I cupped my hands and peered through the most translucent part of the stain glass windows and saw that the church was empty, save two older people kneeling toward the front. The parking lot was quiet and I didn't see anybody nearby so I sidled up to the donation bins, pulled out the wadded up sheets and pajamas and shoved them in.

Why not just throw them away, you ask? My logic seemed Christian enough. If they could be cleaned then somebody would have been ecstatic to have them. I was doing a good deed. I was that kind of guy.

When I got home, I decided that, strategically, the best thing to do would be to give the principal's note to my mother. I would be punished either way, but given the choice I'd rather be punished by her. She'd use the belt too, just like my dad, but she wouldn't hit as hard. Whether that was because of her compassion, or simply because she lacked my father's monstrous upper body strength, I can't be certain. Either way, it was going to be easier on my butt.

As expected, she yelled for a good ten minutes, just long enough for my sister to get home. Mom didn't pause on her account; she kept on going. Finally, it was belt time.

Now, *you* may remember that I wasn't wearing underwear that day, but I sure didn't remember. When I pulled down my pants for the beating, I don't know who was more shocked, me or my mother. Or my sister. She was there, too. There was a silence that lasted an eternity, broken eventually by a merciful, if perplexed, "Go to your room." Apparently, I had discovered one of the very few ways to avoid a beating. It wasn't such a bad day after all.

CHAPTER 5

THAT MARKED THE official end of corporal punishment in our household. From that moment onward my parents had to devise more creative ways to punish me. That night, my dad thought of something that was more deviously cruel than any spanking could have been.

It wasn't just because of the note. The note didn't help. The fact that I'd apparently spent my entire day at elementary school walking around sans underwear didn't help. But those things were just icing on the cake. The real crap hit the proverbial fan when there was a knock on our door around dinnertime.

As you may have guessed, I had been sent to my room without dinner. I nonetheless crept to my familiar spot at the top of the stairs and listened. The front door was significantly closer to that top stair than the kitchen, so I could not only hear what was going on, but I could also see.

It was our Pastor.

Father Barret.

He was carrying some sheets. My sheets. In his other hand, more sheets. Sheets of paper. Apparently some of my schoolwork had gotten crumpled in with the sheets and pajamas, schoolwork with my name on it. Ours was a small parish. Of course he'd recognize my name. Of course he'd know where we lived. Of course he'd come, in person.

Again, the tread of grown-up feet on the stairs, but this time it was only one set of feet, lighter and more deliberate than parental clomping. I retreated to my room and moments later there was a knock. I opened the door and standing before me was Father Barret.

"May I come in?"

"Yes, father." I was suddenly and painfully conscious of how rarely I cleaned my room.

He stepped inside. "The lord is with you."

"And also with you," I replied automatically.

"Yes, my son," he sat at the foot of my bed and looked me in the eye, "but know that the lord is *always* with you. Even when you sin, when you lie, he is there, ready to forgive the pious."

"Yes, father." All I could think was that if I had just closed my closet door then a significant portion of my room's ungodly mess wouldn't have been so apparent.

He placed his hand on my shoulder and said in his aging tenor, "Is there anything you'd like to confess?"

"Here? Now?" I asked, horrified. Confession was something to be prepared, rehearsed, and performed weekly in a small wooden booth to an anonymous and forgiving audience, not improvised spontaneously and delivered eye to eye, even by so practiced a liar as I.

He was a sympathetic pastor, and he could see my discomfort and fear. "On Sunday then," he said, rising. "I'll see you on Sunday."

"Yes, father," I squeaked. He gracefully departed.

Sunday. Plenty of time to think of a good lie.

My parents, however, were mortified, confused and angry. As spanking me was suddenly passé, dad unveiled his coup de grace.

For Christmas the previous year my Aunt Polly gave me *The Lion, The Witch and The Wardrobe*. By New Year's I had read it three times along with *Prince Caspian: The Return to Narnia*. *The Silver Chair* and *The Horse and His Boy* were, by then, old news to me. *The Magician's Nephew* was already cracked and worn. What Ms. Franco didn't know is that I was a voracious reader of things that I cared to read. I was addicted to *The Chronicles of Narnia*. I loved disappearing into that world. The characters were so familiar to me that sometimes, if I had trouble falling asleep, I'd conjure them up in my head and invite them to have conversations with each other. If I had somehow woken up and found myself lost in the land of Narnia, with no map or compass, I'm fairly certain that I could've found my way to any palace, grotto, island or cave mentioned in the books. Sometimes I'd imagine that me and my friends took a wrong turn after school, stepped through a wardrobe in some old attic or were swept by a gust of Narnian wind and found ourselves in the woods outside Cair Paravel, and my knowledge of all things Narnia helped me save their lives. "What's that you say, Mr. Tumnus? The native Narnians wish to crown me King? Well, if they insist…"

The Last Battle sat on my dresser, unopened. It had just been published, the last of the series. I scraped, begged and borrowed to buy that last book. New book smell practically effused my entire room; I couldn't wait to rip into it. First I would read it fast, start to finish, probably in one gloriously fevered day. Then I'd read it slowly, savoring every moment, speaking certain parts aloud to hear the magic words ring in the air. It was going to consume at least the next week of my life, every waking hour, and I intended to savor every minute of it.

At bedtime, my parents marched up the stairs. Another tucking in, perhaps, like last night? A kiss on each cheek and a happy send-off into dreamland? No, not that night. Dad opened the door, marched straight to my dresser, picked up the book and marched out, slamming the door as he left. It was a jarring sound; the door slam echoed through my house. It was quiet thereafter, save my muffled sobs into the night. My pillow was wetter than my sheets had been the night before and all I could think as I cried and cried was: How did she do it? How did she do it? How did she do it? Comforting thoughts of revenge finally lulled me to sleep.

CHAPTER 6

I'M A FRIENDLY guy and I like companionship, but I function better one-on-one or in small groups. I've never been one for large crowds and I've always tended to have one close friend at a time. At eleven, my chosen compatriot was David. He was a collector's item: our school's only Jew. I gravitated towards him despite, or because of my parents' consternation. In actuality, he fell more into the category of demi-Jew, or Jewish Light. He didn't wear payos or a yarmulke, but he was nonetheless distantly responsible for the crucifixion of Jesus Christ and therefore some kind of rebel. My bad-ass Jew friend, who wore ties to school even though there was no dress-code and knew as much Yiddish as I knew Latin, was fiercely loyal and a lot of fun. I figured that my dad was a pilot in the war against Germany that helped save his people, so David's friendship was something I had vicariously earned.

In adopting him I also adopted his family. The smells in their house were foreign to me and their customs were an interesting combination of familiar and bizarre. Because of him I developed a taste for rugalach and the thought of it made my mouth water as I sat in church that Sunday. I'd be having dinner with his family later that evening, an exception to my week of being grounded since we already had plans, and apparently cancelling on a dinner date is a more serious crime than defacing pajamas and being sent to the principal's office.

Crispy, flaky, chocolaty sweet Jewish goodness consumed my thoughts as my butt ached on the bare wooden pew. Roman Catholic starkness didn't allow for any fancy Protestant cushions and so my bony backside shifted painfully during the entire service. I could only hope that Father Barret had a hot date and would do the abridged version.

"The Lord be with you."

"And also with you." Our voices rose in unison like zombies in a movie that, en masse, suddenly smelled fresh brains. This was an auspicious beginning though. There were several long, drawn out ways he could have said, "The Lord be with you," but he jumped right into the speediest and shortest. Thank you, Father, bless your expediency. Now say, "Go in peace," and our collective Catholic hearts would love you forever.

"Lord God almighty, hear the prayers of your people..." Here we go. Hopes dashed. The proximity to Easter meant that Father Barret would deliver a whole slew of prayers. I settled uncomfortably in my seat and began staring off into space. Perhaps I could conjure up the plot of the Narnia book that my father had unfairly purloined as punishment. But I lacked the inventiveness of a fantasy writer. I still do. I can tell a good story only when it happens to be real.

The large wooden beams that crisscrossed above cast ominous shadows in the high ceiling. I used to peer into those pockets of darkness and imagine I could see glowing eyes. Then, winged bat-like creatures with clawed feet and scowls etched on their beaks would screech horrendously and launch themselves at the crowd. Old women would run for the doors, grown men would shriek like little girls, my sister would wet herself in full view of the entire congregation and Father Barret would stand there stammering, too afraid to speak. Then my father and I would stride casually to the pulpit. From two holsters under my arms I'd pull my twin water guns, one green, one red. With my thumbs I'd pop the caps open simultaneously and I'd dip the guns into the well of holy water. With an incongruous click, the sound of a gun magazine being inserted, I'd close the loaded guns and leap into a roll, dodging a dive-attack by one of the demons. Then I'd unload. Squirt after squirt, the powerful jets of holy vengeance would send the demons careening against a wall, sinking to the ground as smoke rose from their evil bodies and screeches of pain escaped their unholy beaks.

I'd take a moment to check on my dad, who by then would have climbed the rafters to get the now fearful beasts, trying to retreat to the shadows. He'd leap from the beams, grab the monsters in mid-air, land comfortably on his feet, and then tear them apart with his bare hands.

Barret droned on. "May this water remind us of our baptism, and let us share the joy of all who have been baptized at Easter."

I prepared to drift off into another fantasy when Barret fixed me in his gaze. "As we prepare to celebrate the mystery of Christ's love, let us acknowledge our failures and ask the Lord for pardon and strength." He was speaking directly to me. I strapped on my penitent face.

On cue, his flock began reciting in unison, in the rhythmic monotone that haunts me to this day.

I confess to almighty God,

and to you, my brothers and sisters,
that I have sinned through my own fault,
in my thoughts and in my words,
in what I have done,
and in what I have failed to do;
and I ask blessed Mary, ever virgin,
all the angels and saints,
and you, my brothers and sisters,
to pray for me to the Lord, our God.

Thus begins the singing. Although I do believe in God, I don't go to church anymore. I don't bother because if there's one place on this earth that God would choose not to visit it's a room full of tone-deaf white people "singing." God is more likely to hear me pray if he doesn't have his holy fingers shoved into his ears.

Ancient hymn of praise, opening prayer, gentle reminders of civic duties, first reading, second reading, Alleluia, then bring on the Gospel, baby. Matthew, Mark, Luke or John: who would it be? The suspense was absolutely not killing me. The pain of the seat, the fact that Father Barret kept me from daydreaming by fixing his eyes on me, my growing hunger, the proximity of so many old women wearing such noxious perfumes, all of that was killing me.

"The Gospel of the Lord." Sounds like an ending, doesn't it? No such luck.

"Praise to you, Lord Jesus Christ!" We responded. "We believe in one God, the Father, the Almighty, maker of heaven and earth, of all that is seen and unseen." The Nicene Creed, our profession of faith. We'd all spoken it so many times that there was no excuse not to have this endless creed memorized. Nonetheless, everyone buried their heads in their books and recited. This gave me my first good opportunity to let my gaze wander.

"For our sake he was crucified under Pontius Pilate; he suffered, died, and was buried." That made me wonder what David's mom would be making for dinner that night. My eyes trailed to the windows. While hardly a cathedral, our modest little church boasted a beautiful set of stained glass windows that represented the Stations of the Cross, fourteen windows depicting Jesus' suffering and death. Every day, light from the sun careened down hundreds of thousands of miles through the atmosphere and collided with those windows, projecting bright glowing images of the insults Jesus endured during his Passion.

In the first window, Jesus is condemned to death. As I squinted one eye to get a clear look at the glass, my view was slightly obscured by my sister's head. Suddenly the subject of my upcoming daydream was clear: The Passion of Joan. First, my sister is condemned to death. At the second window I could clearly see myself handing her the cross, with a smile etched on my face. In the third window, sweaty and bloodied, she falls for the first time and scrapes her knee. The story would only get better. I resisted the urge to skip directly to the eleventh and twelfth windows, where my sister would be nailed to a cross and die. Patience is a virtue.

The creed was ending. "We look for the resurrection of the dead, and the life of the world to come. Amen." It was probably for the best. If I had continued to the fourteenth Station my mind would've inevitably leaped to the next chapter in the story. Joan is resurrected. The world rejoices. For thousands of years, there are churches in Joan's honor and all worship and love the Holy Perfect Sister of the Demon Boy.

The Eucharistic Prayer ended with Barret proclaiming somberly, "Christ has died, Christ is risen, Christ will come again."

In my mind I heard, "Joan has died." Hurray! "Joan has risen." Err, what? "Joan will come again." Boo!

Communion! The home stretch. "Let us offer each other a sign of peace." For those of you lucky enough not to know, this is the part of the service where you are expected to smile and shake hands or hug everyone around you. Some people approach this a little more vigorously than others. On a good day, I could take up the entire time with curt handshakes. On a bad day I'd be smothered against the withered bosoms of every biddy in the shadow of the cross. Today, I merely wanted to avoid hugging my sister, so I energetically sought handshakes from the adjacent gentlemen. The demographics of the day, the watchful eye of my father, and the judgmental glare of my mother made a brother-sister moment unavoidable. Knowing that a handshake might suffice, but a hug would fill my mom with feelings of hope and love, I went in for the hug. Now, you might expect I'd squeeze her real hard, maybe stomp on her foot, pinch her, scratch her, spit on her, but I was beyond such childish trifles. She deserved so much more.

So I hugged my sister gently and sincerely, but with my lips so conveniently close to her ear I took occasion to whisper, "I don't know how you did it, but I'm going to get you back ten times worse."

"Lamb of God, you take away the sins of the world: have mercy on us."

To my delight, she looked a little distressed as Barret broke the bread.

We lined up to receive the communion wafer. My stomach was grumbling as the thought of rugalach made my mouth water while I was on line to receive the Body of Christ. For those of you who haven't had the pleasure, it tastes a bit like cardboard. It melts in your mouth, to be sure, but not in the good way like M&Ms.

"Truly, truly, I say to you, unless you eat the flesh of the Son of man and drink his blood, you have no life in you; he who eats my flesh and drinks my blood has eternal life, and I will raise him up at the last day. For my flesh is real food, and my blood is real drink. He who eats my flesh and drinks my blood abides in me, and I in him."

Truly, truly. I wished he would abide in me as a cupcake. Yet my hopes of a quick post-service meal were in vain for, "One who is to receive the most Holy Eucharist is to abstain from any food or drink, with the exception only of water and medicine, for at least the period of one hour before and after Holy Communion." Truly, truly.

Most congregations have different ways of receiving communion. Father Barret was a purist. You'd shuffle your way to the front of the line. He'd say, "The body of Christ." You'd reply, "Amen." Then Barret would place the wafer directly into your mouth. Even in those days before the spread of germ phobia it still struck me as a questionable activity. This man had stuck his fingers into every penitent Christ-loving mouth that lived within ten miles. Forty years before Purell was invented and I was still craving its like. Not only that, but afterwards, most people would proceed to the cup and drink of the wine. One cup, hundreds of people. The germs that must have been spread in that church, oy.

Something happened that day when I reached the front of

the line, something that led to me finally cracking my sister's mystery.

"The body of Christ," said Barret, looking down on me.

"Amen," I replied. He took a communion wafer and placed it on my tongue, but he did so in such a way that his finger pressed against my tongue. I could see his thick, yellowing fingernail entering my mouth and feel it against my tongue. I also believe that he ventured deeper than was necessary. That combination made me gag. It was a brief reflex, not a calculated defiance, but the result was abominable. When I gagged, the wafer went tumbling out of my mouth.

In that brief instant a quote from Sunday school leapt into my head. "Whoever, therefore, eats the bread or drinks the cup of the Lord in an unworthy manner will be guilty of profaning the body and blood of the Lord."

This would be serious. As I understood it, if the body of Christ was defaced in any way, including being spit up onto the dirty well-trodden church floor, the priest would have no choice but to eat it himself. It would be the only way to reclaim it, showing respect and penance. Sounds silly, I know, but I'm not making this stuff up.

Father Barret would have to eat the wafer that had fallen on the filthy floor. This would be accompanied by God knows how may additional prayers and we would all be stuck in the church for even longer. My mom and dad would be mortified and embarrassed in their church community, and Father Barret would likely take it upon himself to beat me later. A lack of underwear would earn me no respite from him.

All this flashed through my mind in the brief instant that the wafer plummeted from my mouth. Something else happened in that instant. I heard a whispered voice, a familiar voice, speaking hurriedly and closely to my ear. It said merely, "Close your mouth and chew."

I followed the instructions, imagined or no. I closed my mouth and chewed. There was no wafer in my mouth, but I did it all the same. Barret had, by this time, stepped back in horror. He looked towards the floor, scanning for the fallen wafer. Everyone else stepped back as well, but there was no wafer on the floor. He looked all about, but there was nothing.

Then he looked up at me. My mouth was closed. And I was chewing.

Since apparently nothing was amiss, I peeled away from the front of the line and headed back to my seat, grateful that the wine was optional for us young'uns.

Back in our seats, Barret said the Concluding Rite. "Bow your heads and pray for God's blessing."

Everyone bowed their heads except, of course, me. I always liked to take that opportunity to peer over the sea of lowered heads. It was like being momentarily invisible. I scanned the crowd and suddenly met the eyes of my sister. Joan wasn't bowing her head either; she was looking directly at me. She reached over and handed something to me. It was my communion wafer, still slightly moist from having briefly touched my tongue. She wordlessly mouthed, "Now we're even."

After a lifetime of going to church, something magical had finally happened there.

CHAPTER 7

THE LIKES OF fabulous film star David Niven could only have dreamed of acting at the level I achieved inside the confessional that Sunday. I constructed lies with enough truth in them that they could hardly be denied. I sounded remorseful, hesitant, and then relieved when it was all over. Although I couldn't see his face in the opposite box, I'm certain Father Barret bought it. I was sentenced to eight Hail Marys and I was fully forgiven.

I emerged from the confessional, penitent face still plastered on, and crossed to the back of the church where my family waited.

"I have to say three Hail Marys," I announced, then added, "and an Our Father." I can't say for sure what possessed me to lie and reduce my sentence. I was on a roll. Since my family couldn't leave without me, and each prayer is another piece of currency in the lifelong journey to Heaven, they each pulled out their Rosaries and joined me.

"The family that prays together stays together," said mom at the conclusion of our prayer. In a flash we all piled into the 1952 Packard Mayfair Hardtop Coupe and were on our way. The car was my father's indulgence. It was Packard's failed attempt at luxury, essentially a mid-priced model like a Buick or Mercury but with a grille and ornaments that tried unsuccessfully to set it apart. It was the poor man's Lincoln. Dad paid $2,900 for it, used. "A steal," he'd explained to my mom, who wanted a less showy Chrysler. "And it's a Mayfair, like the ritzy neighborhood in London!" She wasn't impressed, but she appreciated the effort and acquiesced.

In the backseat, surrounded by vinyl, nylon, leather, carpet and chrome, I looked out the window. I didn't want to see my sister's face because I was completely and utterly clueless as to how she could have pulled that stunt in plain view of the entire congregation. It was breath taking and I wouldn't let my face betray any hint of admiration. Nor would I allow her to see me confused and clueless. She had a secret, some delicious, devilish secret, and I had no inkling what it was. The balance of power was entirely in her favor and that was utterly unacceptable. My anger for her sheet stunt the other night had been replaced by burning curiosity. So many different ideas were popping into my head that I couldn't process a single one of them. Most of them involved painting my sister in an enviable light, and I couldn't handle that. So instead I feigned interest in the world that sped by outside my window.

I had almost forgotten the rugalach when Dad pulled up outside David's house. I kissed my mom and wordlessly stepped out. I walked up the driveway past the well manicured lawn and knocked on the door, gazing suspiciously at the mezuzah.

"What's that thing you have on all your doors?" I'd asked, when I first visited his house. There was something nailed or stuck to the right side of the door frame at the entrance to the house and to each of their rooms. It was shaped like a Twix Bar.

"A mezuzah," David replied.

"What's a mezuzah?"

He just looked at me, blinking his eyelids and processing the question, looking mildly incredulous. Finally, he said, "What do you mean?"

Fair enough, I thought. I let it drop, because if someone had asked me what a Rosary is or how come we drape our house with lights on Christmas I would've first thought they were making fun of me, and then I would've tried to formulate an answer realizing that no answer would make sense to the uninitiated.

David opened the door and I stepped into the Bernbaum household. My nose was assailed and I took a moment to process. Chicken. Yes, chicken, certainly, who could mistake chicken? And I was probably the only Goy within a hundred miles who could identify the smell of Potato Kugel. It's sort of hard to describe, but I'll try. Imagine a gigantic pie sized potato pancake only fluffier. And it smells exactly like a potato pancake, only less Christ-like.

David's father, a more jovial and garrulous man than my father, led the conversation at dinner. Topics ranged from the Palestinian fedayeen fighting in Eretz Yisrael about some stripper called Gaza to top picks for the Academy Awards. I wolfed down three helpings before David and I were excused. I was technically only released from my punishment long enough to have dinner, but since I ate like it was a timed Olympic sport, he and I had an opportunity to chat.

The moment we were alone, David and I played Doctor. Before you jump to conclusions, you filthy people with your gutter minds, I will explain. I had a problem that needed a solution. Playing Sherlock Holmes was a little passé at that point and this was years before House, M.D. revived the concept of Doctor as Investigator, so I switched into analytical scientist mode and David and I attempted to diagnose the situation.

"First, she crosses the yard in no time at all," I laid out the facts. "Then she takes off her bed sheets and puts them on my bed when there wasn't any time to do it, without being seen. And finally, she whispers in my ear and scoops up the communion wafer as it falls, without anybody seeing her."

"Hmm," pontificated David, "curious."

"Quite."

"Indeed."

"Mmm."

"Curious."

"You already said curious," I objected.

"Quite."

"What could it be? Throw out some ideas," I demanded. "We haven't much time."

David pondered for a moment. "She's a witch."

Once the requisite giggles wore off, I continued. "But what's a witch? Which witch is which?"

David chewed on that slowly before saying, "Quite."

"What if," I speculated, "she is not my sister. What if my sister was abducted and that girl there is an alien reproduction sent to spy on my father for military secrets?"

David didn't like that idea. "If she was an alien, why would she have had any incentive to catch the wafer and save you from the priest?"

"Because," I said confidently, "she knew I was going to get

her back, she was afraid of what I would do, so she did something nice for me to save her own butt."

"That would be true whether or not she was an alien."

"Unless she used her alien powers to *make* me gag and drop the wafer."

"If somebody tried to put Christ's body in my mouth, I'd gag too." David put things into perspective for me. He was good at that, and at making me laugh, as all best friends should be. He was my height, only chunkier, with dark curly hair and round rosy cheeks.

"Okay. So the first thing I need to do is verify that she is actually my sister. How should I do that?"

"Torture."

"Yes," I liked that idea. "Torture."

"Or you could ask her a question that only she would know the answer to."

I scowled at him. That was probably more practical, but the brief vision I had of Joan, hanging upside down over a bathtub filled with electric eels as I tossed hungry leeches at her made me grin.

"And if it actually is my sister…" We sat in silence for a moment, pondering.

Whatever it was that she was doing, she was being sneaky about it, and trying to keep it secret from me and from our parents. She seemed unlikely to slip up, although she apparently didn't mind me witnessing her demonic powers when it suited her purposes. So the only solution I could imagine was that I had to trick her into revealing her secrets. I would have to be more devious than she.

I was more than up to the task.

I heard a honking outside. Dad had come to pick me up.

"I have to go. I'll find out if it's really her, then we'll take it from there."

David saw me to the door where Mrs. Bernbaum waited to say goodnight. As I departed, beautiful Mrs. Bernbaum, kind Mrs. Bernbaum, wonderful Mrs. Bernbaum wordlessly handed me a paper bag heavy with rugalach.

CHAPTER 8

THE WIND PICKED up that night. The chime in our backyard was audible from my bedroom window. I remember that detail not just because it was ominous and functions well dramatically as I record this memory, but for a particular reason that will become clear shortly No spoilers. For now, just know that a storm was brewing.

I knocked on Joan's door that night. I might normally have barged in, but this was a delicate situation. It cracked open and she peered out.

"What?" she asked, brusquely.

I mustered up the gentlest voice I could fathom without seeming uncharacteristically kind. "Mrs. Bernbaum gave me some rugalach. I don't know if you ever had them before. They're pastries. I love them. Want to try some?" I held open the bag so she could see the flaky goodness.

Suspicion suffused her reply. "What did you do to them?"

"Nothing. I just wanted to share since you saved me at church today." She looked at me without moving a muscle, boring a hole through my eyes with her distrustful gaze.

Joan snatched the bag from my hand and walked into her room, leaving the door slightly ajar. Taking that for an invitation, and completely unwilling to simply forfeit my half of the remaining rugalach (I had already eaten three of them in the car on the way home), I followed her inside, into the lair of the girl-beast. She sat in the chair that faced her dresser mirror and pulled out a rugalach.

It struck me as strange that she would choose to sit in a chair facing a mirror. In my room I always plopped in the center of the bed, or on the carpeted floor if it wasn't too cluttered with laundry and toys. Perhaps she wanted to keep an eye on me in the reflection. Perhaps it wasn't my sister at all, and the mirror was essential to her shape-shifting abilities. Perhaps she just liked looking at herself. No, it couldn't be that.

She turned it over, this way and that. She caught my eye in the mirror and said, "I just brushed my teeth. This better be worth it."

"It is," I assured her, relieved to tell the truth for once. She bit into it.

"Say Joan," I continued casually as the good taste registered on her face, "you remember when mom was in the hospital three years ago?"

"Why are you bringing that up?" she asked, the crumbs of Israel spraying from her mouth.

"You know why she was there?" I watched her carefully.

"Of course I do, idiot."

My eleven-year-old voice, while not full-on accusatory, took a hard edge to it. "Then you won't mind telling me." This was about the moment when, if she actually was an alien, the tentacles would erupt from her spine and try to grab for me, at which point I'd have to fight them kung-fu style or just shove a grenade down her gullet. If only I had thought to bring grenades instead of pastries.

I did in fact have a Hoffritz Coin Knife back in my room that suddenly felt very far away. My father had brought it back from one of his flights. It was a French 5-Franc coin that hid multiple tools. If I had had it at that moment I could file her or prune her. The knife part, despite my mother's concerns when I received the gift from my beaming father, was too dull to cut butter on a warm day. It was one of my prized possessions.

Joan hesitated before gently saying, "She lost the baby."

So the body snatcher had done its homework. "Well, obviously she lost the baby because there's no little brother or sister in this house. That's common knowledge. But tell me what mom and dad were going to name it." I stood defiantly before her, ready to flee and hide should anything slimy emerge.

"Barbara, if it was a girl, and Edward if it was a boy." We sat there in silence and she looked at me compassionately. "Was this bothering you, Squint? Thinking about sad memories?"

"Not really," I said with a sigh of relief. "I just needed to be sure that you weren't an alien."

Ok, so I was wrong. THIS was the point where, if she had tentacles, they would have reached out and smacked me around. As she was in fact my sister and though she resembled a squid in many ways, she was tentacleless. She did, however, hurl the bag of rugalach at my head. The waxy paper wasn't particularly aerodynamic so it turned over in mid-air, spraying crumbs all over her carpet.

"What's the matter?" I managed to squeak out as she bodily ejected me from her room. "Couldn't catch all the crumbs like you caught the communion wafer at church today?" Hah! This was the moment, surely. I had her cornered. The grin on my face must have been intolerable.

"I didn't need to," she said, slyly, just a moment before she slammed the door in my face. "They all landed in your underwear." The door shut with a bang, scant millimeters from my nose.

I stood there for a moment, afraid to look. But when I took a step away from the door the contents of my underwear shifted and I could feel a crumb or two tumble down my leg. I pulled open the front of my pants and peered inside then let the elastic snap shut again as more crumbs tumbled into dark and unholy places.

What I did next wasn't perhaps the brightest idea I'd ever had, but I was acting more on instinct and anger than anything else. I inhaled deeply and shouted at the top of my lungs, "Mom! Mom! Mommmmmmmmmmmmmmm!"

Enough time passed before mom rounded the corner for me to begin to regret my impulsive yell. She was wearing her night robe with her hair pinned up and she looked out of breath. From the bottom of the stairs she called up. "What's this then? What are you going on about?"

She was not pleased, and her British accent sounded shrill and haughty at that moment. To top it off, my father appeared behind her, shirtless and fuming.

He grunted impatiently, exasperated, and for some reason in a hurry to condemn me. "What stunt are you pulling now?"

What stunt was *I* pulling now? This was completely and totally unfair. Joan had pulled the stunt. Joan, who was at that moment digesting a delicious Jewish treat meant for me had filled my tighty-whities with crumbs. I had been assaulted. I had been accosted.

I realized that I couldn't say a thing about it. It would sound insane. So I said the only thing I could think of.

"I thought I saw a spider."

My mom supplied the comeback. "I'm going to lock you in a box full of spiders and cover you in honey if you don't get in your room and shut it!"

Dad, not one to give up the last word, shouted, "I don't want to hear a single peep out of you for the rest of the night!"

"Not a peep!" Mom punctuated the scolding, stealing the last word. She and my father rounded the corner again. They were impatient to return to whatever it was that they were doing and didn't bother waiting to see me go back to my room. All in all, I think their response was rather harsh. A few years earlier, the fearful cries of their offspring would have elicited some sympathy, perhaps even a late-night cookie, or an invitation to spend the night in their room. Eleven-year-olds have outgrown compassion, apparently.

So I walked across the hall into my room and with each step I felt dry flaky crumbs working their way deeper into my crevasses.

I pondered, as I pulled off my crumby underwear and tried to contain the spillage, why she had gotten so upset merely because I suggested she might be an alien. David and I both agreed that that was a perfectly logical suggestion. Nonetheless, she had proven through her intimate knowledge of my family history that she was (for better or worse) actually my sister. I continued to reason as I opened my window then got down on my knees and tried to push the fallen crumbs into a pile on the floor. My open window let in the cacophony of windblown chimes. Why hadn't the neighbors ever complained? Surely it annoyed them from time to time. It seemed like an obnoxious decoration. The storm was picking up. It hadn't rained a drop yet, but leaves were whipped about and the trees shivered in anticipation.

I scooped up the bulk of the crumbs then scattered them to the wind. Unfit for human consumption, there was no reason some lucky birds shouldn't find them in the morning. Once again, I had turned my own misfortune to the benefit of the poor and less fortunate. I was a good person for giving my butt crumbs to the birds. I hoped some bird priest wouldn't come knocking on the door the next day to complain to my parents, like Father Tattletale had about the yellowed sheets. I carefully carried my underwear to the window and shook them out, kosher crumbs and thoughts of priest birds carried away on the wind.

At that moment it occurred to me that, regardless of what witch magic she used to accomplish this feat, my sister had been inside my pants. I was so horror-struck by the idea that I didn't immediately notice when a feisty gust of wind tore the underwear from my grasp. Once I realized it I nearly leaped out the window after them.

Too late.

I watched as gravity and the wind fought a furious battle, until my bright white undies landed on a bird feeder in my next-door neighbor's yard.

Well, the birds would get their crumbs after all. I slumped down against the wall. For the second time in a week I was sitting furious, underwearless, and hopelessly confused in my room.

I shut the window, lest the mocking sound of the chimes drive me to despair. My only hope was that the wind might kick the underwear up out of the bird feeder, up, up in the air, launching it into the outer reaches of the atmosphere where they might burn gloriously, a beacon of hope for all mankind.

I shut off my lights and kneeled at the side of my bed. My prayer would have to wait because an idea was forming, a sudden flash of genius that was convoluted, extremely dangerous and completely necessary. If it worked, I would have my sister's secret.

"Dear lord," I whispered, "please bless mom and dad, and Joan." I thought once more of the question I asked when I quizzed Joan. It had stirred up pain that had probably settled for us both. "And God, please bless Barbara or Edward, if he or she is up there with you. I know he or she wasn't actually born, but he or she might be there anyway. Oh, actually, I guess he or she wasn't baptized so he or she would be in limbo. That's not so bad, right? Not so good, either. Well, I guess you're in charge there, too, so please look after him or her. God bless Grandma and Grandpa. And God, forgive me because I'm about to lie a lot, but it's for a really good reason. You'll just have to trust me on this one. Amen." I threw in two Hail Marys, since I cheated at church and deprived Him of several. This would not be a good time to have the lord feeling cheated.

I climbed into my sheets and, for the second time, slept without underwear.

CHAPTER 9

STEP 1: IN the darkest part of the night, as my underwear swayed on the neighbor's feeder and the wind pum-
meled our wooden house like the breath of a hungry
wolf, I crept out of bed. In my pajamas and bare feet I opened
my bedroom door, careful to turn the knob fully before slowly
swinging it far enough to slip out.

Down the stairs I skulked, once again careful to avoid the
third, fifth, and eleventh step. At the foot of the stairs I turned
right and came to a complete stop in view of my parents' bedroom. The door was cracked open and I could hear my father's
snore, a distant rumbling like tectonic plates settling at the
dawn of creation. Otherwise, there was silence. It was as safe as
it was ever going to be. I tiptoed past their room knowing that
at any moment the floorboards of our old house could betray
me with a telltale squeak and wake my parents.

The first thing that would happen, I was certain, was that
my father would grab the axe handle he kept beside his bed in
case of an intruder. It was just the handle, mind you, no cum-
bersome sharp point, but it was still a heavy thick piece of wood
that would easily brain someone who was foolish enough to try
to steal any of our paltry belongings. He'd burst from the room

in a groggy violent fit, swinging carelessly and furiously, and would surely kill his second-born.

This was not part of my plan, so I walked even slower.

I was a ninja.

I was a moving statue, progressing as the earth turns, inaudibly, imperceptibly. I reached their bathroom, which thankfully open. I couldn't risk shutting the door behind me, as it might squeak, and I certainly couldn't turn on a light that would spill into the hallway and surely wake one of them. Still, my eyes were adjusted to the darkness and I had no problem finding my way. I knelt down, close to my goal, and opened the cabinet under the sink. In one bin there were my mom's myriad cleaning products, stain-busting innovations for every occasion and scrub brushes of all sizes.

In the other bin were first-aid products. Johnson & Johnson Band-Aids overflowed one tin. Having a son like me meant that my mom needed to have more of those around than the average household. There were all sorts of things in that bin, including some things my dad had kept from his days as a soldier. There was an unused tourniquet. There was another little military issued gem that my father brought back with him: A tin of sulfa powder.

Sulfa has anti-bacterial properties and was widely used at the time to treat wounds. When my dad was injured in the field once (he'd told us it was a shallow slice in his leg while performing maintenance tasks, though I suspected that was a cover story for something much more exciting), a fellow soldier covered his wound in sulfa powder and wrapped it in clean bandages. My dad's wound didn't get infected and he healed up as good as new. So, when I was six years old and I sliced my arm from elbow to shoulder on a nail protruding from a feebly designed playground, it seemed perfectly reasonable that my father would cover the wound in sulfa powder and wrap it up.

It was perfectly reasonable, except for the fact that, as it turns out, I'm horribly allergic to sulfa. I try not to think about the excruciating pain I endured in the weeks that followed. I had all but blocked it from my memory. Yet that night it would be the key to my plan.

I needed two other tools to complete task. In the first-aid kit there was a scorched needle that mom had used to remove many a splinter from my fingers and feet. I set that on the counter. I pulled out mom's box of Baby Gays, an unfortunate brand name dropped in later years for the less ludicrous "Q-Tip."

And I was ready.

I took the needle and stuck myself in the neck, far from anything that looked too important to be poked. It was a shallow wound, but it did the trick. A little bead of blood began to slowly rise up.

Ok. Next up, I cautiously and slowly opened the tin of sulfa powder. I couldn't let any of it touch my hands or the illusion would be spoiled and I'd be found out.

Success. With the tin open I dipped the cotton of my Baby Gay into the powder. I brought the poisoned tip up to my bleeding neck wound and smeared it all together. That should do the trick.

I replaced the instruments of my deceit, wrapped the cotton swab in toilet paper and quietly trekked back up the stairs to my room. Once in the safety of my lair I disposed of the Baby Gay by pulling up the edge of the carpet and sliding it underneath.

I could feel my skin tingling and beginning to itch. Only time would tell if my plan worked. I climbed into bed and shut my eyes.

CHAPTER 10

"**B**REAKFAST!"
I woke to the smell of eggs frying and bacon sizzling. Sunlight streaked through the blinds. The ominous storm had blown out to cause problems elsewhere. My stomach growled and I leapt out of bed, eager to get the crunchiest pieces of bacon for myself before getting ready for school. I nearly started loping down the stairs when I remembered the scheme I set in motion the night before. So I detoured to the bathroom and checked out my handiwork in the mirror.

It was beautiful. It was a masterpiece of deception. I had a welt on my neck that was about the size of a nickel. It was red, swollen, and leaking. Perfection! Hives surrounded it, diminishing as they distanced from my little hot volcano of lies. At the top of Mount Evil was a small, scabbed hole, my magnum opus.

To top off the effect, I ran my hands under cold water and dabbed my face. Then I climbed back in bed and prepared for the performance of a lifetime. The bacon would have to wait.

"Breakfast, I said!" My mother shouted from the foot of the stairs. I didn't reply. And a moment later I heard the "angry climb" up the stairs. It was easy to recognize; I had heard it so often before. She opened my door, and as she walked from window to window throwing open the curtains and flooding the room with light she said, "Get up out of bed this instant. You're going to make yourself late."

I groaned ever so slightly and said, "I don't feel good."

"*Well*," she corrected me. "You don't feel *well*. I'll have no lies this morning. You're on thin ice as it is. You feel fine. Get up!"

It's then that I executed the reveal. I pushed the covers back and angled my creation towards my mother. She let out a yelp then crossed the room slowly, bringing her face to my neck. Her eyes were wide, simultaneously concerned and repulsed.

"What's the matter?" I asked, innocently.

"Jack!" She called to my father, not masking the concern in her voice. "Come up here!"

Immediately I heard a second set of angry feet climbing the stairs. He, too, assumed I was causing trouble. How unfair.

"Your neck," she said, before my father had made his way up. "You've got a welt; it's monstrous." She placed her hand on my head. "You haven't got a fever but you're clammy and cold and sweaty. What on earth…"

My father walked through the open door into my room. Though it was early in the morning, I couldn't help but notice he already had his pants on, pants that were held up by a leather belt that I knew all too well. It was a risky thing I did that day. The momentum of his anger pivoted to suspicion when he saw my mother using her hand to take my temperature. Suspicion melted to wordless concern when he spotted the swollen welt.

"Let me see it," I said, careful not to overact the part of the stricken child. I got out of bed, slowly, carefully, making perhaps too much of a show of how difficult it was, and moaned my way to the bathroom. I was definitely overacting but I couldn't help myself. The audience was rapt, and I was an attention hog.

I stood in front of a mirror. In the reflection I saw mom and dad stand behind me, worried, helpless. It was time to bring on the coup de grace.

"I know what it is," I said, as if realizing for the first time.

"What?" spat my father.

"Well," I began slowly, as if piecing together bits of an unpleasant and hazy memory, "last night I saw a spider and I yelled. You remember? You both got so angry. I'm sorry I made you both angry. But then when I was in bed, late at night, I thought I saw it again. I wasn't going to yell." Was I milking it too much? Probably. "I didn't want to make a peep because I didn't want to get in trouble. So I ignored it. But then later I woke up and I felt a pinch on my neck. I didn't want to make a noise and disturb you." Insert knife, twist. "So I slapped my neck and in my hand was a dead spider. I killed it. Smooshed it with my hand. It was really gross so I washed my hands and went back to bed. And when I woke up I didn't feel good." Cue applause.

My father looked at the welt and nodded seriously, "Yup, that's a spider bite alright."

"Maybe," I said, hesitantly.

"Definitely," my mother confirmed. "And you're having a bad reaction to it. Look at him, Jack, he's pale and sweaty."

The mystery solved, and the minutia of family care falling squarely on my mom's capable shoulders, my dad replied in the most reasonable way. "I need more bacon."

"Go eat," said my mom. "I'll take care of this." She was on the job.

As dad walked down the stairs to finish off his heart-stopping heap of greasy artery cloggers, mom walked me back to bed. Once I was lying down she looked down at me with now watery eyes. I felt something in that moment. A sharp pang of guilt that stung at least as much as my falsified spider bite.

"Baby. My baby," she cooed. "This is my fault. You said you saw a spider and I didn't listen. Oh I'm such a terrible mother, can't you forgive me?" She hugged me and in doing so her head pressed against my bulbous welt, causing a burst of terrible pain.

"I'm fine!" I cried out, tears springing to my eyes that were thirty percent guilt and seventy percent pain. "Don't feel bad." I had hurt my mother. I deserved that pain and more.

"You are staying in bed today, young man. No school," she said with finality while wiping away both of our tears with a motherly finger.

"Are you sure?" I asked, keeping up my wistful demeanor. Staying home was essential to my plan and I couldn't back out now. The stakes were too high. I was committed to my course.

"Yes," she replied. "I'm going to call the school and let them know."

Then she paused for a moment and arced her eyebrow at me suspiciously. "And while I'm on the phone with them I'm going to ask if you had any tests today, or big projects due, because if this…" Her accusations lost steam as she let the rest of the sentence melt into a gentle exhale.

I suppose I deserved the suspicion. I had certainly earned it on more than one occasion. However, I was able to say with complete honesty, "I don't have anything due today. No tests. And I'd be missing a baseball game in PE."

She knew I loved baseball. Missing a game was a hard

choice for me to make. She dropped her suspicion and stroked my hair. "If you had a fever you'd be in the car heading to Dr. Stamen right this minute, but I don't think it's that bad. We're going to sterilize that then put some lotion on it and cover it up. Then you're going to rest. I've got my pottery group today but I had better cancel that so I can be with you."

"No!" I said, much too quickly. Her pottery group was vital to the plan. I needed some time alone that day. If she stayed home, my late night ninjery and early morning suffering would all be for naught. "Really, it's not that bad. I'd just like some lotion, and some sleep."

I paused briefly, my stomach rumbling. Although loss of appetite would definitely have added to the illusion of sickness, I had to add, "And some breakfast. Eggs, toast, bacon, whatever there is."

"Well, that's a good sign," she said, smiling. "You stay in bed, I'll bring you breakfast."

"Mommy," I said, certainly pushing my luck but hey, if a boy is living on the edge, he may as well dance. "Can it be the crunchiest pieces of bacon?"

She smiled warmly and kissed me on my head. "After I call the school, I'll burn you up some of your very own."

Smashing. Everything was going according to plan. In a moment I would hear the rumble of the Packard Mayfair as Dad rolled down the driveway and off to work. Joan would start her solitary walk to school, and I would slowly eat my delicious crunchy breakfast until my mom left for her pottery club.

Then the fun would begin.

CHAPTER 11

MOM SPENT ALL morning in the basement with her Kenmore Washer. Dad got the Packard of his dreams and she got this washer in 1951 from the Sears Roebuck and Company catalogue. It was hardly equitable, but such were the times I lived in. The catalogue boasted, "This washer helps our housewife do a full load of laundry in its porcelain enamel tub! It features agitator washing action (thorough but gentle) and balloon-type wringer rolls." Thrilling. I always thought it would make a good pot for boiling nasty sisters.

Afterwards, mom headed outside to clothespin the well-wrung clothes. For lack of anything better to do, I fell back asleep while she was doing her chores. Unfortunately, when I woke up, she was already gone. How long had she been gone? Would she be back any minute? Had I gone through all that scheming and subterfuge and self-mutilation for nothing? Did she at least kiss me goodbye?

No time to ponder; I had to get going. I threw back my covers and launched myself across the hallway. I burst through the forbidden threshold into my sister's room. It was a rare treat to be in there unescorted. I felt giddy with the possibilities. There was no limit to the destruction and aggravation I could cause.

She was nearly thirteen years old and still had a massive dollhouse in her room. The infant! I scoffed out loud. What self-respecting brother would pass up an opportunity to destroy it? However, that could take all day and cause severe lacerations. The thing was solid metal, the sort of product that would never make its way to today's safety conscious shelves.

I glanced across the room and noted that her most prized possessions were left unguarded: her clothes! Neat pleated terylene skirts, full dirndl and circular skirts, endless nylon and net petticoats, blouses and scarves, all ready for torching. With such a wild mess of choices, I didn't understand how my sister could possibly dress herself in the morning. I always just grabbed whatever wasn't too dirty. Although, as I stopped to think about it for the first time, if I could have chosen my own wardrobe I would have dressed like Marlon Brando in *The Wild One*. Denim Jeans and Black Leather. I'd be the wild one.

I resisted the temptations and set to work. In case you haven't figured it out yet, I was after my sister's diary. I knew she kept one and I had no idea where she hid it. It was the only conceivable way that I could find out what she was up to, and how she was managing to pull off these stunts. I had to find that repository of truth, and I was running out of time.

Under the bed? No, too obvious. Between the mattresses? Again, no. I set to work dissecting her chest of drawers and looking under her unmentionables. She had apparently gone through mine the night before when she was filling them with crumbs, so it was only fair.

Again, nothing. I carefully replaced everything, hiding evidence of my intrusion. There was an entire drawer filled with cream and white-colored gloves. Why did a twelve-year-old need these things? Girls still perplex me. Under the gloves I found something she'd clearly hidden, but it wasn't what I was looking for. It was Max Factor foundation called "Pan Cake," Max Factor eye shadows and lipsticks, lip brushes and scarlet fingernail varnish. I knew immediately that my father would not be pleased to find these things. Maybe a little Pan Cake would be fine, but scarlet? That sounds an awful lot like harlot! I replaced everything and filed that information away for future blackmail.

I rifled through the closet: clothes and more clothes. I flipped through the bookshelf, careful to check for false books. It'd have been ingenious of her to tear the cover off of another book and hide her diary inside; but that wasn't the case. Where could it be? I was starting to get anxious.

I lied down on her bed and imagined her writing in it. "Dear Diary: I'm a stupid cow and I should fall off the world into a pot of boiling lemon juice." Ok, she's done writing for the night. She's sleepy. Where does she tuck the book before escaping into her stupid girl dreams of ponies and stickers? No ideas came to mind until my gaze slipped back onto that monstrous metal dollhouse.

It was within arms reach from the foot of the bed. I went over and inspected it closely. The shutters were closed, as were the doors. Nobody was home in the inhospitable metal fortress. How to open it? I could huff and puff and never blow open that rusty house. I tugged at the roof and pulled the walls but found no entrance. Then I saw a hinge on one corner of the house. Knowing how it opened, I was able to find a small latch on the opposite corner. I swung the entire house open with a jarring creak and intruded on the sanctity of the dolls within, who were all carefully arrayed having a pleasant dinner at home around their toy table. On the second floor, however, was the coveted tomb.

If the world had been kind enough to provide sound effects then in that moment I would've heard a distinct "Yoink!" as I pulled out the book, closed the house, and bolted back into my room. Sweet success! And mom wasn't even home yet so I could crack open the book and find my answers in peace. I was almost as excited to read this as I was for the last Narnia book, which my father was still withholding from me. Perhaps, if this escapade continued to be successful, then I'd have enough time to liberate my copy of *The Last Battle*.

CHAPTER 12

Dear Diary,

Sundays are boring.

Goodnight,

Joan

HAT? MY JAW dropped open as I read the sparse entry for Sunday. Nothing? No mention of what she pulled in church? No detailed explanation of what happened? No deliciously embarrassing secrets? Nothing? What an utter waste.

Saturday was pretty much the same. What a lazy writer! Why even bother to keep a diary? I flipped back to Friday, where it looked like there'd be a little meat.

Dear Diary,

Annie and I got in a fight today because she said something mean about James Dean and I think it's wrong to talk badly about someone who's dead. She said she doesn't think he should win an Oscar for Giant just because he's dead because he wasn't any good in it and I think he was wonderful and beautiful and giving someone an Oscar after they die is a really nice gesture. His family would like to have it, I am sure. It's a crime that he wasn't even nominated for Rebel Without a Cause. Hate is a four-letter-word so I can't say that I hate her but I think I can write it without feeling too bad.

Love,

Joan

What a pile of useless drivel. I scanned back to the night of the sheet debacle.

Dear Diary,

"Rock Around the Clock" is getting a little old.

With Warm Regards,

Joan

Could it have meant so little to her? Could something that utterly ruined my week be unworthy of even a mention in her secret treasure trove of girldom? I flipped a few pages back.

Dear Diary,

I want to live in Heartbreak Hotel with Elvis Presley. I'd do anything he asked me to. I want to polish his blue suede shoes. Except that I'm not sure whether you can polish suede. Maybe you brush it. I would brush it. He is so beautiful. Annie says she's going to find out where he's giving a concert and she's going to

go backstage and she's going to kiss him on the lips. She's an idiot
if she thinks she can do that. He'd never kiss her because she's too
short. He'd have to bend down and men like him don't stoop.
And she couldn't get close because he probably has guards.

I nearly missed the significance of this next bit because I had become so painfully bored by her ramblings. Elvis? Seriously? Hip-gyrating weirdo. The collection of nonsensical teenage fantasies had ceased to have any meaning and her pointless musings were dragging me into a soporific despair. My bed was way too comfortable to read something this boring without beginning to nod off.

"*I can kiss him though,*" she continued, writing of Elvis. Something about her word choice made me perk up and continue reading.

> *You and I both know that nothing can stop me when I*
> *want something. But taking a kiss like that again would be*
> *stealing and… I'd have to really think about it before I tried*
> *something like that again. That first time makes me feel so*
> *guilty.*
>
> *Yours truly,*
>
> *Joan*

"Nothing can stop me when I want something." Really. WHAT DOES THAT MEAN? Why be coy when writing in your diary? Just spill it, sis! "Before I tried something like that again…" Like what? She'd stolen a kiss? That's gross and fascinating. I simultaneously craved details and cringed about the possibility of reading about anything unnecessarily mushy. Yet

I needed to know: How did she do it? I thumbed the book back even further, hopeful that I was on the right track.

Dear Diary,

Today was a big day. I did something wrong and I can't tell Father Barret in confession because it's just too awful so I'll have to confess to you and directly to God in case he's reading over my shoulder (hi God).

Here we go! I rubbed my hands together and braced myself for the meat.

I had my first kiss. Wow, huh? My first kiss ever. It was Keith Butler. I know. I know! You're thinking that he doesn't know I exist so why would he kiss me? Well, he still doesn't know I exist. It didn't happen the way it's supposed to, but it happened. So I have to write it down so I can remember it when I'm old.

Keith Butler? Ralph Butler's older brother? He was fifteen and on the High School Baseball Team. He was like a celebrity in our town. He was tall with blond hair and blue eyes. Heck, every girl within ten miles wanted to kiss him, how could my sister have been the one?

I was in Church and Father Barret told us to greet our neighbor. So I hugged mom and dad, and shook hands with a couple of people and then I realized Keith was in the pew behind me. I turned bright red. I was all flushed. You know how that redness creeps up my neck and there's no way to hide it? I really don't like that. All I could think of was how red I was and how he was so close to me. I swear I almost fainted. We made eye contact and he reached out to shake my hand. I was wearing cream-colored gloves and he took my hand so gently I thought I would die. Those strong hands that hit home runs were touching me! I promise I could feel the heat through my gloves. I think I held on too long and I must've looked like an idiot. But then he pulled his hand away and I had to shake hands with my brother. His hands were sticky. So my gloves got sticky.

Well, we sat back down and I couldn't focus. I felt faint and I needed to get up. So, I did my secret thing that you and I know I can do. I went straight to the bathroom, washed the stickiness off my gloves and splashed cold water on my face. I was feeling a little better. Then I walked back, but I really took my time with it. On the way I stepped outside for a little air. Everything was still and silent, of course. The annoying thing is that there's never any breeze when I do it, which is what I really wanted. So I headed back to my seat. It was really weird how the incense from the burners hung in the air. Father Barret's mouth was open in a really funny way. The candles weren't flickering. What else? I should remember all the details. I need to fix this memory in my mind forever.

And by the way, just because I'm excited doesn't mean I'm not penitent. I am sorry and I will pray, but that's for later.

Anyway, I was feeling better so I went back to my seat. I turned around one more time to look at Keith. His eyes were open, his beautiful blue eyes, as if he was looking at me. His eyelashes were long and thick, some of them blond and some brown. His lips were pink and pouty and they just looked so perfect. He was still leaning forward slightly, having just sat down. He was wearing a beautiful jacket, but his tie was a little bit askew. Well, almost without thinking about it, I did like I do to daddy all the time. I straightened his tie.

But when I was doing that I was so close to his lips. So close. His tie was straight but before I let go, I leaned in, and, since the boy is supposed to kiss the girl and not vice-versa, I pulled a little bit on his tie so he leaned forward just a little and he kissed me. Well, I mean, I kissed him. It was soft. It was perfect. I could've made it last forever.

I know it was wrong. But it was quick. Really, really quick. It almost didn't happen at all. He'll never know it happened.

Please forgive me, diary, and God, too, if you're reading.

Respectfully yours,

Joan

I don't know if God was reading, but I sure was. I scanned a few more pages, but it wasn't likely to get any clearer than this. The diary was a chronicle of girlish exploits: fights with other girls, daring tales involving clothes and make-up, crushes on boys and endless pontificating about television, movies and music. In short, it was a huge and predictable bore. My sister was as disappointingly normal as any twelve-year-old girl could possibly be. Only occasionally, when you read between the lines, did it become apparent that my sister could do something that I thought was impossible.

She could stop time. My sister could stop time.

CHAPTER 13

"**O**R SHE CAN move super fast," David suggested during recess the next day. We paced along the wire fence separating the track and field from Fulton Avenue, one of our town's thoroughfares. A noisy game of handball was taking place against the wall of the school. An army of conspiratorial girls huddled on the grass nearby, out of earshot, and a gaggle of disinterested lunch ladies sat on the stairs by the door, ready to spring up and stop any fights or bouts of kissing that might erupt.

"Well, either way," I shrugged, then turned to David dramatically, fixed my hands on his shoulders and spoke in my most serious tone. "Whatever this power is, she has only used it for evil. She sneaks up on people. She gets them in trouble. She fills their underwear with rugalach."

"She what…?" I guess I hadn't mentioned that bit yet. David tried to interrupt but I ignored him.

"And she steals kisses from boys that wouldn't want to kiss her if there was a gun to their head. That's criminal."

"Why did she put rugalach…"

"Look! She needs to be stopped, can we agree on that?" I barked.

"Quite."

We'd come to rest underneath a tree. We silently pondered, leaning against the bark as the minutes ticked by.

"Where were you yesterday?" David and I leaped up at the sudden intrusion of a girl's voice on our private conspiracy. There was no sisterly malice in this voice, no characteristic nastiness. I turned around and there she was, face to face.

It was Julia. She of the fascinating nape, she whose back I had daily explored with my pencil eraser. She had crossed the entire field, from the safety of her girl caravan to the no-man's land of the fence, just to speak to me. Here was proof: she cared.

"I was out sick," I muttered, looking down. I couldn't tell the truth, and didn't have the time to think of a lie, so I settled for vagueness.

"Your neck is bandaged!" She sounded concerned as she leaned in to look more closely at it, the smell of soap and berries intruding upon my ability to think clearly.

When in doubt, make a wise crack. "I was bitten by a vampire."

I said that with all the earnestness I could muster but David ruined it by laughing immediately and saying, "A vampire spider, maybe!"

"It was a really big spider! A tarantula." I countered defensively. "And I'm allergic. The bump swelled up and I nearly died." She didn't seem impressed enough. "I threw it off of me, but then it started to go after Nivens so I picked up a baseball bat and I hit it across the room where it splat on the wall." I smiled in a way that I thought was valiant but probably fell more solidly in the "goofy" category of facial expressions.

"Nivens?" David said. "Who is…" I bumped his shoulder hard and fixed him with a murderous gaze that I was fairly sure communicated the fact that if he didn't zip it he'd regret it. Some people just aren't good at lying.

"Poor Nivens!" Julia gasped. Then, to my surprise, she said, "Can I see it?"

I paled. "See my…"

"Neck."

Her interest in gross things could hardly be considered a strike against her, so I wordlessly peeled aside the bandage. David shifted around to get a look as well, since when he asked earlier I had said no.

"Gross!" she cried. "It's weeping!"

"Yeah. It hurts really bad, too," I said. "But I'll be fine."

We all endured another awkward silence before she wordlessly turned tail and walked across the field until she was once more enveloped in the girl collective. A tremor of giggling seemed to radiate from the mass, a sound I could hardly hope to interpret.

It was at that moment that I realized what I wanted. Before then, I just wanted to know what my sister was doing, why she was doing it, and how she was doing it. I wanted to stop her, so she wouldn't have the upper hand. I wanted to be able to pull a prank on her without it being shoved back in my face every single time. I wanted to expose her so mom and dad and Keith Butler and everyone else she'd molested would know her for what she really was.

But as I watched Julia cross the field, her slow measured gait may as well have been the speedy lope of a gazelle. She was so close, practically at arm's length, and yet I felt the presence of some invisible and insurmountable great wall between us. I couldn't catch her because I didn't know how.

I continued to study her as she moved away. You could tell she studied dance by the way she moved so gracefully. If I went after her and asked her to kiss me I'd be the laughing stock of the school. News would spread among the girls like a Blitzkrieg and I'd become a walking joke. It wasn't until that moment that I had even thought about kissing her. But just the fact that I knew I couldn't made it somehow infuriating.

And so I knew. I didn't want vengeance for Joan. I didn't want to expose her. I didn't care about what she did to Keith. In fact, I thought I was beginning to understand why she did it. Suddenly, I didn't want to thwart my evil sister.

I wanted… No, I needed her to teach me.

CHAPTER 14

J OAN AND I walked home together that day. It was something I could calculatedly avoid, and I usually did, but I had a reason for breaking my pattern today.

I broke the silence with what I thought was a kind gesture, an open hand, a friendly invitation to talk. "I was watching *Stage Show* on CBS and I saw Elvis Presley perform. He was pretty good."

Nothing. She seemed lost in her own thoughts. Great, I was invisible to yet another girl. Maybe that was *my* superpower.

"He moves kinda funny though," I continued, not one to give up on a plan. "His legs are wacky, like they're not attached, or he's having some kind of spasm."

Nothing.

"I'm going to count down from five and then I'm going to spit on your face."

Nothing.

Well, I'd left myself no choice. I had a back up plan to force the issue, in the likely event that kindness failed, as it usually did. So I walked in silence for a moment as I began producing and collecting what I would need from the back of my throat.

"Five," I began. "Four… Three… Two…"

The words became slightly garbled as my mouth became increasingly full. I was committed to this deplorable act, even though I knew exactly what the outcome would be.

"One," I said, my mouth full of the mightiest loogie I had ever hocked.

Then I let it fly. My well-shaped protuberance arced through the air towards her face, honing in with deadly accuracy towards her infuriatingly pink cheek. Then it continued through the air where she had only a second ago been standing. It splat unceremoniously on the floor. My sister was now walking on my left side, completely unfazed, as if it didn't even happen.

"You don't even bother trying to hide it from me anymore. So why don't we just talk about it?" I begged.

"Fine," she kept walking without missing a beat. "They're not 'spasms.' He's dancing. Gyrating. His music carries him away."

"What? Elvis?! That's not what I meant!" I shouted. "Tell me how you do it. Do you stop time or do you move super fast? Which is it? How do you do it? I need to know."

"Why do you need to know? Why would I tell you?" She smirked as she lorded it over me. She continued walking in even steps, while I trailed her like a bad puppy that hadn't yet learned how to heel. "If you could do it, you'd just go do awful things to people. You'd probably steal and cheat and get in more trouble than you do now."

"And you don't do anything bad with it?" I said, with the hint of an accusation.

"No," she said, simply. "I only defend myself against you. It's the only way I can stay one step ahead of you."

"Fine," I said, coolly agreeing. "You only do good things with it."

I stopped following her. I stopped dead in the middle of the sidewalk. It was time to shift the power dynamic. "If that's the case," I said, a little louder as the distance between us increased, "then I'm going to walk over to Keith Butler's house, knock on his door, and tell him exactly what you did."

I wheeled and took a right down Rhayme Avenue. I had no idea whether or not Keith lived in that direction, but I thought it would add to the overall effect if she believed I was heading towards his place. My forward momentum was abruptly ended, however, when her claw-like grip tugged my hair and sent me falling backwards until my butt hit the sidewalk.

"How did you know about that?" she screamed. "How could you?"

"Nice hiding spot," I spat from the ground, "*Inside* your dollhouse. It only took me like two seconds to find it. But since I read the *whole* thing, I should take the time to tell Keith what I read about him. Can't see why but maybe he'd be happy about it! Although, I doubt Annie would be happy if she knew all the nasty things you say about her. You're pretty vicious, sis."

She stood there dazed for a moment, and then she was gone. She literally disappeared before my eyes. I knew that at any moment any number of things could happen. One hand instinctively reached into my underwear, fearful of what I might find this time: fire ants or molten chocolate or chocolate covered fire ants. I looked above me to see if a piano or safe was hurdling down at my head. I squinted my eye and scanned the distance for any diverted trains or rockets that might be heading my way. There was nothing, just another boring predictable afternoon in my town. So I continued down Fulton towards my house.

As I neared the next corner, my mind still racing with unpleasant eventualities, I nearly jumped out of my socks because Joan was walking beside me, as if she'd never left.

"Cripes!" I cried. Yes, if memory serves I actually said "cripes." I know it's a little *Leave It To Beaver*, but it was 1956 after all. She just kept walking calmly and so I hurried to catch up.

I kept silent as we walked, having said my part. The threat was still there, but clearly I wasn't running off to Keith's house at that moment, in part because I didn't know where it was, but mostly because it was a hollow threat, anyway. I still wanted the key to her secret, and she would never give it to me if I betrayed her like that. Before we turned into the driveway and up to our house, she stopped me and said, "Look, Squint. I just took some more time to think about all this."

"How…"

She interrupted me before I could form a full objection, "I'll come to your room tonight after mom and dad are asleep. I'll show you. But you won't be able to do it. I'm the only one who can."

"Fair enough," I replied, confident that there was nothing she could do that I couldn't do one hundred times better. Except kiss boys. And even that was just because I didn't want to.

So this, dear reader, will be a frustrating moment for you in this story. I need to rob you of some of the pay off you've been expecting because, for the good of mankind, I can't convey to you exactly what I learned in my room that night in its entirety. I should mention first that, just moments after we sat down to eat dinner that night, mid-blessing, there was a knock at the door.

Knocks on the door at dinnertime always portend doom.

I was right, on that account, because my dad answered and in walked our next-door neighbor, Mr. Larson, who carried pinched between his thumb and forefinger a slightly crumby and birdseed bedecked pair of boy's underwear.

There were some polite words exchanged and uncomfortable chuckles. Dad closed the door and returned to the dining room. He sat at the head of the table and, like the Hindenburg, he exploded. He slammed the soiled briefs on the table, scattering seeds and silverware everywhere. He spewed a string of obscenities that would've made devils blush. I was sent to my room with no supper. My father's meal didn't serve to sate his temper because the moment he swallowed his last fork-full of lumpy mashed potatoes he marched up the stairs to continue his tirade. My still swollen "bug-bite" would do nothing to dampen his anger.

He burst into my room in a fury. His hand twitched. I knew he wanted to hit me. He'd even loosened his belt a notch or two, but that may have been because of the potatoes. Thankfully this trend of not hitting me hadn't quite passed, a trend that may in fact have been reinforced due to the underwear nature of my most recent infraction. Mom and dad were still a little shell-shocked from my unexpected bare ass the other day. So my dad looked around my room. Nothing was as readily apparent as my Narnia had been. He looked at my collection of Matchbox Cars, a source of pride but something I hadn't played with in months. Then his eyes fell on my Hornby Dublo 3-Rail Model Train Set. It was a thing of beauty, with a locomotive made entirely of die-cast metal and lithographed tin plate stock. None of that new-fangled plastic injection molding crap here. This was the real thing: powerful, quality, and dangerous engineering. Everything was set up perfectly, with an elliptical track circling a mountain, trees, and a small town in the valley with a beautifully intricate train station. It was the only truly orderly thing in my maelstrom of a room.

"Hit me!" I thought. "Hit me instead. Hit me, hit me, hit me!" It's as if he knew what I was thinking because he stooped down and grabbed the set. He gathered it all up in his arms, bending rails and crushing trees, and then stormed from the room. The empty space on my floor where the train set had been was like a whirlpool, a void sucking the air out of my room. Oh, the thousands of weeds I pulled to pay for that caboose! How many driveways did I shovel with frostbitten hands to get the track extension? The hours I spent painstakingly painting the locomotive in perfect detail before hitching it to the train and turning the dial, sending it on its maiden voyage. The majestic whistle I heard in my mind whenever it turned a corner. It all crashed down on me at once so I shut out the lights, huddled on the floor, and cried while my stomach rumbled.

It was a pure despair, untainted by any bitterness toward my sister. I knew that even she would never wish this kind of pain on me.

I fell asleep like that, on the floor, huddled up. I hadn't even brushed my teeth or said my prayers or even changed into my pajamas. What was the point?

In my dream I was a passenger on the Hornby Dublo, watching the countryside blur by as the model train zipped along at unimaginable speeds. A great giant leather belt smashed the tracks ahead of us and sent the train flying until it crumpled in a catastrophic wreck. A massive wrinkled hand with hairy knuckles reached down to grab the car I was in. My stomach lurched as the entire thing was lifted high into the air and great meaty fingers began to squeeze. The train car buckled with a deafening squeal, which was almost immediately drowned out by a more pleasant sound: laughter and conversation. The crumpling train car suddenly smelled of cranberries and turkey and stuffing. The destruction paused and in the sudden stillness, I saw my sister sitting at one end of the car, calmly buttering a steaming biscuit. The terror of the train crash had morphed into the joy of Thanksgiving.

My eyes cracked open and I saw my sister in the glow of the moonlight, as I hadn't bothered to draw my curtains either. She was sitting on the foot of my bed and in front of me was a plate filled with baked chicken seasoned with every kind of delicious thing we owned. Also crowding the plate were mashed potatoes, peas, and a hunk of bread slathered in butter.

She had actually come, like she said she would. "Thanks," I muttered as I dove into the plate. She'd brought up a glass of milk as well and it tasted better than I thought milk could ever taste.

After I was done eating, she showed me how she does it.

I know you would love me to describe the conversation, to document the guidance she gave in great detail, the hints, the sensations, the process, the images, and the thoughts. Maybe provide a diagram? Write a manual for the *Idiot's Guide to Becoming an Accelerator*? I know you want that information; I would, too. Some of it is technical and some of it is kind of Zen. I could compare it to the sort of experience you might have in an acting class, where the teacher is explaining how to genuinely feel an emotion on stage. It makes precious little sense and you think the teacher is crazy, up until the moment it works.

I know that one of your reasons for wanting to eavesdrop on that conversation is because you want to try it out for yourself. Now, now, let's be honest here. "But this is fiction!" you insist. "I wouldn't bother trying it out for myself, that'd be silly!" Right. Don't kid a kidder, boy (or girl). You and I both know that you would try it. I know that you would almost certainly fail. Not because you're a bad student, to be sure, but because as far as I know, this is entirely unique to my sister and I, and one other person. However, throughout my life I've been blindsided. There are people out there that know a lot more about my sister and me than we know about ourselves. It's perfectly possible that there are others out there. I know first hand what kind of devastation this "talent" can cause, so for your sake, and for the sake of the entire world, I can't tell you how to do it, not specifically, on the remote chance that it might work for you.

Joan was convinced that she was the only one in the world who could accomplish it, which is why she had acquiesced and showed me the process. Clearly she was wrong. At that point in time I had no clue as to its origin. It could have been genetic and uniquely contained in my family. It may be that my dad rescued my sister and I from a Nazi experimentation camp. Or the British Government tampered with mom's eggs. Or maybe she and I were both aliens, switched at birth for my parents' real children, who were at this moment living exciting lives in a galaxy far, far away. There could be any number of reasons that my sister and I are among the few that can do this. But I won't take the risk. You might be like me. And that would be bad for the world.

My sister didn't expect it to work so she talked freely, openly, and honestly. It seemed almost a relief for her to open up about it. She told me how she first discovered it and how she learned to control it. She told me what it feels like and what the downsides are. I honestly had never heard my sister talk so freely to me before. She was more like my dad in that respect, reserved, guarded. I've always been a quick study when mischief was involved, so I listened to her raptly. When I tried and failed I asked more specific questions and I tried again. I tried again and I tried again and she laughed at my failed attempts and assured me that I wouldn't be able to do it. I tried again and maybe it was the fifth or tenth time before it finally happened.

I wasn't sure that anything was happening until I said something to Joan and she didn't respond. She wasn't even blinking. Her eyes were wide open. I snapped my fingers in front of her face but she didn't respond. Success. I had done it.

What would I do with my first venture into the unknown? Fill Joan's panties with chicken bones? Break into a Bank of America vault and make off with rubies and diamonds? Put tacks on Ms. Franco's chair? No. I crept down the stairs, again, careful to avoid the creaking stairs though nobody would hear them anyway. I peeked into the darkness of my parents' room. I knocked once on the door and hid behind the frame, ready to run if they woke up, but they were ensnared in this extraordinary thing I'd done. So I turned on the light. It took a maddeningly long time for the light to switch on but when it did I made a beeline for the end table on my father's side of the bed.

This was his repository of secrets. Anything worth hiding went into that chest. I knelt down in front of it and, scant inches from my father's bulbous nose, I pried open the cabinet. There it was. *The Last Battle*, by C.S. Lewis.

That night, as my sister sat in my room unaware and my parents lied in their arrested sleep two feet away, I sat on their shaggy carpet and read *The Last Battle*, front to back. I don't know how long it took. It didn't matter. I turned the pages, read some parts out loud, doing the voices, laughing, and even took a bathroom break somewhere near the middle. When I was done, I replaced the book in my father's end table, I shut off their light, and I walked back upstairs. This time, I quite specifically hit the third, fifth and eleventh stairs, reveling in the undetectable racket.

I was the tree in the forest.

I sat back down in front of my sister and before I set about restoring the world I noticed that her eyelids had shut. They had been open and now they were shut. She had blinked once, slowly, over the course of the last few hours that I had been downstairs reading. So I had proof that we weren't stopping time, after all. Either we were super fast or we were merely slowing time. Another side effect of this adventure was that, although I got plenty of sleep on the floor of my room after being ejected from the dinner table, the hours of reading had left me tired and ready for bed again. Whatever was happening to the rest of the world, my body still felt the passage of time. I needed some sleep.

I sat before her and was stricken with panic when I tried to return to normal and realized that I didn't quite know how. I imagined having to spend the rest of my life growing old while the rest of the world stood still. This was a few years before *The Twilight Zone* hit the air, but I had divined a perfect plot for a future episode.

After a few attempts at recreating the action that got me started, I was quite relieved when I saw Joan inhale.

She was perfectly and delightfully horrified when she learned that I'd done it. In fact, she didn't believe me at first, but I was only too happy to prove it.

"Close your eyes," I said.

"You can't do it. This is ridiculous," she said, but closed her eyes nonetheless.

"You can open them now," I said with a smarmy grin in what to her seemed like immediate response. She opened her eyes to see me, exactly where I had been, but holding her diary.

"You little puke!" she said, grabbing it and standing up. Well, at least there was no longer any doubt. She and I were in this together. I'm sure that if she had had any inkling that it would've actually worked, she would never have taught me. Since she couldn't unteach me, she only left me with a few words of warning, "If you try to do anything evil, I'll stop you."

"Deal," I said, positively beaming. "And if *you* do something evil…" I stopped to consider, as the idea had some conflicting appeal. "Well… it depends."

"Okay. Say your prayers and brush your teeth," she said, before sleepily heading to bed.

PART II

CHAPTER 15

I
N NEW YORK City there's a soaring red building with absolutely no windows.

Really. It's there. I won't give you the address because I don't particularly want more ill will or litigation than I've already earned, but it's there, and it's not subtle. It's in that building that I saved the world.

I first saw it in 2008. Although I should have been about sixty-three years old, I was actually only twenty-seven. You'll understand why shortly. I had been pursued for decades by an enemy that I did not yet understand, I was searching desperately for my family, and I was hiding in the comfortably anonymity of Manhattan, one of the faceless millions.

When I first saw it, my eyes were drawn up its side along the smooth walls sliding unimpeded to the spackled sky above. I saw it from several blocks away and had no choice but to navigate my way through the crowded streets of Chinatown to find out what it was. Its stone, red like the blood from a fresh wound (if you want something more specific you'll have to consult Mr. Pietrasanta) stood out ominously against the blue sky and delicate white clouds. It was shaped like a single turret of a castle, one tall red rectangle buttressed on each corner by a giant pillar with a fifth architecturally incongruous pillar going from bottom to top in the center. Along the length of the building there were what looked like black vents and mounted on the roof were satellite dishes and something like a cellular tower. I drew closer to discover its nature, but when I arrived I didn't find anything quite so satisfying as a "Federal Reserve Bank" sign or indications that it was an army base or government building. It was as bare at its base as it was to the top. I circumnavigated the entire building, thwarted the whole way by a tall wall made of the same red stone. I couldn't find any signs, any personnel, or any doors. There were, however, security cameras stuck like barnacles to every corner of the building. What struck me as remarkable was that they were big, hefty, bulky cameras, like the kind you saw in banks in the seventies, rather than today's inconspicuous technology. Surely someone who can afford a windowless fortress in downtown Manhattan could afford modern video cameras.

After circling the entire building I saw that the only entrance was a steep driveway obscured behind a thick iron gate. I couldn't see any mechanism to make the gate rise. The driveway turned a corner, its destination obscured. The building's only identifying mark appeared where the two sides of the iron gate met. On one side there was a small "B" and "E" and on the other side there were two "Ls."

Bell. So one would assume that this was a telephone building. That seemed satisfying enough. I immediately pictured it swelling with switchboards, machinery, and innumerable operators with long painted fingernails, putting people on hold and gossiping at the water cooler rather than dealing with the endless billing complaints that poured in from irate consumers. Why would such a building have need of any windows? Perhaps it's like a joyless casino, nature and sunlight would distract from productivity in that 24/7 hive of industry.

Still, that mentality was more fitting for the seventies or eighties, before most of these processes became automated and all customer service was outsourced to well spoken and poorly paid bilingual workers abroad. Why would they need to house anything more than a few computer servers? Why would they take up so much real estate in the most expensive location in the United States?

Yes, these are the sorts of things I think about. I'm also the kind of guy who sits at home and watches the Discovery Channel to find out how tanks work, or the Food Network when they take us *inside* the chocolate factories. My life thus far has existed in short temporal bursts, and so I often have a lot of catching up to do. I think it's remarkable that people are so dependent on technology and yet they have no real concept of how the things work. A smartphone would make more sense in a Tolkien story than in real life, and yet that bit of magic is in everyone's pocket. Now, don't think that I have any idea how a cell phone works, but if there were a TV special on it, I'd sit and watch it.

Absent any answers, I took one last glance up the sleek side of the building before I turned to go. As my eyes once again reached the top I instinctually went for a sharper look, perhaps seeking some emblem or flag that might tell me more. So I squinted my bad eye, bringing both my peepers to full power.

The building suddenly emanated a sinister red. Like Times Square on a foggy night, tendrils of wan luminescence reached out from the walls. The unblinking eye of Mordor, or the moon through a cloud, the glow roiled maddeningly in all directions. The contents of my stomach, which, if I recall correctly, were a bacon (deliciously crisp, of course), egg and cheese sandwich and a cup of coffee, lurched up and spilled on the pavement in front of me. I fell to my hands and knees, scratching and cutting my palms on the pebbles. I looked up again but the building had returned to normal.

I knelt there, spitting the taste of vomit from my mouth, fishing a bottle of water from my messenger bag, and then mopping my moist brow with the sleeve of my shirt. I heard the slightest click and my attention snapped to the gate, where the "BE" was slowly separating from the "LL."

CHAPTER 16

"I DON'T BELIEVE YOU." David sat across from me at the lunch table, smoothing his paper bag obsessively until it was flat as a placemat. He began to arrange his lunch on the rolling pinned bag, converting his corner of the lunchroom into a four star restaurant. "You're making it up."

"Well, I could prove it, but I shouldn't," I grumbled. As we were still five years from *Amazing Fantasy #15*, I couldn't quite say, "In this world, with great power there must also come – Great Responsibility!" So I mentally grasped for a quote to make my point but all I could think of at that moment were the lyrics to "Davy Crockett." No help there. Instead, I casually said, "Wouldn't wanna show off."

My peanut butter and jelly sandwich looked like it had been rolling pinned. The jelly soaked through the Wonder Bread creating a mostly unappetizing lunch prospect. When Buffalo Bob Smith said on *Howdy Doody* that "Wonder Bread builds strong bodies eight delicious ways," he never envisioned the nightmarish result of my mom's morning food prep rituals. She hadn't even bothered to cut the sandwich in half today, so my first bite would have plenty of soggy crust.

David unwrapped a remarkably preserved piece of meat

pie. The scent of it immediately effused the area. He produced a fork and broke through the crust, revealing a glimpse of peas, mashed potatoes and ground beef. Before taking a bite, he looked at me squarely and said, "You can't prove it because it's impossible. I'm not falling for it."

"Look," I said hesitantly as I poked at my unappetizing lunch, "if you want me to prove it, I will. But you can't get angry at me."

He put down his lunch and said with a challenge, "Prove it."

"You agree you can't get mad, no matter what?"

"Agreed," he rolled his eyes.

"Okay," I said with a devilish smile. You probably saw this coming. David sure didn't. It was much easier this time than it was the night before when Joan first taught me. This time I knew how it felt and what to expect, so I made it happen without much trouble. All the motion and hubbub in the busy lunchroom came to a halt. First, I got up off the uncomfortable bench and took a tabletop walk around the lunchroom. My sneakers stepped carefully between trays and lunch bags, avoiding hands and feet as I trekked about the room. There was Julia deep in a protective bubble of girls. Even with this remarkable talent she was still unreachable. In a larger clique, Keith Butler sat like the epicenter of a jock earthquake. Joan sat with two other girls. The blond curly haired one was Annie and I didn't know the other one. I made my way around the lunchroom, snagging a grape from one bag and a caramel from another, kind of the way I'd fleece and piece together meals from many an unknowing table while travelling aimlessly in the years to come. I counted a total of three boys who were caught mid nose-pick, one older couple making out, one girl crying, and a single cockroach scurrying near the trash. Oh, the things I could have done with that cockroach! I wasn't out to start any trouble. Not at that moment, anyway.

I finished my little survey and went back to my seat where I proceeded to devour David's meat pie. I savored it slowly, discomfited by how loud my chewing sounded in the silence of the motionless lunchroom. I would have to compliment his mother next time I saw her. She really was a phenomenal cook. I placed my soggy sandwich neatly in front of him before letting things return to normal.

I saw him blink in confusion. Apparently I wasn't sitting in exactly the position I was before so the effect was a slight blur. His fork continued downward and speared my peanut butter and jelly sandwich. Balked by a decidedly non-pie texture, he looked downward and gasped.

He looked up and I smiled.

I wish that I had thought to burp at that moment, because that would've been awesome, but all I did was smile. He was a bright lad and didn't need to ask what had become of his pie. So he pulled out a knife and cut the pressed sandwich, sad predecessor of the Panini, into little bite-sized pieces before eating them one at a disappointing time.

He wasn't angry, but there was definitely a palpable tension between us. It was the same sort of tension that I felt when I'd first shown him my Hornby Dublo 3-Rail. He had tried not to seem impressed but the fact remained that I had something amazing that he didn't. The tension about my train set had passed and this would soon, too. This new toy could be as fun for the both of us as my train set had been before my father absconded with it. In order to involve him, I suggested we skip our daily antisocial walk about the schoolyard and instead spend the latter half of recess sitting at the table and working out a list of possibilities. As the list progressed he became less dour and more excited.

"Rob a bank," was his first suggestion.

"Risky. And evil," I countered, but wrote it down anyway. "And hard. How am I supposed to open a vault? And where am I going to hide thousands of dollars?" My perception of a fortune has changed over the years. Back then, a thousand dollars would've made me feel like a king.

"So you don't want to be evil," David reasoned. "You *could* use this power for good. Save people. Stop criminals. Like Marvel Boy!"

Honestly, the whole thing just sounded like a lot of work, but I wrote that down, too. "Look, David, if I see somebody in trouble, I'll probably, you know, save them, you know, if it's happening right in front of me and stuff. But I don't wanna make a career of it. And how often does someone get mugged in my presence?"

He nodded. "Go into the girls room," he offered.

I was about to write it down but stopped to ask, "And do what?"

"Steal their toilet paper?"

"Lame," I said, writing it down, but in smaller letters than the others.

"Leave all their toilet seats up!"

I shrugged. "What about reading everyone's diaries?" I suggested.

"Sure, we'd know everyone's secrets!" David took the paper from me and wrote down the idea himself. Our list grew slowly. Most of the ideas were of the prank variety, and nothing too original. My favorite thus far was the idea of putting a sourball in everyone's mouth and watching a roomful of people simultaneously cringe on the taste. We eventually crossed that one off because we'd be the only likely culprits, sitting there and giggling and not cringing along with everyone else.

During the brainstorming session I thought of something I'd like to try. I didn't share it with David, because he might think I was a bad person. I wasn't particularly well prepared for my science test that afternoon, having been distracted by more important things. I'd been present for the lectures and demonstrations, I'd sort of vaguely skimmed the material in the textbook, I'd even gone so far as to make some notes and underline words and ideas that I found interesting. For example, I had learned in my science class that human beings are bipedal primates in the family Hominidae and are of the genus Homo.

Yes, I remembered that because it was funny. Homo. I very much enjoyed hearing my science teacher, Mrs. McNudle, say the word Homo in her Wisconsin accent with excessively round "Os". Say it out loud. Right now. I dare you. I'll wait.

So I carefully underlined it in my textbook and wrote it out in my notebook. On our test that afternoon, where we had to match up a list of creatures with their categorization in the animal kingdom, I didn't have any trouble connecting Homo Sapiens with Vertebrates in the Primate Order. There were some other ones that I had a problem with. Was a reptile an invertebrate? Was a kangaroo a rodent or a marsupial? And what about an octopus? Was it a fish? Did it belong in the subphyla Vertebrata? If so, where would an octopus keep its spine? Don't even get me started on starfish. It had the word "fish" in its name, but fish must have backbones. So is it a starfish or a star "thingy-in-the-water?" Jellyfish? Who knew? Is an earthworm an insect? It sure creeped me out like an insect. I retained another small bit of information from that class, which I learned because it was rhythmic and I sort of turned it into a song.

Kingdom, phylum, class, order, family, genus, species. Uh!
Kingdom, phylum, class, order, family, genus, species. Uh!
Kingdom, phylum, class, order, family, genus, species. Uh!

To this day I remember it. It seeped into my soul like a bad song you just can't forget. I wonder what important knowledge I can't retain these days because my brain is full of:

Kingdom, phylum, class, order, family, genus, species. Uh!

Certainly this bit of knowledge would help me save the world one day? Or at least pass a test? No such luck.

Yes, it was immoral, but I was just coming off of practically two solid weeks of punishment. Every day I had disappointed my parents. There was underwear appearing all over town, shameful visits from neighbors and priests, inexplicable and ungodly jaunts without wearing any briefs, getting in trouble at school, fighting with Joan, and punishment after punishment after punishment. Can you blame me for wanting to do one thing that would make my parents proud? Showing up at home with a good score on my science test would do just the trick. Since the idea of scoring well occurred to me too late to actually study, I had no choice but to cheat. I sat there in class, having answered only three of the twenty questions and I was quite unconfident about the rest. I really had no choice but to shift into that special state that my sister taught me.

Every vigorously scribbling pencil paused. I got up from my desk and walked to Kim Yang's paper. She was notorious for acing every test she'd ever taken. If this were a better school she'd have been put in a separate class, but we were all heaped together, good and bad alike. The slow learners suffered and lagged behind while the smarter kids went bored and unchallenged. That's the American way, equality for good or for bad. The problem was that Kim had positioned herself so as to guard against prying eyes. Her arm was wrapped around her paper, her head hunched over it, and her hair draped over the other side. It was probably a wise choice since I could see David, one desk behind and to the left of her, trying to casually peer across the aisle at her paper.

She left just enough of a gap for me to learn that worms were Annelids, not insects, and that our friend the octopus was a Mollusk, just like a snail. The only other thing I could see was that mice were in the order "Rodentia," which was something I already knew and that insects were in the class "Insecta." Duh.

I felt bad for doing this to her, but I learned from Julia's unguarded paper that starfish were in the phyla Echinodermata and that frogs were class Amphibia while crocodiles were Reptilia. I owed her one.

Not to get too foreshadowy, but there's no question that I paid back that debt years later. Several times, over one long night. You'll have to keep reading for the sordid details.

All in all, I had a productive time harvesting information, an exercise in pre-internet research practices. I had to make a few different stops but in a way, that sort of reduced my feelings of guilt. I hadn't taken all the answers from one person, only a few answers from many people, like the grazing I did at lunchtime. A missing grape here and there won't leave anyone hungry. No one was getting hurt because of it. In fact, I might even say that I knew a lot of the answers but just used other people's papers to confirm what I knew. I might be lying, but

I would say it anyway. I did do one small good deed before I returned to my seat and returned to normal speed. David was doing mostly well but he was clearly stumped by a few questions. I took my pencil and circled a couple of the answers he was struggling with. Because I'm a good person. It was the Christian thing to do.

"Pencils down!" Mrs. McNudle declared in her unique squeaky alto. Groans accompanied the clatter of pencils.

"Sheets to the front!" We passed our exams up the row of desks where Mrs. McNudle collected them all. I think she was as adverse to homework as I was because it was her practice to allow half the class time for actual test taking and the other half for her to grade them. So whenever we had a quiz we had to suffer through an additional thirty minutes of sitting in silence while she judged us. After she completed and recorded our grades into her book, she handed each stack back to the row leader, who then passed them back. That part of it was always humiliating. I could handle getting a bad grade, but her system allowed others in my class to find out how I did, even before I knew.

There were two zeros on my paper, preceded by a one. I had never seen such a collection of digits on one of my quizzes and it took a moment for me to process that I had gotten a one hundred, which is to say a perfect score. It's funny that although I knew I had cheated horribly and didn't deserve it, I still felt proud of that grade. Whereas I usually would have mashed my exam into the bottom of my bag before anyone else could see it, this time I left it on my desk, in case inquiring minds wanted to be nosy.

On the walk home I thought of the best way to reveal my success to mom and dad. A casual mention at dinner? Leave it out for them to find it on their own? Preemptively stick it on the fridge with a magnet, supplanting some of Joan's redundant good grades? Of course, I decided to go with something a little bit more devilish.

In a tri-fold my test looked like every other disciplinary letter I'd been sent home with over the years. So I folded it carefully and professionally, donned my most sheepish and apologetic look, and stood before my mother.

"Mom," I said, donning my biggest and best Walt Disney Cartoon eyes, "I have a paper from school you should see."

"Oh Lord in heaven above, what now? *What now?*" She shrieked. The poor woman was on the brink of losing it. "Your father can't handle this anymore, you know. What did we do wrong? Where did we go wrong with you?" That's it mom, dig it in deeper, and you'll feel that much worse when you find out how awesome I am. I forked over the paper and she unfolded it roughly.

I mustered the saddest eyes I could and awaited her apologies. She merely said, "Oh."

"That's it?" I said.

"Give me a minute," she replied. She looked it over, shook her head slightly, and finally spoke, tasting the words in her mouth as if they were a new and foreign flavor, "I'm proud of you."

"Thanks mom," I beamed.

"Your father will be delighted." She was still blinking as if trying to shake off a bad dream.

"I hope so!" I said cheerfully. To add to the effect, I kissed her on the cheek and headed upstairs, saying as I went, "I've gotta go get some homework done!"

When I opened my door and marched triumphantly into

my lair, Joan was waiting for me. "What are you doing in my room?" I shouted. "Get out of my room or I'm telling mom."

"Or maybe I'm telling mom you cheated on your test." Her accusing face channeled all the ugliness of the universe. One witchlike finger pointed at me. "You're not allowed to cheat. It's wrong. That's not why I taught you how to do that. That's not why we have this gift."

"You don't know I cheated. I didn't cheat." I said defiantly. "Get out of my room!"

"Of course you cheated," she shrieked. "You never got a hundred on anything in your life, then suddenly you're a great student without spending any time studying? Liar. Liar! LIAR!"

"Don't call me a liar!" I cried. "And if you won't get out of my room, I'm going into yours."

I turned on my heels and marched across the hallway, determined to leave a Converse sized sneaker print deeply indented in her precious metal dollhouse. But suddenly the door was closed in my path. I turned around and she was still there with her arms folded.

"No fair!" I accused her.

"How isn't it fair? If you do bad things, I should stop you. If you try to go into my room, I'll stop you. If you try to cheat on a test, I'll stop you."

I may have had to put up with that kind of abuse a week ago, but things were extremely different now. She couldn't run circles around me like she could before. We were on equal footing. There was no way that someone with my extraordinary talents was going to put up with her crap.

My mom came to the foot of the stairs and called up, "What are you two shouting about?"

"Joan's in my room!" I called down to her and pointed across the hall to my room. No sooner did I look than I realized that she wasn't in there anymore.

"No I'm not, you're crazy!" Joan opened the door to her room and walked out.

"What are you playing at?" Mom yelled at me. Joan was playing me, and I was getting in trouble, again. I was going to end up grounded or beaten or worse. Dad would take away everything I had that made me happy. All because of Joan. She was evil and she had to be stopped. So even though my mom saw me walk across the hall into Joan's room, I went anyway.

"Don't you dare come in my room!" Joan shrieked.

"Or what?" I cried defiantly.

I could recognize at that moment that she was focusing on engaging her power, activating it, and that in the briefest of instants I'd be frozen again and subject to whatever awful malicious prank she chose to inflict upon me. So I raced her to it, I engaged, I focused, I set it in motion, and in that precise instant we both unleashed our power at the same time.

There concludes the strictly linear part of my existence.

CHAPTER 17

DECADES LATER IN New York, kneeling on the ground outside the sinister red building that had inexplicably caused me to vomit, I waited for my stomach to settle and my head to clear. With nary a creak the thick metal gates slid apart, followed shortly by echoing footfalls coming from around the curve of the drive. A genial looking old man, with a full head of thick white hair and a wrinkled, tanned face, turned the corner and continued up the long drive. An unfiltered Marlboro materialized in his stained hands and soon he was gaily sucking down smoke. He was wearing a tan polo shirt and khakis. He looked unhurried as he continued towards the now completely open entrance. There was a slight hop in his gait. He was limping almost imperceptibly.

I'd picked myself up, shouldered my bag and fished out a mint. I was tempted to squint again and see the sight all over again, but I was afraid the result would be the same. Vomiting on an empty stomach was even worse than losing one's breakfast.

Smoke accompanied each word as the white haired man spoke. "Y'alright there, kid? Too much to drink?"

I was far from a "kid," but I guess all things are relative.

He had a New York accent, gravelly with countless years of smoke breaks.

"Fine. Thanks." Then I looked down at the chunky mess I'd deposited at the foot of their monolith. "Sorry about that. If you have a hose…"

"My knuckles tell me rain's comin', so I wouldn't worry too much about it." He looked up through the city's canyons and glimpsed at the sky.

I, too, looked up at the clear blue sky and shrugged. "Okay, if you say so," I said, and started away.

Five swollen but surprisingly strong fingers clapped me on the shoulder and stopped me from continuing. It could've been a friendly gesture but for the unexpected power in the old man's grip and the sudden hardness in his eyes. "Before you go," he said, making sure every inhalation was through the tube of a lit cigarette, "I need to know what happened. Accident reports, liability, and all that."

"No idea," I replied. "I was checking out the building, just looking at it, and I… I lost it for a minute. Or maybe I had some bad eggs this morning, who knows. Really, no big deal."

The cigarette hung limply in his mouth, clinging to his lower lip as his jaws fell open. "How… uh… how old are you?" Suddenly his fingers were preoccupied with unzipping a leather fold he'd pulled out of his pocket. Unzipping was no easy task when one hand was still firmly affixed to my shoulder.

"Old enough to know that this is weird." I shook off his grip and stepped back a few paces. His fumbling arthritic fingers had finally opened the fold, which swung open and spilled dangerously close to my vomit. A yellowing photo landed at my feet.

It was my sixth grade yearbook photo, replete with bowtie

and goofy grin. I was immobilized by the unexpected sight of it. "What the hell…"

"It's him," the man choked, cigarette falling from his dry lips.

"Him who?" Then I realized he was trying to pull a heavy, ancient looking walkie-talkie from his belt. He pushed a thick button and repeated himself. "It's him!"

This was much too weird, much too frightening, and so I did what anyone in my position would have done had they the remarkable ability to do so. I tried to stop time, or speed myself up, whatever. But the moment I tried to evoke that unique power and extract myself from that potentially dangerous situation, the building blurred out of focus, reaching out with the colorful tendrils that I thought I had hallucinated before, and once again triggered my nausea. I dry heaved violently and doubled over, stomach constricting.

Suddenly, I heard multiple sets of heavy boots running up the drive and rounding the corner. Younger men in khaki and tan covered the inclined drive in long strides. The one leading the charge reached out his arm and fired what I thought was a gun. He was halfway up the drive as two wires launched at me faster than sound. They uncoiled audibly and I could hear them whizzing past me, like the snap of a metal whip, but crackling with electricity. It was close. I didn't wait for another shot. I sprinted away from the building as fast as my legs would take me. This was not that fast, since I've always been notoriously lazy and the idea of spending hours in a gym running like a hamster on a wheel along with thousands of other miserable New Yorkers was never particularly appealing to me. Adrenaline, fear and confusion can be powerful motivators. At least I was faster than the Marlboro Man, with his limp and smoker's lungs.

The younger men were the problem though. I cut across four lanes of traffic and headed for the winding streets of downtown Manhattan. I wasn't the sort of stand-up citizen who could run to the cops for help. So I figured I'd lose them in the serpentine and crowded streets. I pushed, bumped, and elbowed my way through immobile window-shopping hordes and past slow-walkers. I skirted construction, dodged pamphleteers of every variety, and leapt over homeless people lying prostrate in the sidewalk.

Two of the tan-shirts were keeping pace with me. I considered jumping in a cab, but traffic was so slow that I could walk faster than any taxi. I thought about descending into the subway system and hoping I could jump a train before they arrived, but if I couldn't, if the subway angels weren't there to perfectly time my escape, what then? Would the tan-shirts have a nice, pleasant conversation with me on the platform while I waited for the delayed F train? Would they offer me some Pepto Bismol for my upset stomach? Would they explain why that gnarled old smoke machine carried a picture of me in his pocket?

No, my best chance was to lose them on the streets. The crowds were thick now and the blocks shorter, and I was able to lose them for minutes at a time, but they always managed to find me again, spreading out and closing in on me with military precision. I felt hunted, not a new sensation for me admittedly, but this was somewhat more immediate than I'd have liked. I had always had my failsafe trick to fall back on. Not this time. After two misfires, I was gun shy and feared pulling the trigger, lest I end up doubled over on the ground again. I was sweating through my clothes and eating air like I was starving. My heart was pounding like never before and I felt a sharp pain in my stomach. I redoubled my efforts and crossed the street, making two lefts to double back the way I came, hoping the line of buses and trucks would obscure me.

Then I saw one of NYC's many little psychic shops in a narrow storefront between a vintage clothing shop and a pizzeria. I was on Bleecker Street, the prime location for anyone who needs a bong, porn, or their palm read. I hopped down the stairs leading to the shop, lurched open the door, jangling the sleigh bells tied to the knob. I found myself in a small parlor with a large window that allowed all of Bleecker Street to see the goings on. What a stupid idea! I considered leaping out and continuing my gazelle run until the predators caught me when the beaded curtain parted.

"I am Black Esmerta," said the psychic. Blood red lipstick, dark eyeliner, and a black wig did nothing to hide the fact that this was definitely albino. "Sit and we shall gaze into the future."

Black Esmerta would have her five minutes of fame but not for another six years or so. Working under a different pseudonym, and in a new shop in Times Square, she would be arrested for bilking some poor believer out of $427,963, by convincing him his lack of appeal with the ladies was spiritual in nature. The truth was that he was just an idiot, a trait that most women found unappealing. But not Esmerta. That was her favorite quality in men.

"Uhh, listen, uhh… Black…"

"Esmerta," she supplied with an affected European accent. It had hints of Russian, Polish, German and Saturday Morning Cartoon.

"Esmerta," I stammered, gasping for breath. "This will sound weird but I'm being chased and I need somewhere to hide for a few minutes. Can we go behind the beaded curtain just for a little while? I'll give you twenty dollars."

I held out the twenty as if seeing it would make her more likely to go along with my insane plan. Crazy man bursts into your place of business and asks if he can be alone with you in your backroom for twenty dollars, what would you do?

"I have been expecting you," she said slowly.

"Look, can you drop the act for a minute, I'm in trouble and I need…"

"Sit!" She said sternly, snatching the twenty from my hand, tucking it into a small satchel that hung across her waist and forcibly nudging me into the creaky wooden seat. I sat at a small stone table with my back facing the window. Esmerta pulled a long scarf off her head and wrapped it around mine. It was patterned silk and billowed down over my shoulders. She whipped off a black wool shawl and wrapped that around me as well. Underneath the shawl she had on a well worn faded gray t-shirt with what I was almost certain was a ThunderCats logo. She sat across from me looking like a relatively normal pale woman in an ill-fitted wig getting her fortune read, while from behind I must have looked like the house Psychic. This woman was clever.

"From cabinet pull out crystal ball," she said, still maintaining the accent. I guess for twenty dollars I'd bought more than just a respite from my run. She would go through the motions. I always did respect a professional. I reached down to the cabinet to do as I was told, and only then did I realize that what I had heard as "crystal ball" was actually her trying to say "crystal bowl" in her colorful muddled accent. I set the ornate shimmering bowl and its rough-hewn stone base on the table.

"Are they…" I began to turn around when Esmerta dug a long black fingernail into the back of my hand.

"They are outside still and they are looking for you."

"Crap." And again, the finger dug deeply into my hand.

"Ow!" I cried. "What was that for?"

"Language." She released me. "Twenty buys you escape from bad men. But you cannot sit at Esmerta's table without for to read your fortune."

"Ok," I said. I'd never actually had my fortune read since my taste for entertaining lies could be sated at the movies. At this point, I should probably mention that she filled out the ThunderCats t-shirt quite well, and that despite the mixed first impression, Black Esmerta was quite easy on the eyes. The costume and makeup seemed designed to make her look older, but I suspected she was barely into her thirties. Older than me by enough to make it a little taboo and therefore a little exciting. In fact, the Albino thing was also kind of…

"Or I kick you out?" she offered, interrupting my reverie.

"Yes. No, please. Go for it," I stammered.

"Crystal ball is fifty."

"How much for the bowl?"

"What?"

"Bad joke. Fifty! Really? Just read my palm or something, how much is that?"

"Crystal ball is on table. Fifty. Or you go join friends up there."

"Fine, fine," I caved. "Let's do the bowl."

"You pay after men leave, or it look wrong." She was quite adept at this. "Place one hand inside crystal ball."

"Aren't you supposed to…" And I was kicked under the table. I hadn't been kicked under the table since my sister gave up the practice when she switched to open toed shoes.

"They are looking, and you must be Esmerta. Hand in ball."

"Great. Fifty bucks to read my own fortune." I slapped my hand unceremoniously into the crystal bowl, allowing it to flop as it landed like dead fish.

"From cabinet, please to take decanter with blue oils and pour over hand."

I did as she said, noting with distaste that the blue liquid I had begun pouring over my hand into the glass bowl reminded me of a popular toilet-disinfecting product. I splashed it around a bit, unsure of what to do.

"No!" she cried. "Pour slow. Like rain drizzle. Style. Yes. Then move both hands in bowl. Gentle, swirling motions. And look into it, gaze, seek, find…"

I found it hard not to giggle as she made each of those words sound profound and essential. I was also quite amused to find myself unexpectedly acting out the part of the Psychic. I wanted to say, "You will find what you seek in the basement of the Alamo!" but I was afraid she wouldn't get the reference and then I'd look stupid.

"Relax your hands and let fate guide their movement. Like Ouija, do not decide, allow." Great, for my fifty bucks I was also getting an instructional tour. Maybe I'd set up my own business. I tried to follow her instructions. She continued, encouraging, her voice more sincere than I would have expected in such a silly situation. "Soft focus, until something catches your eye, then follow it, deeper into the crystal."

The room was lit with a single candle, but the majority

of the light was spilling in from the street. The crystal captured and refracted it, creating a cloudy glow. "Clear the mind of unwanted thoughts," she continued, finally relaxing in her own chair as she witnessed me follow her directions. "Let images take you into the trance. Good. Yes. Now: like in subway, you see something, you say something. See a chair, say chair, then let image go and find next."

I think the mere fact that I had been sprinting moments earlier and my heart was then veering from "arrest" mode to "things might be okay," helped put me in a more relaxed mood. I was perfectly willing to shut out the pursuit and the glowing building and the tazers to have one perfect moment of calm relaxation. Something inside the bowl shimmered. It must have been a tiny flaw in the crystal. Or a reflection of a passing headlight. Or the candle's flicker. Or something inconsistent in the oil. Or Esmerta with a penlight. Who knows? I followed the shimmer and tried to focus on it. Of course, when I focus on things we all know by now what I do. So I squinted my eye and gazed at the spot.

It was a star. A dark star. I knew immediately where I had seen it before.

"Julia's tattoo. On her neck," I whispered. Not just the impression of it. What I saw in the bowl was the real deal.

"Good, let go, seek next." As she spoke my vision softened again, the heady aroma of incense making me sleepy. My mind was wandering and picking up memories. The incense brought me to church and my butt momentarily ached in remembrance of the pews. My subconscious continued to meander. Then I caught another shimmer and again I focused in on it.

It was Joan. This bowl had tuned in to The Women of My Life: A Tour. A television station with nothing but painful memories. Next would be my mother, no doubt. When I squinted and peered deeper into that image I saw something was wrong.

"My sister," I spoke, nervously.

It was Joan, certainly. She was pale, her head wrapped in gauze. She looked to be in her late thirties or forties, delicate crows feet stretching from her eyes. It was unquestionably her, but not as I had ever seen her.

"Old," I said aloud, wanting to keep Esmerta in the loop.

How could that be? Must have been my fears manifesting themselves in an image, but this image seemed so lifelike. She was frozen in a moment of pain.

"Still trapped," I said, realizing the moment I said it that it was the truth.

Although she was mostly in darkness she seemed to be surrounded by a soft rolling fog. Her skin looked pale and white. Her eyes unblinking, she stared through the mist at a stainless steel wall across from her. I imagined myself taking a step backward to see the bigger picture, and the vision obeyed. The greater room was bare, lined with a familiar red stone. As I stared at it, squinting for details, goose pimples rose all over my body. I felt a painful chill pass over me. The room where Joan was trapped... It was cold. I could tell. Painfully cold. As the image sharpened the stone began to shine and glow, like flares erupting from the sun, and my stomach lurched in response, filling up poor Madame Black Esmerta's crystal bowl.

CHAPTER 18

F ROM MY MOTHER'S perspective, this is what happened. This is the story she told the police. Her son and daughter walked home from school together. Her son gave her a test that he'd received a perfect score on. She was careful to provide the test, to show them how her son had gotten a perfect score. Then she went into the kitchen to start dinner. Her husband would be home in about two hours, plenty of time to fix a nice meal for the family, as she always did.

Then she heard her children bickering upstairs. They were always bickering, she explained; it wasn't anything to be worried about. It wasn't at all unusual. But still, as a proper mother, she went to the foot of the stairs and asked what was happening. Her boy was yelling about his sister going into his room. He had always been territorial, she explained. It turned out that she wasn't in his room; she was in her own room. Maybe she had been in his room earlier. Maybe not. Then her son stormed across the hallway and entered her daughter's room. There were some words shouted. She couldn't be sure but she thought she felt a breeze whip through the house, and there was a little bit of reddish light bouncing off the white walls of the stairwell. Again, she couldn't really be sure if any of that actually happened. It was all so quick. But she thought so.

Then there was silence. She called up to them but there was no answer. So with a big pot on the stove beginning to simmer, she walked back to the kitchen, tossed in a pinch or two of salt, then she left her dinner prep and walked up the stairs, calling out to them again. Her daughter's room was empty. Her son's room was empty. She called out to them. She opened the back window and called into the backyard. She looked in the bathroom. She looked in the closets in case they'd decided to gang up on their poor mother and play a trick on her. She went back downstairs and walked through the living room, the downstairs bathroom, the backyard, the garage, the front yard, the basement. She kept calling out. She probably said things like, "This is not funny you little bastards!" She still couldn't find them.

She turned off the boiling water (the potatoes could wait) and sat on the couch in the living room for a while. She sat silent and immobile, the butt of some joke that she could not quite understand. Another woman might have cried, but this one wouldn't be made a fool of. Her husband would be home in an hour and a half. She wanted to call him but didn't want to disturb him at work. Still, she felt abandoned and anxious.

So she went to the neighbor's house. Hank wasn't home but Peggy was, so she sat with her in their kitchen, drinking tea while Peggy fixed her own family's dinner: boiled pasta with melted American cheese, broccoli, and chicken breasts. She relayed the story to Peggy who assured her that the kids were probably just playing a joke and they'd show up once they got hungry for dinner. That made sense, so my mom thanked her then went back home and tried to make up for lost cooking time. The water reached a boil again in no time, and she proceeded to make potatoes and eggs, which was a quicker meal than what she'd originally planned. She had just about finished cooking right when her husband returned home. Still, there was no sign of her children.

She told him what happened as she set out the four places on the dinner table. She also told him what Peggy had said, that the kids would come running once their bellies were rumbling and they smelled dinner. The house was eerily quiet.

When dad got home he took his own look around the house. He started upstairs and hit some places that hadn't occurred to Joan. The house didn't have an attic per se, but there was a hollow spot where the roof angled downward. He checked in there. Then he looked under the beds and in the closets. In the backyard he looked in the shed, he looked in the garage and he looked in the fireplace. He couldn't find his son and daughter.

Dad had an idea. "You know that broad who makes the Jew cookies?"

"David's mother. Mrs. Bernbaum," mom replied. "I have her number." Despite my father's unfortunate phrasing, that was actually a decent idea. It might have explained where I disappeared to, but certainly not Joan. I suppose at that point they were still clinging to the idea that their kids had been disrespectful and uncommunicative. So rather than calling David's mother right away, he and his wife sat down to dinner and ate their potatoes and eggs. He slathered his with ketchup and she was generous with salt and pepper. Butter was spread on toast. After they had their fill, mom wrapped up the two plates for Joan and I then she put them in the fridge. She cleaned up the table while my father smoked a cigarette on the porch.

Then she called David's mother, who answered the phone almost immediately. David was home, and they'd heard neither hide nor hare of me that night. They exchanged assurances and well wishes, and then hung up.

After the dishes were clean she joined my father on the porch and smoked a cigarette, as well.

Then, despite the nagging belief that their son was merely playing an embarrassing prank on them, they called the police.

After four days my mom took the leftover potatoes and eggs from the fridge and scraped the plates into the garbage.

The first month was grueling.

The second month was crueler.

The third month was harsher still. The town's uproar and the support of the parish and police began to shift from militaristic searching to condolences.

By the fourth month Father Barret stopped mentioning the missing children and instead spoke of the "grieving" and the "ones we lost."

And somewhere around the fifth or sixth months, when mom and dad were sitting down to a barbeque dinner on a balmy summer evening in their empty house, they heard the sound of bickering coming from upstairs.

CHAPTER 19

"**K**EEP OUT OF my room or so help me!" Joan shouted.

"Why would I wanna go in your dirty room?" To emphasize "dirty" I grabbed a handful of soil from the potted plant in the center of the hallway and tossed it at her door. If I had pulled that stunt a week earlier I'm sure all the soil would've ended up in my underwear, but I was finally on even ground with her, so she took a different route.

"You. Are. SUCH. AN IMPOSSIBLE BRAT!" she screamed and lunged at me. It had been quite a while since my sister and I had had a no holds barred physical fight. There's something unseemly about having a throw down with a girl, but the fact remained that she was older and bigger than me, so she had the advantage. Let's not forget that she was the one who attacked me! Her harpy talons gripped my hair and pulled me in one direction while I took my free hands and gave her a fierce Indian burn. Is that politically correct? Native American burn. Snakebite? Well, it was the fifties, so let's go with Indian burn. She screamed and I screamed and we ended up on the floor of the hallway at the top of the stairs pushing and scratching and pinching and kicking until the sight of both our parents watching from the hallway below froze us mid-brawl.

"Dad?" Joan gasped in surprise, disentangling herself from me. "You're home early."

"It's… it's six o'clock," he looked confused and hesitant, an altogether unfamiliar countenance on his face.

"Nuh-uh," I countered. "We just got home from school like ten minutes ago."

"It's summer." My mom's voice sounded distant and small.

It wasn't like my mother to joke, but that's what she must have been doing, right? Summer, huh? I was warm, that's true, but I'd also just been wrestling. It was more likely that my dad was home early from work and my mom was being quirky for the first time in her life. The Q&A was put on hold because my mother bounded up the stairs, loping up, two or three steps at a time. I closed my eyes and braced myself for what I thought would be a powerful British backhand.

Instead I felt a fierce hug. She gathered Joan and I in her arms, both at once, and hugged us so tightly that I could barely breathe. Her chest was heaving and I suddenly realized that the muffled sounds she was making as she pressed her face between ours were sobs. My mother was crying with more abandon than I had imagined anyone was even capable of. My strong mother was a British icon for stalwart behavior, from whom I had only ever seen a limited range of emotions, mostly love and anger, occasionally hunger, if that counts. That strong woman was bawling like a baby, her fresh tears wetting my cheek. Then something even stranger happened. My father climbed the stairs and took the entire family in his broad arms.

It was our first full family hug. In that tangle of familial love I made eye contact with my sister. She seemed just as baffled as I was. Then I looked across at my father, and I saw, for the first time in my entire life, tears streaming from his eyes. It was a beautiful if utterly incomprehensible moment.

The outpouring of love would be short-lived, however. My parents wanted answers, but the questions didn't make sense.

"Where were you?" Joan and I had no awareness of going anywhere. One moment we were fighting, then we both tried to one-up the other by being the first to speed up. It seemed to us that we both failed at that, maybe from lack of concentration. I tossed dirt into her room. We wrestled briefly. No real harm was done. Then suddenly our parents were hugging us and crying.

"It's August?" I asked, disbelievingly. "Are you serious? That's impossible. It's April."

Dad hit me. It was his first and last exception to our new house-rule about corporal punishment. I don't suppose I blame him. He was confused, scared, and the only real possible explanation, the only sensible, logical conclusion was that I was lying. Only a moment after he smacked me across the face, and before I could cry or yell, Joan came to my defense.

She told them the same thing. "Dad, we just got back from school." She said it slowly, with conviction. He wasn't about to strike her. Joan was daddy's girl, and if she was saying it then it must be what she believed.

There was nothing to say. No more questions were asked because the answers simply weren't there.

We were a family practiced in faith, every Sunday reaffirming the supernatural: transubstantiation, reincarnation, parting waters, afterlife, and etcetera. But this was beyond comprehension. If there was a precedent in our little black Sunday guidebook we weren't aware of it. So the questions were put on hold and mom ushered us all downstairs. Although she'd only cooked dinner enough for her and her husband, she quickly resurrected a cornucopia of leftovers from the fridge and filled the table with a variety of mouthwatering food.

After a curiously silent dinner, mom warmed some milk on the stove and made hot chocolate. It was an incongruous treat since apparently it was suddenly late summer. Chocolate, however, is always welcome around my taste buds and we all had our fill. On the plus side, the homework in my bag was long past due so there was really no sense in doing it. Joan was in the same boat. We took turns in the bathroom brushing our teeth. Mom, dad and Joan joined me for my prayers. All four of us knelt at the foot of my bed and prayed.

"Lord thank you for giving us our children back," mom whispered, her eyes clenched and her hands clasped. "Please help us understand why you took them. Please don't take them again."

I got a genuine tuck-in that night. Mom and dad both kissed me on the cheek. They wrapped me in my covers, which I would have to kick off in a moment because it was hot as sin in my room. Dad gave my hair a quick tussle and mom squeezed my foot on her way out. They went off to Joan's room to do the same for her. They left both of our doors open, and before I dozed off I saw my father sitting in the hallway at the top of the stairs, a sentry to our imminent slumber.

Having gone to bed early, I woke early. Mom beat me to rise though, as she had to run to the market to stock up. A married couple required significantly fewer groceries than what a family of four with two ravenous children needs. So when she returned I sat in the kitchen as she cracked egg after egg into a large glass bowl. She poured in some milk, butter and cheese and began whisking. Slabs of thick bacon were beginning to sizzle on the thick iron skillet. My father was slicing hunks of bread off a fresh loaf and sliding them into the oven to crisp. Dad's coffee was on the burner, just beginning to percolate. In another pot, water simmered, destined for mom's steel cut oats and English Breakfast Tea. They'd even unwrapped a frozen concentrate of orange juice and dropped it into a glass pitcher with water to thaw. My job was to stir and mash the OJ cube until it was uniformly orange and only slightly lumpy.

Joan was reading a paper that my mom had picked up. "I can't believe Marilyn Monroe married Arthur Miller and Grace Kelly got *The Prince of Monaco*. It doesn't seem fair. They should switch."

Joan was upset that she'd missed out on so many important events. I was livid that I had missed my summer vacation, practically every minute of it. What sort of cruel God would cause me to miss my summer vacation? I thought wistfully of all the fireflies that went uncaught, all the baseballs that went unhit, the piles of ice cream that never melted down my chin, the sand that didn't get stuck in my bathing suit… There was no end to it. We were scant weeks from the beginning of the next school year. To top it off, another subject of debate was whether I would have to repeat the fifth grade, or if I could just go ahead and join the sixth. There was no question that Joan would merely join up with her classmates and nerd her way back to the top of the class. But my fate was uncertain. I was resolved: repeating a grade was not an option.

The big questions remained, however, and since Joan and I couldn't blab about our shared ability, and we had both silently resolved to avoid using it again any time soon, it seemed unlikely that any satisfactory answers would surface. After breakfast dad took us all to church to see Father Barret. As best as he could, Dad explained what had happened. Mom told it from her perspective, which was mostly the same. Barret questioned my sister and I, arcing a suspicious eyebrow at answers that made no sense whatsoever. Then he spoke alone with my parents while we waited outside, and we all left the church feeling disappointed.

Religion hadn't supplied any answers. The best Barret could do was talk about "faith" and "God's will," although I think that he secretly thought I was somehow to blame. Then we stopped off at the police station and weathered a similar event. Questions were asked and answers were disappointing. The police chief was accusatory as we sat in his office and he had a right to be, but what could Joan and I say but that the months that we were supposedly gone didn't seem to happen for us? Short of shipping us off to Washington to be interrogated by Dwight D. Eisenhowers's cadre of nuclear scientists, there was nothing to do. First, the chief insisted that my sister and I had run away and then we had a change of heart but lacked the creativity to at least make up a good story to cover our absence. Then he turned on my parents, raising his voice as he suggested that they might themselves be somehow responsible, hinting at a malicious act that he could not even articulate. At that moment I heard a tone in my father's voice that was usually reserved for me when he caught me doing something nasty to my sister. All at once he became commanding and frightening as he stood and glared at the paunch-bellied police chief. "Just exactly what are you saying that me and my wife did to our children?"

The chief sunk back down into his chair like a deflating balloon in the face of my father's smoldering fury. He changed his opinion on a dime, suggesting next that we'd been through some kind of trauma, perhaps brainwashed, and recommended we see a psychologist. Of course, that would involve appointments and bills, so the idea was filed away for a more prosperous day. As we left, the chief made it quite clear that the case was most certainly *not* closed, but that he had no idea what his next step should be.

What was left of the summer passed in the blink of one eye and soon we were back at school, subject to the same interrogations but from all of our hundreds of classmates. Two missing students were the talk of the town and to have them mysteriously reappear with no explanation was more than the curious cats could handle. Even David grilled me, and when I gave him the same dissatisfying response as everyone else, he withdrew from me. He thought I was withholding something from him and he began to distrust me. Our friendship began to fall apart after that.

When Julia and I finally had an auspicious moment alone, she merely said she was happy I was back. And she asked about my cat Mr. Nivens. I told her that Nivens (whom I had previously described as comically fat) had lost upwards of twenty pounds in my absence, abstaining from his beloved kitty chow because he missed me so much. She was distressed, but I assured her that he ate nearly an entire chicken once he saw that I was okay. Apparently my ordeal hadn't dulled my appetite for lying.

After much bargaining and promising and whining I was permitted to stay with my class and join the sixth grade on the condition that I take tests and finish projects from the end of fifth grade. It was a necessary sacrifice and I devoted much of the early part of the year to studying like a Jesuit. There was no way that I was going to be left back! Along with this newfound studiousness was a tacit understanding between Joan and me. We both knew that, somehow, our abilities had caused that terrible thing to happen, so we formally forbade ourselves from using it. It's a tragedy to discover such a wonderful talent, so powerful and full of mischievous potential, and be forced to abandon it, but we just couldn't take the risk. The devastation that it had caused our family was too much to risk again. From that moment on we were strictly mundane in practically every way.

For about five years.

CHAPTER 20

I T IS TIME for us to leave my eleven-year-old self behind, the impulsive troublemaker relegated to my id where he belongs. As he tries to claw himself free, with sticky fingers and simple swears, let's tune that out and turn our attention to the pubescent world of tenth grade. Remember my earlier allusions to Earth Science shenanigans with Julia? That's about where we need to pick up this story. It's not that nothing interesting happened in the years between eleven and fifteen. I was hardly a saint but my relationship with my sister was somewhat more amiable, and we both managed to avoid disappearing for months at a time. I wish I could say that I strictly adhered to my disavowal of the extraordinary but I definitely made exceptions to that rule. It was rare, only when absolutely necessary, and always entirely discreet.

I think that my guilt for putting my parents through months of distress combined with the effort of finishing my fifth grade assignments while keeping up with my sixth grade work challenged me to become slightly more industrious and focused with my time. So by the time I was caught up, I continued at that level of diligence and my grades were better than ever. Without cheating! That's why I was able to join Julia in that Earth Science class when some of my other friends were consigned to more remedial studies. With my sister and I getting along, and my grades notably improved, my mom and dad were in heaven. The closer our family got to *Leave it to Beaver* wholesomeness, the happier they became. We were all still haunted by what had happened, but it was easier to occasionally forget it, and to laugh around the table while we talked about the news.

1960 was a pivotal year for the entire world, myself included. John F. Kennedy began his campaign for president of the United States. Right about the time my classmates and I began fretting over whom they'd choose as a Valentine, France began detonating nuclear bombs in the Sahara and the BERN Particle Accelerator fired its first beams of high energy particles to inquire into the dynamics and structure of matter, space, and time. Elvis returned from his tour of duty just three days before the Vietnam War began. I was too young to fight in the war but old enough to be annoyed by every teenage girl's devotion to the aforementioned Memphis crooner. While he had the obsessive attention of every girl in the world, I suffered through that particular Valentine's Day without even a peck on the cheek, a badge my eleven-year-old self would have worn with pride but that felt somewhat different as a hormonal fifteen-year-old.

It seemed like every month another satellite was launched into orbit. They were ostensibly for weather and navigation, but as the Soviets continued to lob missiles at our U-2 spy planes, as their MiG fighters shot down our RB-47s, as Sputnik 4 was rumored to carry high-tech Russian weapons into space and Sputnik 5 returned to earth with astro-dogs and space-mice, we were all fairly resigned to the fact that Nikita

Khrushchev and Dwight D. Eisenhower would soon be retreating to their cozy and safe bunkers while nuclear missiles began pummeling us common folk to ash. If they didn't happen to rain from satellites above the clouds they'd certainly leap like killer trout from the sea, or burst from hidden silos in our fields of amber waves of grain.

The nuclear submarine USS Triton circumnavigated the earth, an accomplishment we were supposed to feel proud of but which only added to the fear, because if we could do it, then they could, too. The UGM-27 Polaris missile was successfully tested just before summer break was over. It was a submarine-launched, two-stage solid-fuel nuclear-armed ballistic missile. The USS Seadragon surfaced at the North Pole and oddly enough, their crew played a game of polar baseball on the same day that I played my last game of the summer before school started. All this talk about nuclear war began to feel a little low-tech since in 1960 my dad read aloud to us from the newspaper an article about the first operational laser. Not only did we have to worry about the skin being blown off our bones, but now tiny beams of light from the heavens above would bore holes into our skulls. Ah, progress.

Oh, and we got Hawaii! That's right. Hawaii became a state that summer. Hurrah. New flags for everyone.

It was in this climate that I began tenth grade. David and I hadn't officially ended our friendship, but things had gotten weird and for no real justifiable reason we weren't that close anymore. There was palpable tension that others could pick up on, and since I couldn't very well try to explain by saying, "Well, I can move faster than thought and David's a little jealous," or, from David's point of view, "That ass may or may not be able to move superfast, but if he can then he's selfish about it and if he can't then he's a liar," people began to assume that we were enemies.

Somehow, over time, people's perceptions sometimes begin to shape the truth, and so our mutual dislike festered. He had a group of friends that slightly overlapped with mine, like a social Venn diagram, so we'd sometimes find ourselves at the same events or parties but we rarely interacted, save for cold glares across a crowded room.

My new friend du jour was Alan Canyon, an unfortunate last name considering the extent of his pockmarks. He had blond hair, hazel eyes, and once he discovered the gym and shook off his bad adolescent skin, he'd turn out to be a gorgeous adult. At the time, however, his bad skin, slight lateral lisp, tendency to talk much louder than was really necessary, penchant for drawing naked sword-wielding women, and his ability to use large words and form complicated sentences made him a bit of an outcast. He was the perfect addition to my small menagerie, so we became fast friends.

I was in the driver's seat of the friendship, figuratively and literally. Since my dad travelled a lot for work, his eight-year-old Packard Mayfair, no longer flashy with its peeling paint and bent antenna, was mine for the taking. Joan enjoyed being chauffeured. Not by me, but by the hordes of greasy young gentlemen that knocked on our door. Every morning she got a ride to school, often from different boys. They'd roll up in their turtle-waxed sex-mobiles with their collars popped and their hair as greased as their engines, and she'd skip out when they honked their horns. True gentlemen.

To her credit, she had added Keith Butler to the list of boys who fawned over her. Frankly, it was easy to empathize with him. If she wasn't my sister… I shudder at the thought.

Objectively speaking, she filled out her sweaters in a way that made other girls envious. Keith, the object of her scandalous journal entry, drove her to school the year before on many occasions. He even took her to his senior prom. She cried for practically a whole week after that because after the last dance he had to get on a bus to basic training. He had joined the Army. There were other boys waiting to take his place next year when school started again and she began to move on.

When one of his consistent letters revealed that he was being deployed to Vietnam, the waterworks began again. It was hard to watch, because she was normally so composed, in public anyway. My sister carried herself with poise. She was a leader among her clique of girls and that's partially why the boys pursued her. She was the alpha girl and the prize of the pack. It was strange because she had started out along such a meek path. Perhaps her latent unused power gave her confidence. We both were presumably refraining from using our ability, but the mere fact that we could gave us both a certain confidence. For me it could sometimes be a negative, a swagger, but for her it was something that made her irresistible to the bumpkins in my town.

It was a few days before Halloween when Alan met me at my Packard in the school's parking lot. Cheerful students were fleeing for home, jocks were suiting up for after school practice, theatre nerds were vocalizing in the auditorium in preparation for their rehearsal of *The Music Man*, marching band nerds were arranging their reeds and flipping their drumsticks, and the anti-extracurricular like myself were starting their engines.

Alan hopped in the passenger seat as I revved the V-8 and fiddled with the radio.

"Shouldn't you be at wrestling?" I asked. Alan was a member of the wrestling team, the most devoted bunch of psycho-jocks in the school. Every day one of them showed up with a chipped tooth or a dislocated shoulder. They were constantly training not only to be proficient at their sport but to make weight. I remember one instance where Alan was trying for a weight class and he was a few pounds over before the weigh-in, so he not only starved himself but he wrapped his body in rubber and sat in a sauna for hours. He'd have pulled out his hair and teeth if it meant making a weigh-in.

We were an odd match for friends. I thought he was bonkers for doing that to himself but it was also part of the reason I liked him. He didn't do anything in small degrees. He was a guy who put everything into whatever stupid thing he was trying to do. Elvis's overplayed single, "Stuck On You," started to play and I quickly reached again for the dial. No Elvis in my car.

"Coach is out," he explained. Well, that was good news, one less day of torture for the wrestling team and one more day to air out their stinky singlets. "So," he continued, whistling his "s," "we need to figure out what we're going to be for Halloween."

"Nothing," I laughed. "What for? Going trick or treating?"

"No," he replied. "There's a party and I need to go so you need to go cause I can't go alone. So we need to figure out costumes."

"Why do you need to go?" I scoffed.

"Drunk girls." His reply was simple, eloquent, and convincing. Enough said.

"Who's throwing the party?" I asked.

Alan hesitated a moment then said, "Everyone's going to be there."

"Okay," not allowing him to dodge the question. "Who's throwing the party?"

"David," he said grudgingly. I looked away. "But look, it's not like it's his party. It's a party that happens to be at his house. It's not *David's* party, it's *the* party. His parents will be away. And everyone's going. So it doesn't have anything to do with him."

"No way," I said as I backed out of my parking spot much more quickly than I should have. "I'm sure there are other parties. Or we could just hang out. Or see a horror movie."

"We can't miss this. We won't miss this." If he hadn't been sitting, Alan would be putting his foot down. "You never want to go to parties."

"*Thirteen Ghosts*," I countered. "It's supposed to be really cool. There are ghosts that you can only see through a special kind of glasses—"

"We can wear whatever you want," Alan was not one to back down. "We don't even have to wear costumes. We can just go."

"—and they give you the glasses at the theatre so you can see the ghosts." In a contest of wills, I usually won. But not necessarily when girls factored into the equation. "You can't see the ghosts without the glasses."

"I don't want to see ghosts," cried Alan, "I want to see boobs, human boobs, and there will be boobs at this party."

"Rosemary DeCamp is in it."

"Rosemary DeCamp is like fifty."

"And Margaret Hamilton."

"The Wicked Witch of the West?" Alan scoffed. "She's even older!"

Alan continued to berate me as we waited in the line of cars trying to exit the parking lot. I rebuffed everything he said, which was not easy since every third sentence somehow incorporated the compelling word, "boobs." It just came down to the simple fact that I hated parties and I hated David. I hated dressing up and looking like an idiot and giving people fodder to make fun of me.

And why would I go to David's house? It's not like I got an invitation. There were better things to do. I went on and on until Alan pulled the trigger on the one thing that gave me pause for thought.

"Julia will be there," he said with finality. "I know that for sure. She was talking about it to Frymouth."

Frymouth was Julia's best friend. Frymouth was Julia's Alan. Her name was really Fran Fremmoth, but the unfortunate thinness of her lips combined with her somewhat jaundiced and oily complexion led to the moniker Frymouth. It had been invented years earlier, no one remembers by whom, and it stuck. Children were cruel. I think the main purpose she served was to perpetually make Julia more attractive by comparison. I had heard that Fran was a dancer, just like Julia, though I don't know if she was any good at it.

We drove in silence. He looked at me expectantly. After an uncomfortable silence during which he stared at me with the saddest blue puppy dog eyes, I finally said, "You're Nixon, I'm Kennedy."

"Why do I have to be Nixon?" he objected.

"Fine, I'll be Roosevelt and you be Hitler."

"That's not funny! David's Jewish."

After a moment of racking my brain, I finally I came up with an idea that would work for the both of us. My dad, as you may recall, had been in the Army Air Force and Alan's had been a Navy man. At fifteen I had roughly the same build my dad had at eighteen when he first enlisted. Alan was a little more muscular than his dad because of the wrestling. Once we dug into their respective chests of memorabilia we found two pretty cool outfits. If my sister was any indication of how girls react to a man in uniform, Julia would be quite smitten.

Dad had mixed feelings when I asked if I could borrow it. First, he was curious about whether it would fit, so he let me try it on. Then he was sort of wistful when he saw me, a younger version of himself, standing there in his tan USAAC jacket and cap. As an officer, he'd begun wearing the olive drab uniform, which was replaced with dress blue when the US Air Force became its own branch in 1947, so dad had plenty of uniforms in his collection. I think he also felt a little patriotic and hopeful for although my mother would have sooner died than allow me to join the army voluntarily and risk my life, my dad wouldn't have minded if I followed in his footsteps. Still, Halloween wasn't the most honorable way to parade his hard-earned stripes. It took a little convincing but in the end he agreed with a smile.

"Don't puke on it," was his only stipulation.

Alan's dad, on the other hand, couldn't care less. "Do whatever the hell you want" was the motto at the Canyon household. I found this out the first time I visited and his father offered me a beer.

And so it came to pass that on Halloween night, Alan Canyon and I, dressed like two soldiers on Fleet Week, arrived at David Bernbaum's household. I looked quite sharp, if I may say so, and Alan's sailor outfit was comically tight. He looked kind of like Daffy Duck, with the buttons stretching and the material agonizingly and futilely trying to contain his wrestler's bulk. I stole a quick glance at the still mysterious mezuzah as we knocked on the door. Party sounds emanated from the house and our knocks went unanswered so we just let ourselves in. Luckily there were no other soldiers walking about, but there were several skeletons, ghosts, vampires, Eisenhowers, Nixons, Russians, Barbies, and even a few party-poopers who opted for no costumes at all. As promised, his parents weren't home and we were left to ourselves.

It was pretty standard party fare as far as I recall. Parties with mostly mid and post-adolescent teens sans parental supervision tended to be the same, at least in my admittedly limited experience. There was the perennial debate: beer before liquor or liquor before beer? Alan professed loudly to anyone who would listen that it didn't matter, the important thing was to drink on an empty stomach so you get your money's worth. There was the "Beer before liquor: never sicker; Liquor before beer: In the clear" contingent. There were the High School sophisticates who drank wine; mostly that was the drama club. Since I hadn't found, at that point, an alcoholic beverage that didn't taste like urine, I drank small amounts of everything that was offered. This resulted in me getting wasted that night and suffering from nausea and headaches all the next day.

Two things happened that Halloween that I regret to this day. First, I found myself in the bathroom. Not so bad, right? Well, I found myself in the bathroom… with Frymouth. I don't know how it happened. I don't even remember talking to her. But we were in there. And her Fry lips were all over mine.

I was snapped out of my oily reverie by a frantic knocking at the door. Someone was calling out "Fran! Fran!"

Finally Frymouth unlatched herself from me and unlocked the bathroom door. "What?!" She called out furiously.

It was Julia, dressed as a cowgirl, and the sight of her was a gust of fresh, cold, flower-and-soap-scented air that caused momentary sobriety. What had I been doing? I bolted from the bathroom, leaving both girls to argue about what had been happening and why.

I got caught up again in the swirl of drunkenness, music, costumes, cigarettes, and dancing. The next thing I remember from that scrapbook of regrets was a shouting match with David. I don't remember what started it, but we were fiercely screaming at each other and drawing a crowd of bizarrely dressed spectators, made all the more peculiar by the dizzying effects of several kinds of alcohol. The more people gathered around the more we both felt obliged to raise the stakes and rip into the other.

"Kick his ass!" Alan shouted above the din, the effect of his fury somewhat diluted by the comic effect of his lisp. "If you don't, I will!"

Alan didn't wait for my response. My faithful terrier was off his leash. Alan assumed a wrestling stance that looked fairly ridiculous in the context of a High School costume party. Then he lunged for David's legs. The brawl escalated and despite my best efforts I was drawn into it. One of the costumed devils must've lost control of his trident because my uniform got skewered. David was pinned in a matter of moments in the most homoerotic of wrestling moves.

Once people started shouting, "Hey! Canyon's raping Bernbaum!" Alan disentangled himself from David, removing his crotch from our host's face, and retreating into the crowd.

The melee was forgotten moments after it began. When I retreated to the backyard to lick my wounds and survey the damage, the fact that my father's uniform had been shredded came crashing down on me. I was going to be in really hot water for that. There was a messy jagged hole all along one side of it. Two of the buttons had torn off and were completely missing, and the entire thing hung open exposing my bare chest. Not only that, but someone had splashed something pungent on it... whiskey or gasoline for all I knew. I couldn't tell which since they both smelled the same to me. So I decided it was time to abandon the party. I couldn't leave without Alan. I searched high and low for him to no avail.

Finally it was Julia who guided me to the bathroom where I had previously lip locked with Frymouth and found Alan in quite the same predicament. That girl wasted no time. Julia and I grabbed our respective friends and exited the Bernbaum household. Before Alan and I left, I pulled Julia aside to say... something. Anything.

I stood before her, my military uniform in tatters, like a soldier after a battle. Looking down I saw tall pointy boots and blue jeans that both collaborated to accentuate her dancer's legs. My gaze travelled all the way up to her pink cowgirl hat. The fourteen different varieties of booze currently battling in my system gave me enough gumption to grab that cowgirl by the waist and kiss her, my partially bared chest pressing against the softness of hers. She let it linger a fraction of a second before pushing me away and slapping me hard across the face.

I stood in silence for a moment, flush with shame, before

she simply said, "You taste like medicine." Her actions made more sense than her words. Medicine? She walked to her car, where Frymouth was weeping loudly for a reason I couldn't quite put together, and she drove away.

I walked Alan back to his house in silence, my soggy mind trying to piece together the evening's events. I was unsure of practically everything except for my redoubled certainty that drinking is completely stupid. Alan took an eternity fumbling for his keys. Once he'd pulled them out of his too-tight sailor pockets, he handed them to me then opened the door, which hadn't been locked in the first place. The whole thing had been an infuriating drunken charade. His parents were out, probably drunker than he was, and he was pretty damn wasted. With one arm over my shoulder and the other hand bracing against the wall, I got him to bed. No sooner did his head touch the pillow than he leaped up from his bed and sprinted towards the bathroom with energy I hadn't seen since he launched himself at David.

He managed to get the door open before vomiting with the force of a Soviet missile. It had roughly the same accuracy because only a small portion of it landed anywhere near the toilet. He doused every pristine inch of his parents' bathroom with a mixture of alcohol, potato chips and stomach acid. Then he stumbled back to bed and fell unconscious.

He was my best friend, but friendship has limits. Since I had no intention of going anywhere near that bathroom, except to close the door, I found a sheet of paper and a thick marker and I wrote "CLEAN THE BATHROOM BEFORE YOUR PARENTS GET HOME, YOU FILTHY DRUNK." I left it by his bed then started my walk home. My parents weren't like Alan's. They'd be home. Not only would they be home but they'd be awake, and since I should've been home an hour ago, they'd be pissed.

I was right on every account, except that my sister was still out at the party. She was slightly older, but a girl, and therefore our curfews balanced out. I got home first, which should have put me in a better position, except that they were in a yelling mood and I was the only one there to bear the brunt. My father immediately saw what I'd done to his uniform and he shouted till his voice was hoarse. He also forcefully stripped it off me and pushed it into mom's arms, continuing to yell as I stood there in my underwear. My punishment became hers when she was compelled, after midnight, to go to the basement and start up her Sears Roebuck Kenmore Washer. It was the same one from 1951 but it still washed a mean load of laundry. She set about cleaning the uniform probably to escape my father's rage but also to "stop the stains from setting in."

The booze in my system, the sting of Julia's slap, the lingering taste of Frymouth, the smell of Alan's vomit, all of it made me fairly immune to my father's ranting. I could deal with it tomorrow. Since they were determined to wait up for Joan and give her what-for, I left his ferocity downstairs and crashed on my bed.

CHAPTER 21

LAS VEGAS IN 1960 had precisely nothing to offer a non-gambler under the supervision of his parents. So it came to pass that, as part of a larger punishment plan earned by our Halloween transgressions, Joan and I were made to accompany our parents to Sin City. It was partially punishment for Joan's behavior as well, since she got home hours after her curfew and she smelled like smoke and booze, though she insisted she hadn't been smoking or drinking. Our parents hopped up on the cross and professed that they couldn't trust their children to be home alone because they'd throw parties and destroy the house or some such nonsense like that. Actually, it was probably true. Despite my aversion to parties, the idea of hosting one appealed to my latent delight at being the center of things.

Dad had a business trip scheduled and mom wanted to go with him. He almost never brought her when he went away for business so this was truly a unique occasion. Mom's brother, Uncle Bertram Llewellyn, was going to be in Las Vegas for the same meeting my father had to attend. He worked for BERN, the particle physics laboratory in Switzerland, and my father had been a military liaison for Lab Majorana in Chicago.

There was some facility in Nevada that was opening or closing or whatever. Oddly enough, mom let slip that she didn't want to see her brother, but dad was insistent. He thought it was a good idea for them to reconcile. Come to think of it, among my relatively large collection of uncles, Bertram was one that I couldn't remember ever having met. Dad had his conference and his mission to bring mom and Bertram together, and since he wouldn't dare leave us alone in the house, we all piled into the car and drove hundreds of miles in the age before iPods.

It was a grueling journey, made worse by the knowledge that that weekend, Joan and I would both have to miss another pivotal party. What sort of trouble would happen in my absence? How many teenage trysts? How many fights? How many alliances against me? What sort of trouble would Alan get into? Who would David turn against me? I stared out the window and watched the landscape transform from green to gray, from lush to dry, from alive to dead. Time after time we stopped to refill the tank, stretch our legs, and brave the gas station bathrooms. Joan sat next to me and occasionally wrote in her diary. She'd started keeping it with her at all times, precautions against my prying eyes. Not that I was particularly interested anymore. If I wanted to know her secrets all I'd have to do is keep my ears open for rumors. I bet there were forty pages devoted to her heartbreak when Keith left for Vietnam, and forty more pages about forty other boys who took his place. That would be a sappy romance novel worse than anything I could be assigned in school.

Mom was cheerful. The fetters shackling her to the stove and laundry machine had been cut and she was off on an adventure, albeit with her kids in tow. My father made it clear that once we checked into the Tropicana that Joan and

I would be confined to the room. Furthermore, if we ordered room service instead of eating the sandwiches mom packed for us, then we'd have to hell to pay.

After what felt like an eternity we pulled up along Las Vegas Boulevard to the glitzy hotel, only three years old at the time. It stood out in stark contrast to the rows of dusty pastel cars that lined the street and the squat gambling halls that surrounded it. Dad navigated the Packard up to the opulent entrance, beaming as he stepped from the car.

Moments later, we drove away. Dad refused to hand his keys to the valet so he set off in search of free parking.

"Bull," he said. "Why would I pay someone to park my car? I can park it myself. We're in the middle of a goddamn desert; it's not like space is at a premium."

After nearly an hour of driving around in circles looking for a non-existent free parking spot, dad once again pulled up in front of the hotel and grudgingly handed his keys to that same valet. It was dusk by the time we dropped our luggage in the two-bed hotel room. My sister and I looked at the bed situation and simultaneously cried, "No way!"

"Mom!" Joan cried.

"Dad!" I protested.

"Shut up," he declared percussively. And that was that.

"Now listen," he continued. "You two are here for a punishment. You're not here to have fun. And you won't have fun. Not if I can help it. But you *are* here. And it's almost time for… well—" Was my father actually smirking? What nefarious fatherly secret was bringing him joy at our expense? "—there's something you may as well see."

Despite our prodding, that's all he would say. Even my mom didn't seem know what he had in store for us. He had us follow him out to the elevator, which we rode to the top floor of the hotel. On the penthouse level there was another set of stairs leading to the roof. There was a deck, which gave us a 360-degree view of Las Vegas and the surrounding deserts and mountains. The "Garden Tower" terrace, it was called, and it was spectacular. Despite it being November, it was warm and dry up there. In the center there was an unattended tiki bar and stools. Dad took a minute to orient himself before he pointed and declared, "South."

We looked in that direction, at hundreds of miles of nothingness, and we stared. "You may not have a chance to see this again," he said, a smile creeping across his face. "Damn international treaties with weaker countries are going to push all this underground. Oh, it'll keep going on, you can be sure of that. But we'll have to keep it quiet starting in a year or so."

"What are we looking for?" I asked.

"Just watch," he said, calmly.

So we did and we waited. And waited. And waited until my feet were sore from standing. Mom pulled over a tiki stool. Joan stared up at the clear sky, probably daydreaming about Keith or one of his clones. I leaned on the rail, wishing I was back at home so I could try to smooth things over with Julia. She must've thought I was a terrible person for kissing Frymouth and then for grabbing and kissing her that same night outside David's house. It was not something that made me proud. Just as I began to get lost in the memory, there was a flash of light on the horizon. A giant geyser of ash and smoke spewed into the sky and bloomed outward.

At the very same moment that I realized I was seeing my first mushroom cloud, the entire building began to shake. It felt like an earthquake and from that height I could really feel the tall building sway.

"Almost one megaton," my father said, proudly, "one of the largest detonations in the Nevada Test Site."

My mother, on the other hand, was appalled, and took a step back. "I didn't know they test those things so close to where people live. What about the radioactive fallout?" She continued to inch back towards the stairs, as though a few feet would make any kind of difference if her fears proved well founded.

"That's about one hundred miles away, sweetheart," he said. "Perfectly safe, unless you're some poor schmuck who took a wrong turn in the desert." He laughed, quite excited by the sight, and I was absorbing his enthusiasm like radioactive fallout. "The wind might carry some gunk this way but it'll be no more radiation than you kids get from sitting in front of the television all day."

My mom and my sister joined me at the rail. My dad came up behind us and put his arms around the whole family. We all continued to watch in silence as the cloud ballooned outward. Dad, noting his family's rapt attention and not one to waste an opportunity to lecture, continued his narration.

"This is nothing," he said. His voice rang with passion. "Castle Bravo. 1954. We were in the Pacific Proving Grounds in the Marshall Islands. It was the first deployable dry-fuel hydrogen bomb and we didn't really know what to expect. It detonated at fifteen megatons, twice as powerful as we predicted, a thousand times more powerful than Hiroshima. Li-7 was supposed to be inert in the deuterium-tritium fusion but it sure wasn't. That bomb decimated the atolls, set fires twenty nautical miles away. It was a beauty."

That was probably the most I had ever heard my father speak about anything before. It was rare for him to talk at all, much less to go on about his cloak-and-dagger military work. I hadn't heard him talk so technically about anything since our discussion about the mechanics of the football draft. I didn't quite understand most of what he said, but that just made it all the more enticing. I decided to try to incite a little more talk from this strange and stirring man my father had suddenly become.

"Is that why they test in Nevada now? Because the Islands were destroyed?" I asked.

He laughed. "No. We're still testing in the Pacific. The poor saps that lived nearby can't live there anymore so now we have more freedom to do… Whatever we want." He paused for a moment, considering whether or not to continue. I gave him my rapt attention and wide eyes, hoping that would keep up his momentum.

It worked. "Two years ago," he continued, still looking out at the billowing mushroom cloud, which by now looked like a giant ashen tree with a rapidly lengthening trunk. There was a hushed quality to his voice, which made it all seem that much more important. "Operation Hardtack. You'd know about it if you'd read a newspaper once in a while. It wouldn't kill you, you know. It was top-secret for a while but you can't keep something like that under wraps forever. We detonated thirty-five weapons. Crazy new designs. With this ban on the horizon, we don't have much time left for open air testing so our labs are pushing out all sorts of things. A lot of them fizzled, but some of them were beauties: airborne, underwater, missile-born. Each mushroom cloud looks different. You'll never see another one like this again." He gestured to the horizon.

I silently hoped I wouldn't *ever* see a mushroom cloud again, period. Despite the novelty of witnessing a controlled desert test from the luxury of a Vegas hotel, most people of my generation had a fear of nuclear explosions that rattled us to the core. Anyone that ever had to practice hiding under a school desk when the warning sirens blared inevitably had an unpleasant and sobering realization: nothing would protect you, certainly not a flimsy desk. Like it or not, we were completely at the mercy of the politicians who had their itchy trigger fingers on big red buttons.

My father, however, was on a roll. "And at the same time those thirty-five firecrackers were popping in the Pacific we were running Operation Argus off the radar. About a thousand miles off Cape-town, a Navy task force with nine ships launched three nuclear missiles into the atmosphere, creating the first atmospheric radiation belt."

And a partridge in a pear tree. I had no idea what he was talking about. Radiation belt? Sounds like a superhero accessory. Captain Fabulous dons his Cape of Wonders and his Radiation Belt! That would be a good comic book. I had actually heard about Operation Argus. Not from the papers but I distinctly remember a TV anchor discussing it at some point. To me it just sounded like the Russians could destroy our atmosphere as readily as we could destroy theirs.

"Can we go to dinner?" Joan finally weighed into the conversation. "I'm starving."

My father snapped out of his nuclear reverie, finally looking away from the dissipating cloud. "Your mother and I are meeting your Uncle Bertram for dinner. You and your brother can eat in the room. And don't leave or I'll know about it. Don't think I won't."

Despite not having seen our uncle since I was too young to remember, mom and dad abandoned us in the room and went to eat somewhere exciting on the strip, leaving us with flattened boloney sandwiches and warm coke to sustain us. At least there was a television so Joan and I didn't have to make conversation. I amused myself by reading through the room service menu and examining a magazine that boasted about all the exciting things to do in the greater Las Vegas area that we would not be allowed to try.

With nothing exciting on TV, and having read everything available in the room, I drifted off to sleep on one of the two comfortable hotel beds. I woke an hour later when Joan shoved me out of the bed. Blocking the narrow space between the dresser and the two full-size beds was a tiny metal cot, the sort of uncomfortable device you might expect in a prison cell.

"I called down for it," she said, proudly. "It's for you."

I was too tired to argue so I rolled onto the springy thing and dreamt of endlessly expanding mushroom clouds.

CHAPTER 22

D AD WOKE US up early, escorted us to the free
breakfast buffet where we were encouraged to stuff
our faces quickly with burnt toast, jelly, soggy fruit,
and some bitter liquid vaguely reminiscent of orange juice,
then he piled us into the car. I didn't know what he was planning but I didn't really care. It would be over soon enough and
we would be on our way back home.

He drove for about an hour and a half into the desert,
which piqued my curiosity but I remained silent. It was better to let the drama play out however my dad had planned
it. Air conditioning in a car was still a somewhat new concept at that time, and while the option was available when
dad bought the Packard, it was an expensive upgrade. For
the man who refused to valet park his car, you can imagine
that he would likewise refuse a luxury like a Frigidaire system inside his automobile. "Takes up too much trunk space!"
he said, when I pointed out how much nicer this trip would
be if he had splurged on it. With our windows cracked, a mixture of sweltering air and the occasional granule of sand circu-
lated throughout the cabin. Finally, he pulled up at the edge of
a precipice and we all stepped out to stretch our legs.

"This is a subsidence crater," he declared, proudly. "There are hundreds of these around here. Each one was a nuclear detonation."

"Dad," I asked, my patience having long since been sweated out, "where are we going?"

"Here!" he enthusiastically replied. "I wanted you to see this. You all seemed interested last night."

"We drove all this way to see a stupid hole in the ground?" I spoke impulsively. That was a moment where the ability to think before I spoke might have been an asset, because my father seemed a little hurt by my glib dismissal of an activity that he obviously though was profound. So I shut my mouth and took in the sight.

It looked as if God had pulled his Godly ice-cream scoop out of his Godly drawer in his Holy Kitchen and taken a goodly scoop from out the earth. The crater was smooth, and the stone within had a dusky reddish hue, like blood. The incline wasn't so steep that a person couldn't enter the crater, and that's just what Joan attempted. I'm not sure what possessed her to do it, as she's not normally impulsive or adventurous, but I wouldn't have the chance to ask. Like Alice following a rabbit, she descended into the pit. She was probably just curious. I might have done the same, but she beat me to it. I supposed there was nothing inherently dangerous about the site or it would have been cordoned off. My father, who was no doubt informed in these matters, didn't seem overly concerned as Joan explored.

The redness of the stone was kind of unique and really, how many people could say they've stood at ground zero of a nuclear explosion? I considered following her in.

Two or three careful steps down into the crater and she

tumbled down, as if her legs had given out. Her body limp, she began to roll down the steep incline. My mother shrieked and my father and I began to run after her.

"Stay back!" My father pushed me backwards, not wanting to have to rescue two of his children instead of one.

He carefully edged his way into the crater, almost to the bottom where Joan had come to a silent rest in a position that looked agonizing, cheek pressed against the earth. He knelt by her for a moment as my mom shouted, "Is she okay? Is she okay!?"

Finally, he picked her up, cradling her in his arms, and began sidestepping his way up out of the crater. He had trouble towards the top where things got steeper and I had to help. I reached out to take Joan from him.

As I leaned over and took her I felt a wave of dizziness and nausea pass over me. I hadn't been aware of my fear of heights, but what else could it be? I felt immediately better as I left the ledge and carried my sister to the car while my dad made his way up. She was unconscious but breathing, and her normally impeccable clothes were covered in the red dust from the crater. Her face was bruised and scraped. She had deep scratches on her forehead and cheeks, which were both speckled with drops of blood and caked with the red dust. There may have been something broken or internal injuries but we couldn't tell. There weren't any bumps on her head so it didn't seem as though she'd tripped and been knocked unconscious. It looked more like she fainted while climbing and then simply slid down to the bottom, getting cut and bruised along the way.

We quickly piled into the Packard, mom in the backseat with Joan, and dad peeled away. He drove like a maniac.

On the desert roads so close to a nuclear testing site there was nobody to stop him from speeding. Finally, after perhaps a half an hour of my mother fussing over Joan, we pulled up at a simple one-story brick building surrounded by an unremarkable link fence. I had assumed we were heading back to Vegas, but lacking any directional skills I really had no idea where we were. I supposed it made sense that my dad was familiar with the area and would take us to the closest place where he could find help.

Wherever we had arrived, it was a shorter drive than to the city. The building was fairly squat and inconspicuous, constructed of cinderblocks and surrounded by a tall fence with barbed wire. There were a few vehicles parked outside and some antennae and satellite dishes on top. I also took notice of the preponderance of security cameras and uniformed guards patrolling the perimeter.

"Medic!" my dad cried as he stepped out, holding open his wallet as two unfriendly looking military men approached carrying M14 service rifles. They checked his credential then one of them spoke in his walkie-talkie while my dad opened the rear door and lifted my sister out of the car. Two more men in the same uniform came out wheeling a gurney and in a matter of moments she was ushered inside, followed by my dad, who left my mom and I instructions to stay outside in the sweltering desert heat.

We waited silently, dazed, under the watchful eye of the soldiers that had greeted us. It seemed like an eternity before he returned, accompanied by a portly balding gentleman who was severely over-dressed for this climate. Who wears a three-piece suit in the desert?

"Bert!" mom cried, running into his arms and squeezing

him tightly. "Thank goodness. How is she?" I suddenly realized that the stranger she was hugging was my uncle. He was an aged version of a man I remember seeing in our photo albums.

"A little the worse for wear, I'm afraid, mostly bumps and scratches. Come in and see her." I had become so accustomed to my mom's fading British accent that I barely noticed it, but his voice rang of Brit like Big Ben. It was a rich, unapologetically upper class sound, dancing from high to low pitch in an instant.

Once inside, soldiers restricted our path and flanked us so we could only go directly to the infirmary. As we were hurried down the stark white hallway I peeked down an intersecting corridor and saw what appeared to be a giant freight elevator with some fierce metal doors. I tugged on my dad's shirt and asked, "What is this place?"

"It belongs to your uncle's company." He spoke with an air of finality; that was all he would say on the subject, though I desperately wanted to ask why a company outpost in the desert would be guarded by military. I took the hint and followed them into a small room that held two beds and an array of medical equipment. Joan was bandaged and immobile, but overall she looked like she was resting comfortably. Mom fussed with the pillows and inspected the bandages while dad spoke quietly with the doctor and my uncle at the door. They began to raise their voices and I saw my uncle take my father by the arm and pull him farther down the hallway. I'd never seen anybody assert himself over my father in that way before, with the possible exception of my mother when she insisted he take her to the theatre. It was disconcerting. The voices rose to shouts and a guard shut the door, isolating us in the infirmary and muffling the details of the argument. Finally, dad returned looking extremely ruffled and announced that we were leaving.

He seemed reticent as he said, "Bertram and I both agree that Joan should stay here for the time being. Moving her might not be safe, and the doctor can look after her. He'll call us when she wakes up."

My mom ferociously leapt into the battle, pointing an accusatory finger at his face. "Don't you dare. You swore... You swore!"

What had he sworn? This situation had become as intriguing as it was frightening.

"Yes," he replied, "but circumstances..."

"Don't," she said with finality. "You swore that my brother would never be alone with either of them!"

I couldn't make any sense of what she was saying. Was there a more sinister reason why Joan and I hadn't been allowed to join them at dinner last night? Was Uncle Bert's conspicuous absence from our lives on purpose? It seemed too far-fetched. I supposed she was overwhelmed at that moment and talking incoherently, although now I know better.

*

She took a deep breath and slowly said, "I am absolutely, positively not leaving her side. We will stay here until she wakes up."

My father simply shook his head. So mom continued on, "I *will* be by my daughter's side when she wakes up. Is that clear? I'm not leaving her in this *place*." She spat that last part with disgust. Did she know more about this desert building than she let on?

Dad took her rigid hand and tried to soften it between

two of his. "It's not really my choice. This is a sensitive facility and we can't stay here. We just can't."

"Bertram!" my mother marched towards the hallway where her brother waited. She pointed her finger at him and said with finality. "I am not leaving my daughter here."

"She'll have the best care," he said in a soothing tone. "You needn't worry at all. The moment she wakes we'll bring you back, or we can fly her back home."

"Bollocks. Not an option, Bertram. I won't leave this building and I certainly won't leave Nevada without my daughter."

The argument continued and the entire thing began to feel wrong. Why would Uncle Bert insist on us leaving? Why couldn't we just take Joan with us? Just what was this mysterious place, so inconspicuous and small and yet so heavily guarded? A random little outpost staffed with doctors and soldiers... The whole thing made no sense whatsoever.

It had been quite some time since I'd used my special ability, but I began to consider whether this might be the right moment to break my vow. I swear that it was motivated by concern for my sister and my mother, not by anything malicious or by self-serving curiosity or personal gain, which I'll admit is my usual modus operandi. For the good of my family I needed to find out what secrets this building was hiding. If Uncle Bert was making us leave for our own good, then I would help convince mom. If, on the other hand, there wasn't a good reason for us to leave then I could jump into the fray on her side. I needed to understand.

Things were moving too fast so I slowed them down.

CHAPTER 23

O R, TO BE precise, I tried to. Rather than frozen family, motionless guards, and unlimited license to explore, I felt a strange and violent wrenching sensation and then I witnessed my surroundings transform.

Wallpaper yellowed and peeled in what looked like an amateur stop motion video. Glass cracked inaudibly to let dry gusts of wind blow around the thin layer of sand that covered the once pristine floors. The oxygen tank was still there but rust sprouted around the knobs. One gurney overturned and the other simply disappeared. My mother, my sister, my uncle, the guards… They all vanished, too.

I knew immediately what must have happened, but I didn't know why. Not that anybody really knows the rules to this, but I thought it only should have been possible if Joan and I had tried to do this at the exact same time. She had been completely unconscious. There was no way, no conceivable circumstance where that could've happened, right? Unless she had woken up in that instant and tried to accelerate. I also wondered what would have happened if she had accelerated before being knocked out and remained in that state while unconscious. If that were the case, then why hadn't she leapt forward with me? With all signs pointing to impossibility, the fact remained: whatever had caused our mysterious disappearance all those years ago had happened again to me.

I was petrified. How much time had passed? How many weeks or months? Where was my family? What must they have thought when I vanished in plain sight? If they had left Las Vegas, how the hell was I going to get home? I think I had about six dollars and change in my pocket, which was really quite a lot back then, certainly enough for a bus ticket, not that I had ever ridden a bus before. Perhaps solo travel shouldn't be that imposing for a fifteen-year-old that was almost his father's height, but I had been pretty sheltered by my understandably overprotective parents. These and a million other inane thoughts passed through my head as I turned around and found the door ajar. Sand had piled up, a small dune keeping the door from serving its one purpose. I walked out into the hallway and meekly called out, "Hello?"

I wasn't surprised that there was no answer. The place looked abandoned. My voice sounded small, sucked up by the sand and the sinking fear of being alone.

"Hello!" I cried again, louder this time. Not even an echo in response. I stepped through the front door out into the bright desert sunlight. No cars, no guards, no family… Nothing for miles.

A phone. If I could find a phone then dad could come get me.

No, I didn't reach into my pocket. Lest you forget, this was decades before cellphones made this kind of situation a foreign one. I went back into the building and turned down another hallway that had previously been blocked by burly guards. There was what must once have been a front office: a dingy desk, a lamp, empty filing cabinets with drawers hanging open, a single golf club, some road maps and phone books, and a stainless steel Presto! coffee percolator. I flipped the light switch but nothing happened. No electricity. No phone. Nothing.

I went back down the hallway and this time I hung a right down that intersecting corridor I'd noticed on my way in. There were those same two giant metal doors, but they were welded shut. Had it been an elevator? A vault? I couldn't tell. It was a mausoleum now, sealed for eternity.

There was a normal sized door at the end of that hall but it was barred as well, boarded up. I went back into the office and grabbed that golf club. Wielding it like a sledgehammer I wailed on the boards for several exhausting minutes to no avail. Then I inserted the handle into a gap in the boards and used it as a pry bar. With great effort they came loose, one by one, until I had exposed a door: a locked door.

Nothing makes me want to get into a room more than locking me out of it. I was determined. I went back to the infirmary, heaved the heavy metal oxygen tank onto the gurney and rolled it toward the offending door. I took a running start and pushed my homemade missile across the hall, bursting the door off its hinges and sending door and tank careening down a flight of stairs. I couldn't stop my forward inertia and I, too, slid down the stairway, riding the gurney along a steep incline until I slammed to a halt at the first landing. None the worse for wear, I dizzily climbed back up the stairs and in the light that spilled from the hallway above I could make out a switch.

Fortunately, this part of the building must have had a separate power supply, some old battery that hadn't quite died yet. The fluorescents grudgingly flickered enough for me to continue down the stairs. I descended deeper and deeper, and the air around me cooled to a chill. That was an improvement, at least. I paused to look up at all the distance I had covered; climbing back up would be a chore. Finally, I ended up in some sort of control room. Whatever equipment used to live there had long since been torn from the walls, leaving only frayed wires and twisted metal braces. Vast consoles were empty, devoid of the myriad buttons and displays that must once have lit up the room like Christmas. There was a fire extinguisher, an old cabinet stocked with canned food, and even some magazines. There was also a broad window taking up most of an entire wall that was so grimy I couldn't tell what was on the other side of it.

Well, it wasn't as if anyone was around to object, so I tapped into what remained of my earlier impulsive self and picked up the fire extinguisher then hurled it through the glass. It shattered with a startling crash. I climbed through, carefully avoiding the protruding shards, and found the meat of the place: a vast service tunnel that seemed to go on forever. Aluminum tubes and copper wiring lined the sides of the wide passage and in the center was a thick pipe that ran the length of the tunnel. I began making my way down the tunnel, but piles of detritus made it a difficult path to traverse and I soon turned back. On my way back to the control room I realized that there was an almost imperceptible arc to the tunnel and I began to suspect that the entire thing was one giant circle.

It would be several years before I understood what I had seen that day, and then only because I found a working one: a vast, complex, incredible work of man that vastly overshadowed that prototype I'd smashed my way into in the Nevada desert.

With nothing pressing to do, as I was incontrovertibly

alone and miles from another soul, I took a moment to pull out a can from the cabinet in the control room. It was simply labeled, "Meat." *I like meat*, I thought. Luckily there was also a can-opener. I removed the top and couldn't begin to identify what animals had died to create that grayish matter. I was hungry and sans fork, so I scooped out the salty substance with my fingers and had a disgusting little picnic. With a full stomach, I filled my pockets with more cans of mystery meat and began my arduous trek back up the stairs. In the front office I spread out the maps on the dingy desk and tried to orient myself. If my interpretation could be trusted (I have always had a terrible sense of direction) I was at least fifty miles from Las Vegas, but once I found the main road I'd surely be able to find someone to give me a ride. I wished I had paid more attention on the way there.

So I started walking, fully conscious that at any moment a military research bomb could go nuclear in my face. I must've made it a good five miles before I had to crack open a can of Progresso and drink it down. This was the sort of soup that was supposed to be mixed with a can of water, so it tasted like thick salty paste, repulsive, but at least it was something to replace the buckets I had already sweated out.

Three cans later, having soaked through my clothes and baked my skin to a bright red, I finally found the highway. It seemed that all of mankind had the sense to avoid driving on such a hot day. Not a single car went by for an hour as I walked. On the horizon, heat caused the black pavement to shimmer and intermingle with the pale blue sky, even when I squinted to get a better look.

Finally, a car approached. I stuck out my thumb and I

guess there's nothing too threatening about a teenage boy in the middle of the desert because it actually pulled over.

"Please," I said with parched throat, "can you give me a lift to the next town. I need to find a phone."

"Sure thing, partner," a kindly looking man with high cheekbones and a cleft chin smiled at me. "Looks like you've been through a wringer. Hop on in."

I joined him in what I realized was a kind of car that I'd never seen before. "Nice ride," I said, as he eased back onto the road. "What is it?"

It was a small, bright red, three-door hatchback. I was grateful that it was nice and cool inside the car. This guy had sprung for the Frigidaire in his fancy little red automobile. I gratefully inhaled the processed air and relaxed into the bucket seat, which I noted was covered in some kind of shaggy tan carpet. Strange. The radio quietly sang an unfamiliar tune and the clock… There was something strange about the clock… Instead of hands it had numbers, like you might see on a flip-flap display at a train station. This one seemed to omit some light, like a tiny television.

"What is this?" I pointed at the clock.

"Honda Accord," he said, indifferently. "Ya like it?"

Honda… I'd seen ads for a Honda Dream before. It was a dinky Japanese motorcycle and it was bright red. I didn't know they made cars, too. "Yeah," I said, "I like it, but what's this?" I tapped on the clock.

"What do you mean?"

"The clock."

"What, are you one of them analog fans?" he asked with a smile. "You can get that on this car, but it's not for me. Quartz digital all the way. On my wrist, too." He presented his wrist and strapped to it was a similar device in miniature.

I paled as a sinking feeling grew in the pit of my stomach and I reluctantly asked. "What, uh… What year is the car?"

"Brand spankin' new!" he grinned.

"Oh." That didn't help. "So it's a…" I let the silence linger.

He raised an eyebrow and said, "It's a 1979."

1979.

I took a slow, deep breath as I did some of the most unpleasant math of my life.

I had been gone for nineteen years.

PART III

CHAPTER 24

1979 WAS A portentous year, to say the least. I was never one to stay up at night worrying about ghosts or omens, but it's hard to completely dismiss the preternatural when you yourself are capable of something so completely out of the ordinary. On February 7th, Pluto moved inside Neptune's orbit for the first time in known history. Also in space, the U.S. Voyager was giving us our first look at Jupiter's rings, NASA's Skylab began its return to earth after six years in orbit, and Columbia, the first functional space shuttle orbiter, sat on the tarmac ready to be launched. On February 18th of that year, it snowed in the Sahara desert. A few days later there was a total solar eclipse and Los Angeles passed a bill ensuring rights for homosexuals. There was a tsunami, a coup, a hostage crisis, a Michael Jackson album, and *Star Trek: The Motion Picture*.

And 1979 had something that 1978 didn't have: me. I was sitting in a 1979 Honda Accord being driven to the city of Las Vegas. The driver's name was Duffy. He professed to be some kind of professional gambler, a career option that nobody had bothered mentioning to me in High School. Having come from a world of crazy eights and stickball I couldn't begin to follow the games and strategies he described with such enthusiasm.

"Nah, it's just about knowin' the odds. Important thing is you gotta know 'em when other people don't. If you're smarter than the guy next to you, and patient, you'll clean 'em out. It's the weekend folk, the dads, honeymooners, bachelor party dudes, they stop by Vegas and drop their money in my pocket. I always think, why bother wastin' time at the table, just write me a check!" He laughed and I grinned sheepishly, completely in the dark.

"Where you want me to drop you in Vegas?" Duffy asked. His modest southern twang put me at ease for some reason. It sounded friendly in a moment when I really needed it.

I thought for a moment. "The Tropicana," I said. It seemed as good a place as any to start and for the life of me I couldn't think of a single other specific place I knew about in Las Vegas. Of course it was unlikely that anybody I knew would be there, but it was the only place I knew for hundreds of miles. I had to find my mom, my dad, and my sister. I had to find answers. Lacking any direction, I figured I would start with someplace familiar.

At least, I thought it would be familiar, until Duffy pulled up in front of the site of my family's vacation, nineteen years ago. The building we'd pulled away from in 1960 had been pretty big compared to its surroundings, but it was still a relatively small, compact casino hotel. If what I'd left was kind of a classy, "Dean Martin" suave, where I'd arrived was "Tito Puente" all the way. Duffy had brought me to a monstrous edifice, a shrine to everything bright and tacky. It filled my entire field of vision and I had to crane my neck to try to see the tops of the many attached buildings. "This is… huge!" I declared. "What happened?"

"Well," Duffy explained, "over there you've got the Paradise Tower. That was finished just a few months ago. Twenty-one floors of guest rooms and suites. And over there is the Tiffany Tower, with twenty-two floors. Now, if you ask me, that's the one you want. Not quite as new, but that one connects to the Tiffany Theatre where they show the Follies Bergere."

"Bair chair?" I asked.

"Yup," Duffy agreed. "Do you like French Girls?"

I really didn't know what to say to that. To date the most exotic female I had ever met was my British mom.

"You like French girls," Duffy answered for me. "Everyone likes French girls. We're talkin' feathers. We're talkin' sequins. We're talkin' music, drinks, and just enough tail for you to shake your stick at."

"Oh." I was so completely lost. I pasted a look on my face that I'd perfected in school, the one where a teacher asks you a question and you look like you understand but need time to think, when in fact you'd been daydreaming and have no idea what's happening. Usually it would buy you enough time for one of the nerds in the class to volunteer an answer and pull you out of the hot seat.

"Check it out. You could pass for eighteen," he whispered. "Just walk in confidently, nobody'll question ya." Great. I was getting advice on how to get into some bair-chair girly show when what I really needed was my family, a plane ticket home and a time machine to go back to 1960.

"Well, thanks Duffy," I said as I exited his car. "I appreciate it."

"No problem. I'll probably take a turn at the Tropicana

tables tonight, so maybe I'll bump into ya. Just listen for the sounds of winnin'! You'll find me." His little Japanese future-mobile rolled away from the casino and I was once again on my own.

I walked through the front entrance, now more opulent and flashy than before. Where there had been walls now there were great open passages leading from tower to tower, from casino to casino. Business was booming and everywhere I craned my neck I could see tightly dressed cocktail servers peddling drinks and cigarettes, men in sharp suits at table games and chubby sunburned tourists in Hawaiian t-shirts lugging around buckets of nickels from slot to slot. Just past the check-in desk in the grand lobby I found a row of telephone booths. I sealed myself inside one, carefully pushing away a dangerously full ashtray and fishing a dime from my pocket.

I called home.

One ring. Two rings. Fear and suspense. What would I say? How would I explain? Perhaps I was making a bad decision. What would you do in this situation? It didn't matter. I just needed to find them, and they could punish me, and we'd get on with our lives.

At long last, someone answered. "Allo!" This was not a familiar voice.

"Hi, who is this?" I asked.

"C'est très grossier, appeler quelqu'un et demander son nom avant de dire le vôtre!" An incomprehensible female voice shouted at me. "Who are you? Est-ce la putain qui baise mon mari? Vas vous faire enculez."

After a moment of silence, whomever I was speaking to hung up on me. I knew one thing for certain: my parents had moved. I could call directory assistance, but my last name was fairly common. How long would it take to call everyone on the list? How many dimes did I have in my pocket? No, directory assistance wasn't a good place to start. Who else could I call? I hate to admit it, but the list of phone numbers I had memorized was quite small. I didn't know my grandma and granddad's number, even if they had managed to hold on for nineteen more years. I didn't know my aunt and uncle's numbers.

Then I thought about my friend Alan. I threw in another dime and dialed.

A woman answered. "Hello?"

"Hi, is Alan there?"

"Alan?" I could hear a smile of recognition in her voice. "No, he lives in upstate New York now!"

"Is this Mrs. Canyon?" I asked.

"Yes, dear."

"I'm an old friend of his but I lost touch. Would you mind giving me his number?"

She obliged. Luckily there were Keno pencils everywhere so I wrote the number down on a ticket and said goodbye. I didn't immediately dial the number she gave me. I tucked it in my pocket and picked up the phone again, lest I forget the digits that suddenly came to mind.

It had been years since I called David. In fact, the last time I saw him we came to blows. We hadn't been friends for a long time but his number was apparently still chiseled into my brain. If there was anyone in the world I could talk to about this, it would be him. I had already confided in him once before. It hadn't worked out all that well, but at least I wouldn't have to explain the part about being able to move super fast, and he'd be likely to believe that this wasn't some crazy hoax.

The phone rang once and a woman picked up, "Hello?"

"Mrs. Bernbaum?" I asked.

"Yes?" I paused for a moment. The voice didn't have Mrs. Bernbaum's husky depth. It was still somehow familiar. Very familiar.

"Can I speak to David, please?"

"Whom shall I say is calling?" The voice was nasal, slightly shrill, and unpleasant. A name was on the tip of my tongue.

"Uh…" Being in Vegas, I thought it best to keep my cards close to my chest. "It's about work."

"Hold on."

David picked up the phone, and at that moment I realized. "Fran! That was Fran!"

"Yes…" David replied, slowly.

"Frymouth? Mrs. Bernbaum…" And I put the pieces together.

"Oh my God," I laughed. "You married Frymouth!"

"Who the hell is this?" he spat, and I began to fear that he might hang up before I had the chance to enlist his aid.

"David, it's me," I said.

"That doesn't answer my question." His voice didn't sound all that different.

"For God's sake David, don't you recognize my voice?" I asked. "Please don't tell me you're still jealous because I can do it and you can't. You've had nineteen years to get over that. And I don't think you ever really appreciated that I used it to give *both* of us the answers on that test."

Silence followed and I was afraid he'd hung up. "David?" I asked. Silence. "Hello?"

"Let me go to the study," he said. "I hope you know you're calling at dinner time."

I heard him excuse himself from the table and an annoyed nasal voice scolded him in the background. "Seriously, David? Right now? The roast will get cold!" How could I have ever gotten drunk enough to make out with someone who sounded like that? I've never known anybody who could stretch out vowels and make ordinary words sound quite so unappealing as Fran.

A huskier voice came to his defense, "Leave him alone! It's business." There it was! There was the Mrs. Bernbaum I knew!

"Your mom's there, too!" I cried.

"Just a second…" he said.

"Wait… Do you live with your mother? Still?" I laughed.

"It's *her* house," he retorted. "We're just over all the time for dinner. We live next door." He always was a momma's boy, but with the quality of Mrs. Bernbaum's cooking I guess I wouldn't have moved too far, either.

"What about your dad?" I asked.

"My dad," he said, once he had shut out the sounds of his bickering mother and wife, "he passed. So Fran and I take care of my mom… Or she takes care of us. This is crazy. Where are you? What happened to you? Everyone thinks you're dead."

"I'm in Las Vegas," I said, simply. "At the Tropicana."

"Las Vegas… That's where you… That's where they lost you…" He tried to piece things together.

"Listen," I said, wondering how much conversation time a dime bought you in 1979, "you remember what happened when my sister and I disappeared for a couple of months?"

"Yeah, and you fed me all that bull about…"

"Oh shut up, David, you and I both know it wasn't bull—"

He tried to interrupt, "If you called just to play games—"

"David!" I shouted, perhaps a little too loudly, as a couple of tourists passing through the lobby looked at me strangely. "Please, please, just hear me out, please. I'm scared, I'm alone, and I don't have anyone else I can talk to right now. You're the only person who knows what I can do, who knows for a fact that this is *not* a joke or a hoax. So let's drop all that, please. I proved it to you over and over again *and* I helped you ace that exam about the animal kingdoms. You know I circled the right answers for you. Your welcome! Just please can you assume for a minute that I'm telling the truth so we can move on."

"Fine," he said, clearly not convinced. "So you're telling me that you and your sister skipped forward again, like the summer before sixth grade."

I was suddenly filled with dread. "Joan never came back either?" I asked, certain that I already knew the dismal answer.

"No."

"I don't think she skipped ahead with me. At least, she wasn't there when I came back. I was alone."

"She never came back from Vegas, so where did she go?" he asked.

That was something I didn't know, and it struck me as selfish that I was only just now trying to figure it out. "I don't know what happened to her," I said. "She got hurt in the desert, in a..." What had my dad called it? "A subsidence crater. She was knocked out. We were in this weird building... Look, I can't explain any of it. I just know that my parents are gone and I'm in Las Vegas alone and the hotel I left this morning is suddenly four times as big and... digital clocks and... Hondas..."

Gosh, it was embarrassing, it's even embarrassing to write

about it, but I started to cry. David chimed in with "Shh... shhh... it's going to be okay."

I snapped back at him, lashing out in defense. "You married Frymouth?! You said you had to marry a Jewish girl."

"There weren't any Jewish girls. She converted. She actually makes a really great Jew."

"Do you have kids?" I asked.

"One. He's eight years old. We're trying for another."

"Wow. Gross. Congratulations." I didn't know what else to say.

"Hold on, Fran's knocking," David said. Then he shouted, "Start without me! I'll eat later! This is important!"

Frymouth was pissed. I could hear her shrieking in reply, "If your *mother* had cooked tonight you'd be out here eating it!"

David said quietly to me, "She's right, you know. Mom can cook. Fran: not so much. Her food's as bad cold as it is hot."

"Yeah, your mom's a swell cook. Loved her rugalach."

"Okay," he said, taking a deep breath. "You disappeared in 1960. If you're telling me the truth, which you can't be because this is insane but never mind, then you're still sixteen. What are you going to do?"

"I have to find my family."

"That's gonna be hard," David said, gently. "I don't know if you know this, but none of them came back from that Vegas trip. It was a big mystery in the papers."

I didn't know that. I didn't know anything, apparently. But I still had to find them. Someone must know. If I could find my uncle or someone who was there that day, then they could help me. I just didn't know where to begin. I realized that I had been talking to David as a friend and equal, but he was also now an adult and a father. I needed a father's perspective. "What... Uh..." I began sheepishly. "What would you do? What should I do?" I felt tears coming on again. Embarrassing. I blame puberty.

"Oh God this is... insane!" David exclaimed. "I still don't really know if you're pulling my leg or not. I mean, you sound just the way I remember you, but that was nineteen years ago. I wish I could see you in person. I'd invite you to come here and stay for a while, figure things out, but what if mom or Fran recognize you? How would I explain that one? Okay, well, there's really no sense in coming back here anyway, since you know your family isn't here. I'd like to see you. But... you know, married with kids, I can't just run off to Vegas on a moment's notice. Maybe in a week or two I could work something out... You're at a hotel. That's good. Get a room, eat a hot meal, sleep, you'll feel better, you'll think better."

I thought about it for a moment. "That's some pretty cruddy advice, David. I figured you'd be all wise and knowledgeable now."

"I know," he agreed. "Damn. Sorry. Ok... Do you have any money?"

"No," I said. "A few dollars. But I can get more easily, I'll just do my thing."

"No!" he cried. "Stop that nonsense. You just skipped nineteen years. Do you want to wake up at the end of time? You want some adult advice: stop playing. You're like a baby with a loaded gun. Just... Look, I'll call the hotel and get you a room and put it on my credit." He hesitated. "I can't believe I'm doing this. I'm not made of money, you know."

"Thanks David," was all I could think to say.

"You rest up, relax, sleep, have some food, don't have any fun… and then… I don't know. I don't know what I'd do in your situation. I don't know! Let me think about it, okay? I'll call your room, we'll talk tomorrow, and I'll have some better ideas."

"Thanks, David."

"No problem."

"Hey," I was taken aback by his generosity, "I'm sorry for being a jerk, back then. Not just ruining your party, but all of it. I don't know why we couldn't talk, why we stopped being friends, but I know it was my fault. I always wanted to…"

"This is…" he interrupted me. "I've had this conversation with you in my head lots of times. You know, since you disappeared and everyone figured you were gone for good and I'd never get to say the things I wanted to say. Look, I'm sorry, too. You've been like a ghost haunting me. I can't believe that we get to finally bury the proverbial hatchet."

"That's such a nerdy way to say it but, yeah."

"Okay," David was back to business. "Let me make a call then go eat. Go to the front desk in twenty minutes. Everything should be ready. I gotta go."

"Bye," I said, then hung up and walked back into the expansive lobby.

With twenty minutes to kill, my stomach rumbling, my face filthy, my body dehydrated with a paradoxically full bladder, there were any number of things I should've done, but I had one more dime in my pocket and one last number in my head.

"Hello?" An older woman answered the phone.

"Hi, I'm trying to reach Julia. Is she there?"

"Oh, my, no." She sounded dismayed.

"Well, do you know where I could find her? I'm a friend from High School and I was hoping to track her down and say hello."

"She certainly doesn't come around here anymore," she sounded indignant and defensive. "I don't know anything about the places she goes." The word "places" dripped with disgust.

"Do you have a phone number?" I asked. "Or address?"

"All I know is that she's dancing in Sin City." She said those last two words with disgust, spitting them out like poison, and then she hung up on me.

CHAPTER 25

S IN CITY?

It took a moment to sink in.

Sin City was Las Vegas. Julia lived in Sin City. Julia lived in Las Vegas? Julia was here! Things were finally looking up. If I could find her then I'd have a friend here who could help me find my family.

After a quick and explosive trip to the men's room followed by a long draw on an adjacent water fountain, I navigated the dizzying lobby and found the front desk. I gave them my name and they handed me two sets of keys.

Had I known then what I know now, I might have warned David not to give them my real name. I assumed that anyone that was looking for me had given up a year or two after I disappeared. I also assumed that anyone looking for me was doing so with the best of intentions.

I was wrong on both accounts.

With keys in hand I proceeded up the elevator to the old section of the hotel, the area where we'd stayed nineteen years ago. Apparently David hadn't splurged on one of the newer rooms, but I suppose I should've been grateful to have any place to go, even for just one night. The room service menu had expanded as much as the hotel. I'm a man of simple tastes so I called down and ordered their biggest burger, slathered with cheddar, mushrooms, onions, and bacon, as well as some fries and a coke. For a moment I remembered the sack of baloney sandwiches that my sister and I had eaten in this wing of this exact hotel. It felt like that miserable meal had happened last night, when in fact it was nineteen years ago. I left a trail of my dusty clothes as I made my way to the bathroom. I would have stayed in that steamy shower for hours, watching miles of sand and grime wash down the drain and sampling every complimentary product, had the room service not arrived so quickly.

I jumped out of the shower when I heard the knocking and wrapped myself in scratchy white towels. Still dripping wet, I answered it and a young porter, my age though taller and ganglier, pushed a cart inside. He made comments about the weather that I largely ignored while he set up my burger feast on the table by the window and stood awkwardly by the door as I fished one of my precious few grimy one-dollar bills from my pocket and handed it to him.

I cannot remember the details of the meal because I practically inhaled it, barely pausing to breathe until every fry had been smothered with ketchup and crammed down my throat. I turned on the television, an RCA Colortrak, and while I had no presence of mind to pay attention to the actual program, I did enjoy the swirl of high-resolution color. I knew that NBC was broadcasting episodes of *Bonanza* in color, or at least, they had been in 1960, but I had never had the opportunity to see them. Color televisions were becoming more common, but they were still astronomically expensive. Apparently they were no big deal in 1979. With my stomach full of meat and potatoes, with my eyes dazed by flashing colors, and with every inch of my body weighted down with exhaustion, I lay on the bed and slept.

Don't you just hate it in books when the main character puts his head down on the pillow then you have to endure fifteen pages that describe his deep and meaningful dreams? Sure, the dream probably reflects some important message, emotional state, or they can even help predict what's to come, but what a painful bore. It goes on and on and at the end of it you feel like someone has wasted your time.

So here is a wholly abbreviated version of what I dreamt when I fell asleep after having lost everyone and everything I've ever known, traversed a killer desert, met a gambler, reached out to an old friend, and eaten a hamburger.

It was a running dream. One of those frantic "holy moly I'm being chased" dreams where no matter how hard you try you can't seem to run any faster than a plodding walk. It's as if you're treading through deep water. Screams get swallowed and remain unheard. Every hiding space seems exposed. The unseen but all-seeing enemy gets closer. They take big strides and gain on you with every step. You know those dreams. You've had them. I didn't know what I was running from, but I felt they were after me and they'd eventually find me. The streets of Las Vegas, the rooms of the hotel, the hallways in my High School, the basement in my house, I tried every hiding space but every moment brought them closer.

Finally, I found myself running from them in that giant circular tunnel under the brick building in the Nevada desert. It was there that I finally gained some traction. My shoes grabbed the floor and I gained speed until I left my attackers behind me. I began to feel hopeful. I would escape. Then, coming from the other way, I saw my sister, Joan. She was running toward me as fast as I was running toward her. But it was all happening too fast, and we were going to catastrophically crash. That's when I woke up.

Not so bad, see? Only one and a half paragraphs about my dream. Easy as pie.

Speaking of pie, I was hungry again when I woke up. It was about 9PM. I shook out my dusty clothes and ventured downstairs in search of some dessert. It occurs to me now that I must have looked like a misfit that wandered in from a 1960s costume party. I still looked better than lots of the people milling about down there.

The hotel was designed so that it's impossible to reach the elevators to your room without navigating partway through the casino, a clever way to shake money out of people's pockets. I didn't have more than a few dollars in my pockets anyway, so there wasn't much temptation. I picked my way through the slot machines and card tables until I saw what looked like a coffee and pastry shop. I'd almost made my way through before a strong meaty hand grasped my arm.

"Hey son! You look a lot better now."

I looked at the hand grabbing me and when I saw the digital watch strapped to the offending arm I knew it was Duffy sitting at a semi-circular table covered in green felt. "Hi!" I replied.

"I'm just finishin' up on 21 here, need to back away now that I'm ahead. What're you up to?"

"I'm gonna try to find a shake or something."

"Well now, you come with me then!" he said, gathering his chips and pouring them into his saggy jacket pockets. "I know just the spot for a shake!"

He laughed heartily and walked off. I didn't get the joke, but he hadn't led me astray so far, so I let myself be led. If he was some kind of bad guy he had already had every opportunity to prove that while I was in his Honda. I followed him through the crowd, which was incredibly easy since he was now wearing a bright yellow suit. It was the first yellow suit I had ever seen. He looked like a tall banana in a cowboy hat, stalking his way through the casino with an unlit cigar hanging out of the corner of his mouth.

We reached a set of heavy oak doors, ornately carved and guarded by a large imposing man in a red cap. Above the doors was a sign in an extravagant curly font that read, "Tiffany Theatre."

"He's with me." Duffy slapped one hand on the guards shoulder and clapped the other into the guard's hand. The doorman quickly pocketed a bill. That Duffy was a smooth one. In a moment we were let into the Tiffany and an intoxicating world of music, smoke, booze and women. I kept his yellow shape in the periphery of my vision as I squinted my eye for clarity and took in the sights.

I'll have you know I was no stranger to the world of bare breasts. Not only had I cupped Frymouth's budding boob in one hand at that Halloween party but I'd also accidentally seen my sister bare-chested and, in my room, I had a fully nude large-breasted woman printed on an air-freshener, the kind of thing a perverted trucker might hang from his rear-view mirror. She smelled of pine. I'd found her on the street and hidden her under the rug in my room. For all I know, she's still there.

The Follies Bergere was something else. It was a three-dimensional, fragrant spectacle of lights, feathers and flesh, of slow reveals choreographed to erotic music. An extravagant chorus number with two rows of twelve long-legged beauties with twice as many glitter-capped nipples took the stage. Suddenly, I realized what Duffy must have thought when I said I wanted a "shake." High-kicking, smiling, and laughing, they danced for a rapt audience of men of all ages and sizes. Some customers sat alone, nursing their drinks and focused one hundred percent on the show. Some, in groups, chatted and laughed and only occasionally glanced over at the marvelous spectacle. To my surprise, some men sat with women! What an odd place for a date.

Duffy shouted to me above the din, "They do this great number to an Earth, Wind and Fire song. It's like you're on acid. I hope they do it tonight." He led us to a table in the fourth row and a cocktail waitress quickly joined us. She was a pale imitation of the girls on stage, but with more exposed flesh than I could handle at that hormonal juncture in my life.

"What'll it be boys?"

"Jack, rocks," Duffy said. "For you, son? I'm buyin.'"

"Umm…" After the Halloween party I wasn't too keen on drinking ever again. This didn't seem like the place to order a milkshake. "A beer, please. And do you have any food?"

"Mm hmm, kitchen's open for five more minutes so tell me what you want and I'll slip it in fast," she said with a wink.

"Okay, umm… Just some… uh… fries, please."

"Sure thing, cutie," she said, and then disappeared into the crowd.

Luckily, Duffy wasn't too interested in small talk. He seemed happy enough to have some company but he was no more inquisitive than he was in the car. So I was free to take in the show. My eyes were as wide as a cat staring at a bird in a cage, and these birds were flapping their wings. Duffy noticed me staring and laughed, but I couldn't help it. I didn't see how anyone in that room could act nonchalant with this kind of spectacle happening in the background. It deserved all my attention. A big group number ended and the preponderance of flesh melted into the wings, leaving one woman standing in the center. She was veiled, a thick pink mesh obscuring her face, and she wore a nearly translucent pink bottom and top, with layers of gold and gray netting accented with gold ribbon and feathers. She looked like some kind of fantasy hybrid Egyptian gypsy bird.

"I love this number," Duffy leaned over to me. "I used to watch *I Dream of Jeannie* all the time. Great show. Did you?"

"Nope. Missed it."

"How could you miss that? Everyone watched that show. Anyway, this one does a solo dance to the theme song. You'll know it… Da da, da da dada da… Good song. And she does what you always wanted Barbara Eden to do: take it all off. Well, most of it off, anyway. Course, if Jeannie really got naked she'd just wiggle her nose and 'poof'! All her clothes would be gone. But there's no fun in that. I like a slow reveal. This one does some belly dancing, too. Definitely got some dance training. Legit. Not as young as some of the others, but this one has the talent."

She sure did. Her body undulated in an entrancing way. The roar of the patrons dropped to a hush as her hips pushed percussively this way and that. A pink scarf fell away and her stomach was revealed, a sparkling jewel set in her navel. It danced as if it had a life of its own. Another bit of lace fell away from her hips and her shapely legs caught the light. They were sprinkled with glitter and she shined in the scant light.

Another bit of fabric leapt into the audience and her arms were bare, moving not with the gyrations of her whole body but in an entirely different rhythm with mesmerizing dissonance. Drinks and fries materialized in front of us and I ate and drank, barely taking my eyes off the "Jeannie."

I nearly choked when the final pink netting fell from dancer's face. I couldn't be sure, but I squinted with all my might and I could have sworn that the dancer looked like Julia. Nineteen years is a long time, but if it was her then she had aged well. I knew that she was somewhere in Las Vegas and I knew that she had studied dance back in the day, but the rest of it didn't make sense. What were the odds? Not to mention the fact that Julia never seemed like the kind of person that might end up as a Vegas showgirl. Not that she didn't have looks or talent, but had always seemed more shy and academic. After the last accessory dropped with a click of the mini-tambourines she held in her fingers, the music came to a close and she struck a pose and made a slow, deep curtsy before striding off the stage. It had seemed like all her clothes were going to hit the ground, but she didn't actually strip completely. There were probably tourists out by the pool that wore less than she did at that moment. I wasn't sure if I was upset or relieved. The theatre rang with applause as men tossed bills and chips up on the stage.

I had to know more, and I couldn't very well go up to her, say "hello," and catch up on old times. With a beer warming my stomach and fogging my judgment, I once again thought of my power. What should've been a blessing had turned into a curse. It was unpredictable. If I tried using it again I could end up in the year 3000, completely alone. Would that be so different? Would that be worse? Nobody I knew would be alive so there was at least the freedom of starting over. I'm sure I'd get my standard issue hover-car, moon-wife, and robotic love-slave. How could that be bad? There was also a part of me that suspected that this entire thing was some kind of a dream, or that it was all out of my control. My actions couldn't possibly have consequences if fate was dictating everything. So if I tried to step into super-fast mode and ended up forward or backward in time, or dead, or on top of Mount Everest, it was all completely out of my hands, right?

So I did it. This time it felt right. As if someone had turned the volume quickly down on the riotous scene and paused the projector, everyone silently froze. At last, something had gone right. I practically skipped down the aisle, weaving in between servers and patrons, hopping gaily over a portly man's leg that was rudely stretching out into the aisle, and I jumped on the stage. I looked around for a moment then followed the path the Jeannie took through the curtains.

Just off stage there was another act about to emerge. A completely bare-chested woman with an Amazonian headdress had a python wrapped around her body. Her breasts were slick and oiled and she was painted with zebra stripes from head to toe. The python's mouth was slightly ajar and its tongue was caught mid-flicker. She had two muscular men flanking her, both likewise oiled and wearing nothing but loin clothes. I wondered what Duffy would have to say about this act. I know I certainly didn't want to miss it. Luckily I had all the time in the world.

I continued along the narrow backstage wings of the theatre, past exposed brick, ropes, sandbags, and pullies, to the first dressing room that was cracked open. I stuck my head in and immediately blushed bright red. I saw, in person, for the first time in my life, the act of fellatio. One of the feathered dancers from the first act appeared to be resting her head in the lap of a suited gentleman. Her thick mop of hair and the feathered headdress obscured the action but I wasn't so sheltered that I couldn't discern what was happening.

My gentlemanly fifties sensibility won out over my overwhelming curiosity and the mad rush of hormones I was fighting, so I left the couple in peace. I had more important things on my mind. Nonetheless, I made sure to note which dressing room I was leaving, in case I should pass by that way on my way back for another instructional peek. I stepped into the second dressing room and there she was. The Jeannie. She had sat down on a stool and she was rubbing the thick makeup off her face. I walked up behind her and looked at the back of her neck. If it was Julia, then the many a long hour I had spent staring at the back of her head in class, memorizing the features, would surely allow me to recognize her. It could have been… There was a tiny tattoo of a star right where the hair dispersed on her neck, a delicate enticing little mark. Otherwise, it could have been her. I looked at her in the mirror, where the makeup cloth didn't obscure her face.

Her eyes were familiar… Still bright, still kind. It was Julia. It had to be. I wanted to hug her but it was so odd. She was now, I guessed, only slightly younger than my mom was, but it was *her*. I had found a friend in Las Vegas. I decided at that moment that I would approach her, confide in her, and I'd finally have my help. I'd also be able to ask some burning questions. What had happened after I left? Where had all our friends landed as adults? Who got together after I left? What couples broke up? Who was the valedictorian? Who was the prom king? And how the hell did a conservative Catholic girl end up as a burlesque dancer in the Flamingo Hotel in Las Vegas?

I took the long way back to the house of the theatre, studiously ignoring the temptation to more closely inspect what was happening in the first dressing room. You may perhaps accuse me of trying to see more boobs up close, as the larger chorus dressing room was on my way, and you might perhaps be right. I certainly looked… I may have seen two or six or some other even number, since it's only common sense to pay attention to one's surroundings. These performers were hardly shy, right? I was a paying customer, so why shouldn't I see something tasty?

At the rear of the stage, behind a golden curtain that separated the narrow backstage from the deep space of the stage proper where a python would soon get its moment in the spotlight, there was a man, frozen, mid-slap. His hand had just made contact with a dancer's face. She looked shocked and pained, and he looked like an angry, sloppy drunk. It was safe to assume that a place like this had security and would soon toss a jerk like that out on his butt. Still, hadn't David told me all those years ago that I should do *good* with my power? Having just ogled a parade of breasts and intruded upon a lady using her mouth in wondrous ways that God never intended, it was time to balance things out by doing a good deed. My first impulse was to disentangle the python from the dancer and wrap it around that prick's neck. That was a bit too much, and would've taken quite a lot of work on my part. So I did something that I have to admit was fairly unoriginal. In fact, I think I stole it from *Dennis the Menace*, which was airing new episodes before we left for Vegas. I tied his shoelaces together. I also pulled out his wallet, pulled out the thick pile of cash, and then stuck it back in significantly lighter. I tucked half the wad of cash into my pocket. I wanted to give the other half to the dancer he'd struck, but I could not fathom where she might have any pockets on her skintight outfit. So it came to pass that, while in a Vegas strip club, I tucked a wad of cash into an exotic dancer's G-string.

I felt a little bit better with some money in my pocket. Since I had no confidence that I'd be able to successfully engage my talent again, I decided to take advantage of the moment. If a little cash (four twenties, three tens and four-teen ones) made me feel better (indeed, that was more cash than I'd ever gotten my mitts on at once), I figured that a *lot* of cash would make me feel a *lot* better. It would also help me get through the next few days, as David's assistance was only for one night and I might need to either pay for my own room or finance some travelling.

There's no shortage of cash floating around a casino. I'm sure if you were in my position you'd have the gumption to find the vault and loot the place of millions. I, however, really didn't have those kinds of aspirations. I just wanted a little pile of money that I could use to help set things right, a tool that I could use as I began the hunt for my lost family. I stepped out of the Tiffany Theatre and burst into the stillness of the casino floor. I was tempted by the tables overflowing with chips and cash, but decided that stealing directly from the dealers was a bad idea. I remembered working at the ice-cream shop last summer. If, at the end of the night, the register said that there should be $42 inside and there was only $41, Mr. Rein, my boss, assumed I'd either taken it or I'd messed up. Either way, he took the dollar out of my salary. It was still my fault and I had to pay. So I imagined that if I took money from one of the tellers at the window or one of the dealers at a table that they could get in trouble for it. The last thing I wanted was someone to lose his or her job because of me.

I stalked through the casino floor, looking for an opportunity. Surely I'd come across another injustice, like the wrong I had righted inside the theatre. No such luck. I supposed I couldn't rely on my "rob from the rich mean guy" take on Robin Hood. I did, however, manage to come up with one philosophy that helped me out that day. All of those people in there were gamblers. Gamblers piss away lots of money on the slim, almost non-existent chance that they'll beat the odds and win the jackpot. The people at the machines empty their wallets into those voracious devices, get encouraged by a small return, and then throw the rest away over the course of time. They don't usually realize how much money is in their pocket at any given moment, especially when they're doing well, as it's going in and coming out almost constantly. This was during a time when all bets were taken in cash. I figured that since they were going to piss it away anyway, why shouldn't I skim a little off the top? The casino was going to get that money eventually, so I was really stealing from the greedy corporation, not the individuals, right? It was a bit like the "grazing" I had done in my school cafeteria, when I took a pretzel from here or a carrot from there. I rescued a five from one large woman in a bright sundress, three from an older fellow, and twenty from a cigar aficionado. The slot players carried around buckets filled with their winnings, so I grabbed my own bucket, took an insignificant amount here and there until my own bucket was filled to the brim with quarters and half-dollars. I went at this for a while until I got pretty tired. I stashed a sizeable pile of cash and coins up in my room, which was no mean feat since

I had to climb the stairs to get there, and then I headed back to the Follies.

In the literary world and in the world of movies and plays, when you witness a character do something deplorable, it's fairly likely that he or she is going to pay for it later, mostly by suffering a terrible death. Main character hits his wife but then spends two hours redeeming himself? Not good enough: he falls into a propeller! Heroine of the story cheats on her husband then saves a village of starving indigenous people? Sorry lady: lung cancer! So yes, you just witnessed me steal from hordes of innocent people. I would point out to you that, first of all, they're mostly gamblers and drunks and they'd lose the money anyway. Secondly, I took only a small amount from any one person (except this one guy who looked like a real Nixon). And finally, I've already suffered my tragedy. My punishment had already been meted out, so fate owed me a sin or two.

Once back at the table, the python woman and her two burly men walked out onto the stage the moment I returned to normal. Duffy leaned over to tell me some little known fact about this act when something fell against the back curtain. The jerk that struck that woman backstage had tumbled against the curtain and fallen through, giving the whole audience a laugh. Tied shoelaces. Classic.

I thanked Duffy for the amazing experience and, claiming tiredness, bid him goodnight. In a flash I was in my room, sleeping now not only on a ratty mattress and box spring, but a pile of money the likes of which I had never had before. The power of all that cash filtered out whatever dreams I might have had. I slept as sound as a baby.

CHAPTER 26

I SPENT SO MUCH time dwelling on my life in the '50s and '60s that you must be anxious for the meat of this adventure. I can't help but to tell the story in the way that makes sense to me, because I lived it. I also think I'm dwelling on those parts of my life that I still really need to figure out. For example, writing about David and Julia and my sister helped me grasp how I feel about them. It's closure. It's therapeutic. I guess that's a little selfish and I apologize, but I'm afraid that you're going to have to suffer through a little romance before we get back to the action.

Well, "romance" is kind of a stretch. You can be the judge.

Duffy had departed to shake down another casino. "Never stay in one place too long or they figure you out," he'd said. So the next day I went to the theatre alone, trying out Duffy's palm trick on the doorman. It worked like a charm. Speaking of how I was spending my ill-gotten hordes of cash, I should mention that I took a room in the newest tower. I didn't call David that day as I had promised since I didn't want to listen to him lecture me about how irresponsible I was being. I wore an outfit of genuine 1979 clothing, newly purchased from The Flamingo's finest men's shop. Strapped to my wrist was my first digital watch. Future boy!

At my quiet table towards the back I nursed a beer and sat through many of the same acts I enjoyed the night before. Julia's Jeannie didn't make an appearance that night, but rather it was a flamenco soloist that expertly tore up the stage. Her skill, speed and rhythm made up for the fact that her breasts never made a complete appearance. It seemed that headliners like Julia and the flamenco lady didn't have to go completely topless. She received a standing ovation from the crowd, myself included, and when she took the same flourishing curtsy I'd seen the night before, I knew immediately who she was.

I sat there until the show was over. I sat there as the place emptied. I sat there until Julia emerged, carrying a duffel bag, and walked past me down the aisle. I couldn't think of anything to say and I nearly missed my opportunity. Then she came to a halt scant feet beyond where I sat and turned around.

"You…" she was hesitant, "you look like someone I used to know."

"Maybe I *am* the person you used to know." What a cheeky, obnoxious, and flirtatious thing for me to say.

She laughed. "What are you, fifteen? He'd be in his mid-thirties by now. How'd you get in here anyway?"

"I'm twenty-one." I had lied to her for years about my cat, now I was lying about my age. And my name. "I'm… Well, my friends call me Ace, because I'm really good at cards. I'm a professional gambler." And my profession. From whence spewed this fountain of lies? I was on a roll, and it seemed more digestible than the truth. I held out my hand.

"A *gambler* in Vegas, how exciting," she said, rolling her eyes. "Please excuse me." She walked past me without even shaking my hand.

"Can I buy you a drink?" I hopped up and followed.

"I sincerely doubt that you can, unless you have a fake ID." She didn't slow her pace.

"Please, just one. I'm here alone, I need someone to talk to." Well, at least that part was honest.

"I don't drink with fans." At least she smiled this time, though in order to see it I had to skip around her like a yappy puppy.

"I'm not a fan, I swear. I didn't even like that Spanish thing you did today. I preferred the Jeannie yesterday."

Again, she emitted a heartwarming laugh. "Okay, not a fan, but a stalker."

Perhaps it was my uncanny resemblance to a long lost companion that made it possible to persuade her but she finally allowed herself, despite protestations, to be led to a dark hotel bar that was on the way to the parking garage. At a corner table she sipped Chianti over candlelight as a jazz pianist in the lobby provided atmospheric music. I had bought the whole bottle, which she said was unnecessary since she'd only stay for one glass.

"Tell me about your friend," I said, playing a dangerous game. "The one I remind you of."

She took a deep breath and looked down at her drink. "You really do look like him. I guess you look a little more put together. He was always a mess. He was just a boy," she said, as if that explained everything. "It was ages ago. We went to primary and High School together. He was never my boyfriend, per se, but if he'd have asked I would've said yes."

She looked up.

I looked up.

"Really?" I asked. "You wanted to be his girlfriend?"

"Sure. Well, I wanted him to ask, anyway. Maybe I was a little young for it. But… We did fool around a little." I refilled her glass. "Innocent stuff. Well, not all that innocent. Petting, things like that. Oh," she laughed, "and one time at a party when he was really drunk he kissed me and I slapped him."

"Why'd you slap him?" See? Closure.

"Other people were watching. And everyone knew that he'd been smooching another girl only an hour before. My best friend, no less! What a moron."

"Total, complete moron," I agreed. "So… Why didn't you two end up together?"

She took a sip before she answered the question. "He disappeared."

"Disappeared? Wow."

"His family took a trip to Las Vegas, actually, and they never came back."

"They must've really liked it here."

"No, something bad happened to them. They really just disappeared. Didn't even come back for their things. Their car was never found. Lost in the desert, I guess. Taken by aliens, who knows? You know," she leaned in close. "I never said this to anyone before, but he's sort of why I ended up doing what I do. When I finished High School and all sorts of things were expected of me, I just had it in my mind that at any minute it could all be over. So I vowed to only do the things that make me happy. I always loved to dance. I was a good student and could've done other things, but what I *loved* to do was dance. And even though it made no sense to my parents or anybody else I knew, I moved to New York City!"

"Oh, wow cool…" I beamed. "So you did the whole Bohemian artist thing?"

"Hell no! I got into The Juilliard School and studied dance under Martha Hill."

"Wow." She made it sound impressive, but I'd never heard of Juilliard. Or Martha Hill. "So then you joined this show…"

"No! Not initially. I performed all over the world. I got to travel everywhere. I have had adventures like you wouldn't believe." I figured I'd have her beat in the adventure department, despite her nineteen years of experience, until it hit me that I was essentially still a child. I remembered that my original reason for wanting to talk to her was to get her help, to recruit her as an ally in my search for answers. Instead I was being distracted by this silly role I was playing.

She continued, "As I got older I spent more time expressing myself with my own choreography. I got involved with this Bergere production when it was in development in Paris. I choreographed two tours of it and the show you saw tonight."

"Wow. I just assumed…"

"You're not the first. When my grandmother heard I was going to be headlining a follies burlesque in Vegas she stopped talking to me," she said, wistfully. I refilled her glass. "Most people don't understand. They don't see it as art or as business. There's a stigma attached to it. A dancer over thirty can teach, choreograph, or become a mom. But me? I choreograph and I dance every day. My crowds love it, and I love it. I can do anything I want. Jeannie, Flamenco, it's all up to me. I'll dance until I'm in a wheelchair, and even then I'll turn it into something sexy."

Just like that drunken night, days or years ago, when I was wearing my dad's torn army outfit, I went in for a kiss. But this wasn't an embarrassed girl at a party full of catholic teens. This was an accomplished and confident woman. A woman with a fond memory of a boy she thought she once loved. And there was his carbon copy, going in for a kiss.

This time, she didn't object.

If quality counts for anything, I count that as my first. My technical first kiss had been with Julia anyway, but this one was so much better. Her experience, her longing, my hunger, it all counteracted my boyish clumsiness.

I said before that I've been dwelling too much in the past. So I should certainly abbreviate the lurid details of how I lost my virginity that night. To move the action forward, I absolutely should not breach the gentlemanly trust and describe to you how our kissing at the bar led to us kissing in my room on the velvet couch before the expanse of windows that overlooked the sparkling strip. It would be appalling if I were to explain to you how forceful she was when she grabbed my tie and nibbled on my neck. The story of how that tie landed on the floor and my brand new shirt lost three buttons would best be left for another time. There are things said about dancers. There are things said about older women. I shan't affirm or deny either, that would be in poor taste, but you can be certain that I have a robust and firm opinion.

I would never boast about how, with one hand, and never having done so before, I managed to unclasp her bra in a most expertly manner. Despite that evidence of my dexterity she soon pegged me for a virgin, probably because of my sense of wonder at every step in this process.

I will leave much of it to your imagination, as you are likely to be kind. In reality, there were some areas where I could have used some improvement. The art of working a nipple, for example, doesn't come naturally to everyone; genetic code doesn't include instructions on how to make them stiff and pleasure them with your mouth, so Julia guided me and taught me, telling me exactly what she wanted every step of the way. She was not shy about it and told me precisely what to do. I'd soon memorized the key points and began riffing on the theme like a jazz musician.

The rest of it came fairly easily. It came easily several times, actually. I was sixteen at the time, though I'd told her I was twenty. For those of you that have had the misfortune to experience male adolescence, it is akin to being a permanently aroused sex-machine at an age when sex is forbidden by most cultures. It is ironic and cruel. Suffice it to say, I had a lot of pent up energy. The moment one wave of passion overtook us, another one was building up behind it. I think at around thirty-five, she was at her sexual peak as well. It was a mighty combination and it took its toll on both of us.

She fell asleep in my room. I believe that I could have gone perhaps one more time but she had reached her limit. So I lay awake for a moment, reveling in the memory of it, the smell of it, ignoring the twisted and perverted and unnatural way in which this perfect thing that was destined to be finally had come to pass.

I kissed the star on the back of her neck. I felt a slight rumble course through the hotel, like a distant echo of the one-megaton blast that my father shared with us that night. The sparkling Vegas lights outside my window seemed to add to the atmosphere of this perfect evening so I left the drapes open and snuggled into Julia's warm embrace. I closed my eyes and slept.

When the sunlight from the open window woke me she was already gone.

CHAPTER 27

THE FISTFULS OF dollars I fleeced from bloated tourists weren't enough to keep me going. After four more days at the Tropicana I was running out of cash and ideas. If no member of my family returned from that trip then I had no one to go back to. My uncle may have had some answers, but how to find him, when he usually lived across the Atlantic? This is even assuming he wasn't caught up in whatever catastrophe befell my parents and sister. He could be just as lost as they were. Or he could be sipping brandy back in Jolly Old England. Maybe I'd need to travel there? Maybe I could hire a private investigator. Maybe I should give up the whole thing and follow the Follies Bergere around the globe, practicing my newfound skills with Julia every night. Either way, I'd need more money.

To do that, I decided that I would turn my lie into a reality. I'd become a professional gambler. A gambler with a distinct edge.

I turned my remaining cash into chips and walked boldly up to the craps table, which Duffy had told me offered good odds to the savvy gambler. All the cash I had in my pockets was gone in a matter of minutes and I walked away from the table feeling dizzy and angry, not having understood a damn thing that just happened. I trusted the dealer when he told me I lost and I walked away dejectedly. Loathe as I am to submit myself to education, I realized I needed a tutor if I was going to be successful in Vegas. I needed to find Duffy.

As it turns out, I didn't have to look too hard. I asked the concierge to tell me about a really hot event in Vegas that nobody would want to miss, but I specified that it absolutely couldn't be an Elvis concert. He looked at me like I was insane before informing me that Elvis had died two years earlier in 1977. Perhaps 1979 wouldn't be all bad.

The concierge pointed me to the Sands that evening, where "Mr. Las Vegas," Wayne Newton, would be performing with the "Copa Girls." I'd never heard of him, but I took the man's advice and stalked the Sands. If Duffy wasn't going to see the show, he'd certainly be there shaking down tourists at the card table.

"You bet I'll teach ya," he said with a smile, "but ya gotta have luck, math skills, and balls."

"I've got two of those!" I said with a smile and he looked at me curiously. I think he misinterpreted, as I had meant to imply that I was bad at math.

"I should damn well hope so," he said. I decided not to correct him. I certainly had luck, or something even better. We sat down at a poker table at the Sands, he in a white suit, steel tipped cowboy boots and straw hat, and me in my polo and jeans. I watched him play as he talked me through the logic of his actions. It seemed pretty straightforward and made much more sense than craps. Finally, I anted up and joined the game. After a few rounds losing in order to figure out the flow of the game, I began using my little advantage. Sometimes I'd rummage through the dealers deck and stack it so that I'd be dealt an incredible hand. Sometimes I'd take what chance dealt me and I'd peek at other people's hands to see whether I should fold or raise. Sometimes I lost, through miscalculation or sloppy cheating, but I figured that was okay, as it would help me from appearing too lucky. Duffy pulled out of the game and coached me, clapping me on the back and ordering us drinks when my tiny pile of chips began to grow. It was slow going, but my money gradually multiplied.

"You have graduated Duffy's Academy of Cards," he said, raising his glass to me. After we drank, he said, "On that note, I'm gonna go catch me some Copa Girls."

"But the show must be over by now," I said.

"That's the best time to catch 'em," he winked and disappeared into the crowd.

After a day or two of working the Flamingo, I took Duffy's advice and I tried out the other casinos. A couple of weeks passed and I had amassed quite a pile of money. I kept at it for a while, more than was necessary by any measure. You could definitely say that I was getting greedy and I was not nearly careful enough. Perhaps gambling was a welcome distraction from my real issue, that I didn't know where to begin looking for my family. I spent more time with Duffy as he showed me all that Vegas had to offer. He loved the life of a high roller and he was nothing if not flashy. I didn't start wearing yellow suits, but I did improve my wardrobe with some sharp new outfits.

After a few months I moved into a brand new hotel called the Shenandoah, owned in part by Wayne Newton. I had a swanky suite and was entertained night after night at the theatre downstairs by the likes of Wayne himself, George

Burns, Danny Thomas, Frank Sinatra, and Lucille Ball. This hotel would eventually become The Bourbon Street Hotel and Casino before being bought by Harrah's and demolished. When I was there, however, the paint was fresh and it was the place to be.

I did most of my gaming outside of that hotel, but it was at the Shenandoah that they came for me.

It was nighttime and I was in bed, regretfully alone, as that night with Julia hadn't repeated, though not for lack of effort on my part. I had continued to buzz around her like a fly, but she never let her guard down like she did that first night. She kept me at arms length, happy to have me in her audience, just not in her bed.

The power to my room was cut, a key was inserted into the door, and a flood of men poured in.

I was groggy, and it all happened so fast that I didn't have time to process. I was hooded, gagged and spirited away before I could even shout. My hands were restrained behind my back. I felt a sharp prick in my neck. Someone had stuck me with a needle. My eyes became heavy, and the adrenaline that kept me kicking seemed to seep out as my leaden limbs released. I passed out cold.

I woke to smelling salts under my nose that jolted me into a painful sobriety. My head throbbed and there was a terrible dryness in my mouth. I tried to move but my hands and feet were bound. I was in a featureless room, save for the electrodes attached to my chest, a machine monitoring my pulse, three soldiers aiming their rifles at me, and one soldier that moved away with the smelling salts and then positioned himself behind the beeping machine.

A loud voice shook the room. It was distorted, crackly,

and I traced its source to a speaker mounted in the upper left corner of the ceiling. Next to the speaker was a large security camera. "Are you familiar with electroencephalography?" it said.

"What? Who are you?" I shouted at the speaker, furiously. Then I turned to one of the guards. "Let me go! Please." He was motionless so I tried a different tactic, pasting on my saddest puppy dog face. "Please, I'm scared. Can I have some water?"

"Electroencephalography," the distorted voice continued as if I hadn't said a word, "is the measurement of electrical activity produced by the brain as recorded from electrodes placed on the scalp. An E.E.G. There is one on your head. This one is unique in that the electrodes are bidirectional, not merely passive. They are functional for bilateral E.C.T. That stands for Electroconvulsive Therapy. The electrodes can deliver an electrical stimulus. The stimulus levels are in excess of most individual's seizure threshold. Quite painful and of course there is the risk of catastrophic cognitive impairment. Do you know what polygraphy is?"

My head was still swimming from whatever they had injected me with. The vocabulary lesson certainly wasn't helping. "Writing pretty," I said.

"No," the voice replied with not an ounce of amusement. "That's calligraphy. A polygraph is an instrument that measures and records several physiological responses such as blood pressure, pulse, respiration, and skin conductivity while the subject is asked a series of questions. False answers will produce distinctive measurements. You are attached to such a machine."

"Why?" I asked. "Who are you? Is this about blackjack?"

"We've learned, by studying someone like you, that there are physiological precursors, hints, if you will, that telegraph that you are attempting to… speed yourself up."

This son of a bitch knew who I was! And he knew what I could do! Only two people in the world should know that. They studied someone like me? There was no one like me, except… He didn't give me time to make sense of all he was saying.

He continued, "These devices will detect if you are attempting to speed yourself and they will trigger the E.C.T., which will in turn cause you severe pain and distract you enough to keep you from succeeding in your attempt. You can take my word for it, as I have no wish to see you in pain, but you may try for yourself, if you choose."

He sounded almost hopeful, but I was inclined to take him at his word. Not merely because I didn't want to risk the brain damage or whatever would happen with that machine, but also because, even if I was in super-speed mode, I'd still be handcuffed and tied to this chair and locked in this room. All the time in the world wouldn't change that. My talent was useless in this situation. I was trapped.

"What do you want?" I asked.

"First," he sounded inhuman through that speaker and I came to the conclusion that they were purposefully distorting the sound of his voice, "let's address what *you* want. Some water for the boy, please, he's parched."

A soldier held a cup to my mouth and I swallowed quickly, coughing as it trickled down the wrong pipe.

"Look," I said, "please, if this is because I've been winning at poker a lot, I'm just a professional gambler. I'm good at what I do. And I'm lucky."

He laughed. Through the distortion he sounded like a maniacal robot. "You're more than lucky. You're gifted. You're one in a billion."

"Yes, I'm gifted," I agreed. "That's all. Please, let me go and we can forget all this. I've got money, I can pay you."

"Why would I let you go when it took me nineteen years to find you? I was beginning to lose hope that you'd resurface in my lifetime."

What kind of twisted sci-fi bull was going on? I couldn't understand a word. But I supposed if this villain was intent on monologuing to help me figure out his scheme, the least I could do was to listen.

"It made sense you'd resurface in Las Vegas since that's where you were last seen. Your winning streak finally triggered suspicion days ago in the casino security networks, which we've been monitoring all this time. That's what led us to you." He lowered his voice and said, "Kudos on finding your High School flame, by the way. She's quite spectacular."

"What the hell…" I shouted.

"Please, please… Relax. Don't startle these fine men. I assure you their guns are loaded, and we wouldn't want to give them any reason to feel threatened by you, would we?" He paused. "This is a new opportunity for me. You see, we've had to keep your sister unconscious all these years, so even though I talk to her all the time I don't believe she can hear me. But you, you are the missing piece of the puzzle."

"She's alive," I whispered. "What about my parents?"

My sister, alive. Who were these damn people? I struggled against my restraints. I considered using my power, despite the risk.

"I wouldn't," the voice cautioned, as if he could read my intentions. "It will cause you so much pain, I assure you."

I screamed, "What are you doing to me? Who are you? What did you do to my sister? Is she here?" I blinked furiously to keep my tears from obscuring my vision.

"And here I thought you two never got along. Fascinating… Blood *is* thick. Please now, just relax. They want to take some readings while you're conscious."

From a door behind me, men and women in lab coats came and went. Nobody looked kind or cruel… just indifferent. Nobody looked familiar.

Though now that I rethink the experience, I can connect one of the guards to a later moment in my life. Yes… Wrinkle his face, gray his hair, insert an unfiltered Marlboro in his mouth and one guard becomes the doppelganger of the man that ignited the pursuit outside the red Bell building in NYC. Remember that? It was ages ago and yet almost thirty years in the future. I'm certain it was him.

Time passed so slowly as I settled into a quiet and miserable routine. I would almost rather have been unconscious the entire time. I don't know how many days I spent strapped to that cursed chair or locked to a narrow hospital bed. I have no idea how many times they released a chemical into my IV drip that knocked me out so they could readjust their equipment, or how often they woke me just long enough to ask me how I felt or if I had been dreaming. I had no inkling what kinds of twisted tests they performed on me while I was knocked out. Blood was drawn countless times. They introduced innumerable chemicals through my IV; some gave me raging headaches, some made me feel hyper and desperate, most just made me feel scattered, drowsy and docile. I was fed regularly though my hands were never unbound. Sometimes I had the privilege of swallowing, but most of the time my sustenance was delivered via nose tube. I occasionally drank through a straw, but was more often hydrated via IV. They collected the contents of my bedpan to be tested. Such was my routine: I woke and slept, laying flat on a gurney, with no idea of whether it was day or night.

"It's time to test a theory." The disembodied voice woke me one day, or night. I was strapped to my gurney, as usual. Although this time I appeared to be alone in the room. As my vision cleared I turned my head and saw that a stack of blood-red bricks had been placed in the room, a small waist-high wall of unmortared masonry.

"Your E.C.T. device has been removed, temporarily," the distorted voice announced. "But as an added precaution, the walls have been electrified and there's no way to deactivate that from inside that room. You should also know that the door has been bolted from the outside with steel that is thicker than you are. Also, your hands and arms are still securely bound. Now," he said, finally getting to the point. "I would like you to speed up for us."

I looked at the video camera suspiciously, "You'll shock me."

"No," he said. "That device has been removed. We want you to speed up now, if you please."

Although I was feeling more lucid than usual, I didn't know what he was getting at. Was this a trick to get me to shock myself? But what choice did I have? Perhaps I should go the civil disobedience route and piss him off by not doing it. But I was curious about whether or not I could. What was the worst that could happen? Forgive me if I was feeling a little fatalistic at that point. So I did it.

The polygraph began to whirr and the E.E.G. spiked, but no sparks fried my brain. Instead, I immediately became sick to my stomach. My guts lurched and I threw up my mostly liquid diet. My attempt to speed up had failed miserably and I was left shuddering violently, choking on my own vomit. I was strapped to the gurney, spasming uncontrollably, with my head tilted back. The vomit had no way of escaping my mouth. I would drown on it in an instant.

The door burst open and more lab coats rushed in. One of them undid the strap on my right arm so I could lean to the side and puke on the floor, violently coughing until I could finally draw in air. As he did, and as my muscles began to obey me once again, I had the presence of mind to grab a ballpoint pen from his pocket. While leaning over the side of the gurney, I was able to shift my weight so the balance of the whole thing changed, sending me crashing to the floor. Another lab coat struggled to right the gurney as a guard held my free arm and tried to pull me out of the puddle of puke.

"We'll need to test that!" a lab coat exclaimed, scurrying for a vial to collect what had splashed from my mouth.

The whole thing was like a well-choreographed bit of physical comedy. Throw in a few pratfalls and some slide-whistles and it'd have been regular a circus act.

That is, until I took the pen I held in my hand, flicked off the cap with my thumb, and jammed the point with all my strength into the kneecap of the guard who would one day limp up to meet me outside the Bell building.

Hear a piercing scream and picture, if you will, a melee of lab coats and guards slipping on blood mixed with vomit, and a door that had remained slightly ajar. The gurney was still strapped to me but I launched myself towards the door anyway, using all the strength I could muster after lying immobile for days. The bed caught in the door, blocking the guards and doctors inside and leaving me outside, but still no less trapped. A fresh cadre of broad-shouldered guards began to advance down the hallways towards me.

My little escape attempt would be short lived. With no other option, I decided to give my special trick one more shot. I shut my eyes to focus completely then I felt a mild wave of nausea that passed quickly. Whatever they'd done to foul up the mechanics of my talent inside the room was no longer fully in effect. Maybe it was those bricks or something they had hooked me up to that had kept me from doing my thing. Not anymore though. The advance of the guards halted immediately, as did everything else.

As you can imagine, it took me ages to disentangle myself from the gurney, but since I had one free hand I was finally able to do it. I had to repeatedly slam the frame of the gurney against the door until the welded piping cracked and my restraints could slip off. Having been horizontal for so long, it was difficult even to stand. I felt dizzy, and strangely weak, not to mention exposed in my hospital gown, with my bare ass flapping in the open. I had no desire to go back into the room I'd just escaped from, just in case whatever device they were using might still be able to foul me up. I made my way through what turned out to be a cavernous building. Each door was marked with a letter and a series of numbers and each one was locked with a numbered keypad. My sister could be behind one of those doors and yet I couldn't simply steal a set of keys from a frozen guard's belt loop; I'd need the code.

The mysterious man that had been speaking to me over the monitor could also be behind one of those doors, but how was I to know? The building seemed to go on forever, labyrinthine halls branching off like tunnels in an ant colony.

After an ordeal like that I was less interested in the "Inner Sanctum and Secret Plan" room than I was in the exit sign. I had been too frightened for too long to put on a sleuthing cap. My "flight" instinct was in full force. I wanted out.

I pushed through a set of double doors that led out of the honeycomb of hallways, past a guard at a podium, and into a part of the building that seemed more conventional. It might have been a university, perhaps, or a hospital. More people made their way about, lab coats and guards to be sure, but also regular people in normal dress. Finally, I pushed through another set of guarded double doors and found myself in a cavernous lobby filled with perfectly still people and a door-way leading out to the glorious fresh air.

I burst through the door. Although I was grateful that the sun beat down on my face, the cold air assaulted me. It was freezing! I couldn't stop and gawk for long; I had to keep moving.

Up and to the left, a train had stopped on tracks that were suspended twenty feet in the air. Tall buildings of steel and stone surrounded me. I identified it immediately, since I had been there before: Chicago. Dad used to work there often and we would go into town to meet him for dinner. There were quite a few more skyscrapers than there had been the last time I had a meal in Chicago.

Mmm... A meal. My thoughts were immediately con-sumed with food. How long had it been since I had eaten something that hadn't been pureed first? I was starving. I wanted to find the nearest fast food joint and stuff my face with burgers and fries then find a clothing store and get some pants and a thick coat.

First, though, I turned around to take in the site of my imprisonment.

I didn't have to search to find it. Emblazoned in bold steel on the front of the massive edifice was a single word in all capital letters.

MAJORANA.

CHAPTER 28

B LACK ESMERTA'S CRYSTAL bowl certainly didn't
see *me* coming. I am speaking, lest you forget, of the
vomit that splashed around inside the smooth surface
of the crystal bowl, up over the sides, and through the slatted
wood of the table to splash down on the rug and feet beneath.
Still quite empty from when I threw up outside the Bell building
and exhausted from fleeing the men that chased me throughout
downtown Manhattan, this left me feeling hollow and miserable.

"Is fifty dollar cleaning fee!" Black Esmerta was not amused.
She stood and stormed through the beaded curtain, returning
with a roll of paper towels, some all-purpose cleaner, a sponge
and a bucket of water. She dropped them in front of me and
went back behind her curtain. I heard a television click on and
the sounds of *The Simpsons* filled the room.

I muttered, "If I'm paying a fifty dollar cleaning fee then *you*
should be the one cleaning it up."

"Don't forget between the wood!" she called back. "If any
customer comes and leaves because of puke stink then you
pay double!"

Fantastic. I had navigated the streets of New York, dodged
my pursuers, probably escaped another decade of electrodes

and tube-feeding, and while I should've been putting distance between myself and that ominous red building I was instead trying to perform the extremely difficult task of cleaning up a multi-tiered puking. I'll spare you the sordid details, but suffice it to say that when I was done my hands were dirtier than the floor.

"Mrs. Esmerta," I called.

She appeared and inspected my work. She scowled, mildly dissatisfied but willing to let it pass. "I give you advice."

"Great, how much is *this* gonna cost?" I could dispense with her advice for the time being. This thing had already sucked up too much of my time.

"You are rare. Unique. You have great clarity, you have vision, and yet you are ignorant and you see nothing. Both at once. Exceptional. Stupid. Terrible waste."

"Thank you, very, very much," I said, oozing sarcasm, "Really, but now I've got to…"

"Run?" she asked. "Go hide again for years? Ignore answers right in front of the nose? Go where the wind carries you instead of grabbing this situation by the—"

"Look, there's nothing I can do!" I protested.

"Powerless and powerful, again, both side coin. Stupid. Poor sister," she turned back towards the beaded curtain.

"I can't find her," I cried. "I tried once before. My abilities don't help because they misfire when I get close. Whoever these people are, they know more about me than I do. They're always one step ahead so all I can do is hide." None of this should have made sense to Esmerta. I tried to recall the details of what I had said while gazing into the blue liquid, before I popped my cork. I couldn't exactly remember. I'd talked about my sister. I'd seen a lot more than I'd said, of that I was certain. Is it possible that she, too, saw what I had seen in the bowl? That would explain her insight, but would give her a lot more psychic credit than she seemed to deserve, with her cheap storefront and laughable theatrics.

"When you get close…" she repeated. "They misfire."

"Yes."

"Like just now?" she asked.

Huh. In my effort to ignore my problems and run away from them, I'd stumbled closer to their source. Those people knew who I was. They acted as if they'd been on the lookout for me. And when I tried to speed up, I'd gotten sick. I threw up. It was the same way I got sick when I tried to speed up all those years ago when I was trapped at Lab Majorana. Were they connected? Were they the same people?

I thought back to my imprisonment in Chicago. When they piled those red bricks in front of me and asked that I try to speedup, perhaps they knew that I wouldn't be able to? Many years ago, those red bricks in my prison at Lab Majorana triggered that reaction: failure to accelerate and failure to keep down my lunch. I felt the same way when I was in front of that red building today. Something about those bricks… I thought back to the subsidence crater that Joan had fallen into years ago when this whole mess began. It had been red. Could there be any connection?

Long ago, in Chicago, I stabbed a man in the leg during my escape, a young man, to be sure. Outside the Bell building a man with a limp approached me. Could it be the same guy? And just now when I had the vision of Joan trapped in a red room, I got the same sick feeling. Was that red building some kind of Majorana facility? Could Joan be trapped inside that building?

"Black Esmerta," I said, finally starting to put some

pieces together, "how much would you charge me to use your computer?"

She considered for a moment. "Is high speed, very good connection, and is Mac, very expensive. Twenty."

"Okay."

"For five minutes."

I rolled my eyes and pulled out my wallet, peeling off some bills: bills for cleaning, bills for reading, bills for hiding, and now bills for surfing the net. I threw in an extra twenty, assuming I'd need at least ten minutes online. I'm no whiz with computers like you kids that grew up with them, but considering I'm a child of the fifties I don't think I'm too bad. First stop: Google Maps. I didn't remember the exact address of that red building downtown but I knew the intersection. I punched that into Google and brought up the intersection. I switched to Street View, panned around the three hundred sixty degree view of the street until I saw it again: the stark, unadorned, reddish walls of the building, although in the photo they were partly obstructed by a passing truck. Alright, so I had an address. I entered the address into Yellow Pages Online: nothing. I Googled it and nothing came up. I went to the Bell Telephone website, but the many off-shoots of Bell—Bell Atlantic, Bell Pacific, Bell Canada, etc.-made that a difficult route to take. Nonetheless, there was no listing of a Bell facility at that address.

"Try Yahoo." Esmerta had been looking over my shoulder.

"Google's better."

"Says you. Try anyway."

I tried and found nothing, because Yahoo sucks. Even *I* knew that. I tried the United States Postal Service website but that was as inefficient and user-unfriendly as you'd expect. The only additional information I got was the zip plus four. I went to NYC.gov and clicked around until I found something promising.

ACRIS, or the Automated City Register Information System, was a wealth of mostly useless information. Property taxes, rental agreements, landlord violations, tenant disputes, tax transgressions, water and sewer registers, everything that should probably be private was there for all the world to see. Information about that particular address was still hard to come by. I got a little bit closer once I identified the exact parcel and block number. The only thing that came up was another address in Manhattan, which was cross-referenced as the responsible party. I figured out the parcel number for that second address, entered it into the search bar, and finally it looked like something was going to pop up. Processing… processing. Yes, it had found an owner. His name appeared at the bottom of the screen.

I blinked, taken completely by surprise.

Suddenly, the building's gates made a bit more sense. "BE" on one side of the gate, "LL," on the other. It had nothing to do with the phone company.

I thought of the last man who'd seen my parents, my sister, and I together. A portly, balding gentleman, overdressed for the Nevada climate where I'd last seen him. The one person that I thought could possibly help me find my parents. The man that I had hoped would have the answers I'd craved for so long. The man that I had assumed was sipping warm beer in Jolly Old England.

My uncle.

Bertram Llewellyn.

"BE" and "LL."

CHAPTER 29

THROUGHOUT MY LIFE I've lurched through time, so I am well suited to nonlinear thinking.

Perhaps that is why I like to take things out of turn when telling a story. If this jumping back and forth is bothering you at all, or if you're having trouble following it, well... just imagine how I felt. You can always put the book down and go do something else. If you happen to be listening to the audiobook, listen to it at three times speed so my voice sounds funny. That ought to help to spice things up.

I didn't have any of those appealing options, so now, being the one in charge of this tale, we shall skip back to the moments following my escape from the Majorana facility into the streets of Chicago.

Freezing was the more immediate danger. Hunger could wait. It was damn cold and I was wearing a rather revealing hospital gown with the rear flaps untied. Hello frozen Chicago, please meet my ass... My cold ass, with goose pimples rising. Good day to you, gust of wind. Please don't blow up my gown like Marilyn Monroe and acquaint the entire Midwest with my cold and shriveled private parts. I walked into a Sears, my bare feet grateful to leave the pebbly sidewalk. I skipped quickly past the snow blowers and washing machines towards the menswear section. I caught a glimpse of the omnipresent security cameras and realized how easy it would be for the Majorana people to track me if I wasn't moving so fast that I presumably couldn't be seen. How had Lab Majorana found me in the casino? Certainly not by catching me doing my super-speed-swindle, but possibly by my remarkable success, or perhaps just by recognizing my face as I haunted the places night after night. Could they have been tracking Julia? No. The thought was too frightening to accept.

I suppose I could've had my pick of the Sears underwear collection, but they were mostly in packs of three. To open a pack of three just to steal one pair of underwear would be wasteful. So I really had no choice but to continue my long tradition of going commando. I grabbed a pair of Calvin Klein jeans. Right out in the open and yet in complete privacy, I pulled off my hospital gown and stuck it behind a rack of clothes. Despite the fact that my recent liquid diet had left me bony and gaunt, the pants I had chosen were too small in both the legs and waist. These were my first pair of Calvin Klein jeans, actually, so perhaps the sizing on those was different. They'd just come out and they were apparently really popular, with Calvin Klein's name etched on the back pocket. I first saw them in a commercial featuring Brooke Shields, who was fifteen at the time, saying, "Nothing comes between me and my Calvins." Well, sans underwear, now I could say the same thing. I had to try on a few pairs, going up in size, until I finally found a pair that went to my ankles and closed at the waist.

I grabbed a sweater and a thick coat and, again, struggled to find a good size. I resisted the temptation of an open cash register in the men's section, again thinking of my summer at the ice cream shop. Instead I spent a little time "grazing," taking a one or a five from every wallet and purse I could find. Not too much to be missed, but once I was done I had a decent emergency fund to cram into my new Calvins. On the way out, I also grabbed a thick hat and scarf, partially for warmth and partially for concealment. While on that note, I also stopped to look at their sunglasses. I plucked out a sweet pair of aviators with yellow lenses then glimpsed myself in the small mirror attached to the rack.

The glasses looked fine, but there was something strange and unfamiliar about my reflection. My hair hung down over the yellow lenses and I had to brush it away. That was strange. I had been closely cropped not too long ago. There was a barber on the Vegas strip that I'd visited when I spruced up my overall image in the hopes of repeating my evening with Julia. Now I had a sizeable mop on my head. Could it be the side effect of whatever evil experiments they subjected me to back in the lab?

I shrugged it off and again headed towards the door, stopping once more in front of a full-length mirror to indulge my vanity. Everything about this reflection was wrong, and I suddenly had an inkling as to why the jeans and sweater hadn't fit.

There was no boy of barely sixteen in the reflection. There was a man of perhaps eighteen or nineteen. He looked like me, to be sure. Those were my eyes, sunken but recognizable. I supposed the nose was about the same, if perhaps slightly bigger. The man in this reflection was a good two or three inches taller than I had any right to be. I should have been short, but the man I'd become looked damn near average. I would have jumped for joy but clearly had too much going on, so I filed it away for later. I turned around, slowly inspecting the aged body I now inhabited.

And yes, I certainly did unzip my new Calvins and take a closer look at my new eighteen-year-old equipment. Wouldn't you? Suffice it to say, Julia would be pleased. I could do a lot more with this. This would be good.

It was a momentary distraction from the inevitable conclusion. I grabbed a copy of the Tribune that was tucked under the arm of a passing customer and looked at the date.

I had been held captive for almost three years.

CHAPTER 30

B Y NOW YOU'RE certainly used to me jumping forward in time, usually through the misfiring mechanics of whatever space-time manipulation my sister taught me all those years ago. This time, however, I had leapt forward in time in a more old fashioned way. Unthinkably long stretches must have passed while I was kept unconscious on that gurney. I had been convinced that it had only been a few days, a week or two, at most. But it had actually taken me well into the eighties and past the last stages of my adolescence. Perhaps for that I should be grateful. The body I now inhabited, though weak and completely unfamiliar, was a better one for traipsing alone through a strange city. More closely resembling an adult would have advantages for a man on the run.

I was out the doors of the Sears and on the streets of Chicago. I don't know why I hurried past the motionless figures on the street. They certainly couldn't harm me. I was shaken up and I wanted to put distance between the lab and me. I wanted to go somewhere no one would ever think to look for me. Where was the last place in the world any sane person would want to go? I found myself on Harrison Street, which led to the Greyhound Bus Station. I skimmed the destinations designated on the departing buses.

All of them seemed a little too desirable. Milwaukee was quaint and cheesy, that certainly wouldn't do. Grand Rapids was touristy, and we couldn't have that. Cincinnati was booming, Rochester was quirky, and Ithaca was unacceptably gorgeous. Finally, I found a destination so atrocious and so utterly unappealing that I knew I'd be safe there. I took a back seat in a mostly deserted bus that was about to close its doors and depart to Cleveland. With a feeling of relief I let the world return to its own pace. Nobody seemed to notice that a bundled up stranger had just materialized in the rear of the bus.

I fell into a blessedly dreamless sleep and about seven hours later I was there: The Mistake By The Lake. The Armpit of America. Apologies to Cavs fans and those who have pride in their city, which I know is on a rapid rise, once again. In fact, when I was growing up (the first time around) in the fifties, Cleveland had a wonderful reputation. We heard the phrase, "Best Location In The Nation," and it was true. The Indians won the 1948 World Series and the Browns were dominant in professional football all through the fifties. The population was nearly one million, making it one of the largest cities in the country. Apparently I skipped its quick and abysmal decline. Heavy industry fled the city, residents abandoned it like rats from a sinking ship, fleeing for the suburbs, and violent racial conflict became the order of the day. Riots and shootings weren't uncommon. Cleveland became the first major city to default on its loans since the Great Depression. The sports teams struggled and the industrial waste that polluted the river actually caught on fire, setting the entire river ablaze. On the upside, this led to the name for a quite tasty beer, Great Lakes Burning River Ale.

While the Cleveland of today has quite a lot of offer, no sensible 1980s person would voluntarily immigrate to such a place unless they were fleeing something much worse. We arrived downtown before sun-up and I immediately wished that I had had the foresight to carry a gun. It was a scary place at night. I stayed at the bus station until morning when the RTA began bringing people in from the suburbs and the city took on a semblance of life. Lost amongst the parade of suits, I went in search of an unremarkable motel, preferably one with no security cameras. I found one behind a steakhouse that had been painted bright pink, the color of Pepto Bismol. The clerk at the front desk didn't even ask for my name. He pointed to the cash only sign, then asked if I'd be staying one hour or the whole night.

After peeking into my ratty room, I decided to take a risk and to play the one card I had left. I was feeling very alone and needed to hear a familiar voice. I supposed David was the likely candidate, but someone else came to mind. I hesitated for a moment. Since Bertram obviously knew about Julia, perhaps he knew about my other friends and would be monitoring them. Exercising caution and common sense for probably the first time in my life, I left my room and hiked to a pay phone several blocks away. I had left the Keno card with Alan's New York State number back at the Shenandoah, but since I knew where he was it took no time at all to ask the operator to connect me.

When he answered the phone he was bleary and upset. I explained to him who I was and he predictably scoffed, protested, threatened to hang up, and asked a host of questions before finally accepting the possibility that there was a slim chance I might be who I claimed to be. I reminded him about the "Clean up your puke," note I had left for him the night of David's party, an embarrassment he hadn't ever mentioned to anyone else. I think that's what convinced him. I tried to avoid giving away too much, or supplying details that would make my story too unbelievable. I certainly didn't bring up the fact that, depending on how long I was inside that Majorana building, I was biologically still at least eighteen or nineteen years younger than he was. Recall that I never shared my big secret with Alan, so much of the truth I had to tell would be far too implausible to believe.

"Okay," he said, his characteristic lisp was still detectable, if somewhat smoothed by the years, "What happened to you twenty years ago in Las Vegas?"

My answer was an unsatisfying, "I don't know." I told him my family was missing and that I was recently kidnapped. I escaped and now I was in hiding.

I also told him, though it was perhaps irrelevant, that I had very recently run into Julia in Vegas and took her back to my room and made sweet love to her, over and over and over. I couldn't help it. It was a breach of trust and in poor taste, but he was my best friend. Over twenty years had passed for him, but for me it felt as though it had only been a matter of weeks.

I pulled up a hood to provide warmth and obscurity, scanning the streets for signs of anything suspicious. I didn't see how they could have tracked me, but I'd be damned if I was going to be caught again. With my eyes peeled, I popped in another dime and continued my chat with Alan. I learned that after High School he left home for West Point, the U.S. Military Academy in New York. When he graduated he was an officer, and I smiled brightly at the idea of my best friend in a sharp Army uniform, snapping orders while other soldiers stood at attention. An image flashed through my mind of he and I wearing our fathers' uniforms at David's costume party. Would I have joined the military, if I hadn't skipped through time? Would I be married with kids? Then I started thinking about Julia and immediately snapped my attention back to Alan. The thought of what life she and I might have had together could do nothing but wound me. Alan was still talking about his military career. I paled when I remembered the global political climate I'd left in 1960. Had my best friend gone to war?

As it turns out, West Point graduates were never likely to end up on the front lines. They undergo testing to determine their strengths, and Alan had been assigned to the administrative end of things. He played his part for the country and was no doubt a true American hero, but his skills were in strategy and organization.

He told me about his wife. I was thrilled to hear he'd found someone. Not that I doubted he ever would, but it was just good to hear about good things happening to good people. They had a beautiful little boy named George and a second child was on the way.

"Alan, look," I said, after some of the weirdness passed and we were talking easily, "I know we haven't seen each other in a long, long time. It's totally unfair for me to do this, but I've gotten in trouble, there are some people after me, and I don't have anybody else to turn to. I need some help. Please."

"I'll do whatever I can..." he said, with a tone implying that he had no solutions to offer.

"Great!" I said. "Can you find out everything you can about a company called Lab Majorana?" I was still twenty years away from Google's IPO, and research skills weren't my forte. We take for granted now that we have instant access to the most obscure information at all times, just by reaching into our pockets or whispering sweet nothings into Siri's microphones on our watches. This was a different time, so I was getting information the old fashioned way. Come to think of it, if I had been a better son or just a more attentive person in general, I'd have known more about Lab Majorana. I did recall that my father had been their military liaison in Chicago, but I couldn't remember him ever saying anything else about it. I've never been clear on exactly what my father's job was, since it was so easy to just think of him simply as a military fly-guy. His knowledge and enthusiasm for all things nuclear was made crystal clear from his lecture atop the Tropicana the night before Joan fell into the crater and I fell into the future. Could there be any connection between my father's work and what was happening to me?

"Okay," Alan said, snapping me from my reverie.

"Oh, and can you look up a name for me? He's my uncle and he might know something about my parents. Bertram Llewellyn."

"Can you spell that?" he asked.

"No."

"How can I reach you?"

I thought for a moment. "I'll call you, okay?"

"Alright, tomorrow. But a little later, please," he grumbled. "I don't do mornings."

With my first Cleveland day I decided to do a little bit of shopping, seeing as how I had only one outfit to my name. Having stolen from their Chicago store it seemed only fitting that I make a real purchase from the local Sears, which was just down the road. It was, of course, closed. Shut down. Like nearly everything else in this abandoned city. There were signs indicating that the adjacent Cleveland Play House had just purchased the building and architect Philip Johnson would soon turn it into a gigantic theatre space. A Sears turned into a theatre? I could just picture it: a great big open space with show girls and mannequins, easy listening music, an orchestra, and doorbuster deals on holidays. There was a matinee performance of *A Funny Thing Happened on the Way to the Forum* about to start in the original Play House so I bought a ticket and settled into a warm red velvet seat. It was fun, it passed the time, and who doesn't enjoy seeing a man in drag?

Afterwards, I went to the Pepto steakhouse in front of my motel and sat conspicuously at the bar, the palest person in the joint, and enjoyed an incredible steak and a few beers. I drank until it was dark out then I carefully picked my way back to my sad little room and went to bed.

The next morning I took a bus to a nearby university where I was able to blend in quite easily, then called Alan from a pay phone in the student union.

"Ever hear of Weston, Illinois?" Alan asked.

"Yup, it's a town near where we grew up, near Batavia."

"It *was* a town near where we grew up. In 1966 the town was taken over and completely demolished to provide a site for Lab Majorana."

"That's... uh... dramatic, and evil sounding. So... why? What is it?"

"Well," he began, "officially the board of the town voted their own town out of existence in 1966 to provide a site for Lab Majorana, but the lab didn't officially come into existence until 1967. This whole thing stinks. It raises all kinds of questions."

"Okay, but what *is* it?" I pleaded.

He lowered his voice, "A nuclear research facility."

"Is it top secret?" I asked.

"No. It's in the Yellow Pages."

I whispered, "Then why are you whispering."

"I don't know. Just being dramatic. Shut up and listen! I've got all kinds of notes here. Originally it was called the World Accelerator Project. It was renamed in 1974 for an Italian theoretical physicist named Ettore Majorana. This guy is like a super genius. He had guys like Fermi and Heisenberg coming to him for advice when he was in his twenties. We're talking smarter than Einstein here." My very own blue-eyed pre-internet Wikipedia was providing some stimulating information, but I wasn't sure how it was relevant.

"Ok," I said, "So this Majorana guy is doing what, exactly?"

"Not him," he corrected. "Ettore Majorana disappeared in 1938." Alan didn't wait for me to interject. He had always been a bit of a geek, and he was geeking out about this topic. "Disappeared! He was 32. At first they figured it was suicide but then they found out he took a lot of money out of his bank accounts right before he vanished. This guy was an intellectual giant and everyone figured that if he disappeared, it was for a reason."

"Ok, so what are they working on?" I asked. "Why would they want me?"

"You tell me," he said. I remained silent, trying to put together a puzzle with pieces that kept changing shape. Alan continued, "I really don't know why they'd want anything to do with you. Maybe it's some misunderstanding."

"It *wasn't* a misunderstanding."

"As far as what they're doing, uh… the short answer is… a lot. The main thing is that they're building the Tevatron."

"That sounds like something from a comic book."

Alan was intent on making his way through the notes he had painstakingly compiled on my behalf. He began to get more enthusiastic as he continued. "It's a two hundred million dollar science fair project. It's a particle accelerator and it's going to be the first like it, the highest energy particle collider in the world. Basically, it's going to fling protons and antiprotons at each other, at super fast speeds, in a four mile ring tunnel lined with super magnets."

Several things about what he said resonated with me. Flinging particles at superfast speeds? The mechanics of something like that was way beyond me. I had gotten as far as using a band saw to make a fish-shaped wooden tool in shop class that presumably could be used to pull out a hot oven rack, but actually had only been used to prop open the back door to the shop when I snuck outside for half a cigarette. Superfast speeds? How would someone like me perceive these "superfast" particles as they barreled down a tunnel? Would they appear still to me, or would they move visibly through the air? Could I jog alongside them and catch them like marbles? Or line up my bat and knock one out of the park?

I was also taken aback by the mention of a giant circular tunnel. It was an undeniable fact that Lab Majorana had something to do with my abduction. They were constructing a giant tunnel. On the day I disappeared after my sister had fallen into a crater twenty-two years ago, my father took us to Uncle Bert's desert facility that, unbeknownst to me at the time, was built over a hidden circular tunnel of vast proportions. I didn't know what that facility was for; all I knew was that my uncle and perhaps even my father had something to do with it. The pieces didn't fit together, but they were at least starting to appear.

I couldn't think of any cogent follow-up questions, so simply said, "Thanks Alan. I really appreciate it."

"No problem man. Hey," he continued, "I wanna see you. We should hang out, catch up. You should come out to New York."

"That sounds like fun," I said, knowing it could only happen if I was willing to explain why I looked like a college freshman. "Definitely. I'll try to find some time to do that. I've gotta deal with this situation first though. Hey, if you find out anything else about this place… I'd love to know if they have any enemies, because I need some friends right now."

"I'm on the job," he said, and I imagined him doing a crisp Army salute. "Call me whenever, just not too early. Take it easy, man."

"Bye, Alan." I cinched up my hood tight, scanned the college crowd for anything suspicious, and wandered to find a campus map.

It wasn't hard to find the extensive libraries of Case Western Reserve University, a newly formed collaboration that included the resources of a powerhouse of science, the Case Institute of Technology. With my High School education cut short, I was at a severe disadvantage, but I had to learn enough to at least contribute to these conversations I was having with Alan. Words and names bounced around my head, most of them absent meaning, and I was determined to fill in some blanks.

I spent hours camped out in the library's stacks, researching exhilarating topics such as particle physics, protons, antiprotons, energy policy, and college girls. After only one night I'd abandoned my ratty room next to the pink steakhouse and moved to the hostel right off campus, which was further from the seedy corners downtown. It was a lovely tree-lined area called Cleveland Heights. I had my own tiny room with a wafer thin mattress. The crowd was all students and it was easy to feel anonymous. For three straight days I rolled from my bed to the library and made slow progress. I worked hard to put the pieces of the puzzle together and I continued to gather information, becoming a more informed citizen in the process. My dad, wherever he might be, would have been proud that I got in the habit of reading the paper every day, looking for tidbits that might come in handy. I became a fixture at that library, due in equal parts to newfound studiousness and newfound studiousness of college girls.

After co-eds, the most fascinating topic I researched in the library was Ettore Majorana. He had a suspiciously brief career, but his story piqued my imagination. Here's a quote I found that seemed worth remembering.

There are several categories of scientists in the world; those of the second or third rank do their best but never get very far. Then there is the first rank, those who make important discoveries, fundamental to scientific progress. But then there are the geniuses, like Galilei and Newton. Majorana was one of those.

—Enrico Fermi about Ettore Majorana,
Rome 1938

CHAPTER 31

I T WAS JANUARY 17th, 1982.

    After only a few days in Cleveland, I'd had quite enough. We were four days into a brutal cold snap with record low temperatures, which in Cleveland is saying quite a lot. Not only did we have frigid air blowing in over the lakes from Canada, it seemed to be coming from all directions and converging on this ice-smote city. Dozens of people died in poorly heated buildings, isolated from emergency services.

    Newspapers would record that day as "Cold Sunday." How imaginative. The Cleveland Plain Dealer announced, "Unprecedentedly cold air swept down from Canada and plunged temperatures across much of the United States far below existing all-time record lows." Wisconsin was negative 31 degrees Fahrenheit. Chicago was negative 21. As far south as Florida, the citrus crops were ravaged and destroyed by the cold. It was unfair for me to think of Cleveland as the epicenter of cold weather, but that's how I had come to feel in a short time.

    Also, the more I learned about the scope and power of the organization that had abducted me, the more I thought it was wise to keep on the move.

    I called Alan that night from a payphone outside of the Art

Museum, which was a short and frigid walk from my hostel. "I'm moving on, Alan, any suggestions about where I should go?" My breath turned to frozen fog in the night air as I exhaled. I had pulled up one side of my thick wool hat to press the payphone receiver against it, and already that ear was reddening with pain.

"Actually, yes," he immediately replied. "Long Island, New York. Suffolk County."

"What?" I asked. "Why? Why leave one pit and go to another? I need someplace warm. The Bahamas. The South of France. The inside of an oven. Anything. Come on, you've travelled all over, what's your favorite place."

He thought for a moment. "Wegmans. They have everything. Just opened one up near me. Anyway, remember you asked me to keep looking into this situation of yours. You wanted enemies of Lab Majorana?"

That got my attention. "Yeah! You found someone? Who?"

"No, I didn't. Not exactly. I found a group that fights to prevent their work." He spoke in a hushed voice. "There's a group that only goes by the acronym 'FC.' And they're doing everything they can, legal and illegal, to stop these particle accelerators from coming online. There's ideology behind it, about how the large-scale organization required by huge projects like this erodes human freedom. Then there are other people, including some physicists, who believe that if one of these Hadron colliders was active and two of the right kind of particles smashed into each other in just the right way, it would set off a chain reaction that could result in the complete destruction of our universe."

"Crap," I said.

"Yeah, the Big Bang all over again, except in reverse. It would be like creating a black hole here on earth that sucks in all matter until there's nothing left."

"That's nonsense right? They wouldn't do it if it was dangerous."

"That's what I'd think. But you're painting these people as kind of evil, so who knows."

I asked, "So, you think I should join up with these 'FC' people? Even though they work outside the law?"

"Well, look," he said. "I'm not a physicist but I don't personally think these colliders are bad. A lot can be learned from them, and I think its fear and ignorance that keeps them offline. One of the goals of these things is to discover the Higgs Boson."

"The God Particle," I said. See? My hours in the library hadn't been all for naught. I'd studied a thing or two besides the endless parade of bright young women that paraded through that cathedral of learning.

Alan corrected me, "A *hypothetical* particle that would help explain why matter has mass. Why do you have to bring God into it?"

I began, "I wasn't! It's…"

He cut me off and continued, "The ramifications of that discovery for science would be amazing. But…"

"But?"

"I don't know. If there's a chance these toys might destroy the universe, even a small infinitesimal chance, then it's a stupid risk to take. This FC group is working on disrupting a project on Long Island, at the Stonyhaven National Laboratory. If they succeed or if they fail, their next target will be the Tevatron at Lab Majorana. They've got resources and allies and information… and if Lab Majorana is still trying to get their hands on you, then this group would probably want to keep that from happening."

It seemed promising. More importantly, it was a viable and compelling reason to leave Cleveland! There was no question that my safest course of action was to stay put and wither away into Midwestern anonymity, but I had lost all patience with the cold and I felt compelled to heat things up. Lest you forget, this was long before my revelatory gaze into Esmerta's bowl, when I finally started to piece things together. While I still had a burning need to find and save my sister, I felt certain that any attempt to retrace my steps to Chicago would lead to a one-way trip back to my gurney in that windowless room. However I proceeded, I'd need a strategy and allies.

"So how do I contact them," I asked. I'd been outside at the pay phone for so long that I had begun shivering vigorously.

"Okay. So, they've been building this thing since 1978 but there've been all sorts of roadblocks. Stuff keeps breaking, magnets spin out of control, inspections fail. Good luck for the FC, right? Then there's public opposition in the Department of Energy, in congress. It won't be hard to find them. Go to Stonyhaven, take the tour of the lab, learn what you can, keep your eyes open… You'll find Isabelle's enemies."

"Isabelle?" I asked.

"Yeah, the collider, she's named Isabelle."

"So I gotta go to Long Island where Isabelle might destroy the world and find the people that are trying to slap her around."

"Yup."

"Sounds like a plan. I'm shipping out tomorrow!" I slapped the payphone receiver down, yanked my hat back down all the way, and practically skipped back to my hostel.

Only one more night in Cleveland!

CHAPTER 32

I CAUGHT AN EARLY bus the next morning to New York City where I'd be able to catch a train to Long Island. This was my first time passing through the Big Apple. I'd been to Chicago and Las Vegas, not to mention Detroit and Cleveland, but the scale of NYC put all of those to shame. It was overwhelming. I made a note that if I wanted to disappear again, a city of seven million might be a great way to become anonymous without having to freeze my butt off in The Mistake By The Lake.

My bus let me off downtown and I had some time to kill before heading north to Penn Station. Drawn by the sheer spectacular gravity of the Twin Towers, I found myself joining a crowd that had gathered at the base. As it turns out, I happened to be making my way through NYC on the day that Dan Goodwin was scaling the North Tower of the World Trade Center. He used suction cups to get up the first four stories then he shimmied up the window-washing track. I watched as he ascended until he looked like nothing more than a speck of dirt on the side of the massive building. From another angle I saw the infamous statue and I waved to Lady Liberty. I avoided making eye contact with the plentiful panhandlers that lined my route to Penn Station where I had to dodge many a vagrant and Harry Krishna before I finally caught the Long Island Railroad to Stonyhaven.

The lab was only open to visitors on Sundays. There was a dearth of hotels in the suburbs that surrounded the lab, so I knocked on the door of a cute, two-story bungalow that had a "For Rent" sign in the window. I introduced myself to the diminutive dark-haired lady that answered the door. I told her I was a student and I gave her a pseudonym. She explained that she was hoping to rent out her basement, which offered a cozy room, and private bathroom, but no kitchen or living area.

Something about the whole situation seemed inviting so I paid for a week with cash, without even having seen the room. As I finally stepped through the threshold I realized what my subconscious must surely have already known. There was a mezuzah on her door, as there had been on David's. Much to my satisfaction, my new landlady was delightfully Jewish, and on the first night I spent there she invited me to dinner. Chicken. And Potato Kugel! Ah, the memories. It was too wonderful and welcoming for words. Although she didn't supply any dessert after that delicious meal, I remembered something she'd mentioned during dinner. I practically skipped five blocks to a bakery in a shopping center nearby and bought a box of assorted rugalach.

It was bittersweet, because it made me think of my sister, how I'd shared my rugalach with her once, and how the crumbs had ended up in my underwear. I might have missed an opportunity to find her in Chicago. I couldn't be sure, but the thought haunted me. The rugalach, however, was not bitter. It was mostly just sweet and flaky and chocolaty. I made a mental note that I owed David a phone call. I hoped he wasn't worried. It had been so long that I assume he'd forgotten about me once again.

The next day I took a tour of the laboratory, a gleaming circular edifice atop a massive green hill. The tour guide walked backwards across the campus as she spoke in a nasal voice that reminded me of Frymouth. "Stonyhaven was originally owned by the Atomic Energy Commission and now it's owned by the United States Department of Energy which contracts out most of the operations and research to universities and private research organizations. It's operated by Associated Universities, which includes Harvard, Columbia, Cornell, MIT, Princeton and Yale. Private Institutions conducting research at the lab include Farnsworth Neutron Source from South Dakota, Rand from Geneva, Switzerland, the Universities Research Alliance, and the Midwestern Innovation and Technology Corridor which are both responsible for the Majorana project in Illinois."

Holy crap. I'd have to tell Alan. Lab Majorana had their filthy fingers in this nuclear pie as well. I suddenly wished that I had bought sunglasses for this trip. And a large hat. And a gun. I had put myself in the belly of the beast.

She continued, her voice flat and emotionless. "Stonyhaven National Lab is staffed by approximately three thousand scientists, engineers, technicians, and support personnel, and hosts four-thousand guest investigators every year. The laboratory has its own police station, fire department, and postal code. In total, the lab spans over five-thousand acres."

She walked us through a large exhibition hall and we stopped before an aerial view of the campus. "This giant ring at the top of the picture is our proton storage ring accelerator, which is being constructed and should be operational in less than a year. We call it Isabelle, for Intersecting Storage Accelerator, plus belle, because it's beautiful," she said, dryly. "Do you have any question?"

Yes, I thought. *I would like to know whether Isabelle is part of a nefarious plot to destroy the universe. I would also like to know the names, phone numbers, and addresses of any covert organizations that might happen to be attempting to thwart your little experiment.*

"No questions? Okay, let's move on then." I had to endure the rest of the tour, even though I had quickly lost interest in the myriad experiments she droned on about, none of which provided insight into my situation.

I stepped into an elevator on the last leg of the tour, but the door shut uncommonly quick, separating me from the group. I immediately felt an appallingly familiar prick on my neck. I managed to squeak out a "Son of a ..." before my vision darkened and I collapsed to the ground.

When I woke I was inside a large circular room with great glass walls reaching impossibly high up all around me. A plump man in a lab coat with a handlebar mustache and plenty of stubble on his rosy cheeks stood behind a thick plated window. When he saw me stir he picked up a microphone.

"Don't..." he said, slowly and insistently, "don't... do... anything. You are inside the world's largest Tandem Van De Graaf generator. It's an electrostatic accelerator that will be integrated with our Isabelle and used as a particle accelerator once she comes online. If you try to *accelerate* while inside that chamber then all the electrons will be stripped from your body. Probably."

"That sounds like it might hurt," I said, as I once again shook off the fog of whatever chemical they'd injected me with. I picked myself up off the ground slowly, as I was still unsteady. At least I hadn't been strapped down.

"Yes, you're very funny," he said dismissively. "Look, this whole thing is a little distasteful for me. I'm not the sort of guy who gets involved with this kind of thing. I'm not a guard. I'm not a thug. I'm married! I go to church. Unitarian, but it still counts. I play the ukulele. I'm just a technician. I'm here to operate this. Just please don't judge me." He was pleading with me, and I felt tempted to remind him that he was the one with all the power in this situation.

"What do you want from me?" I asked, blinking away the grogginess and taking in the details of my surroundings. I felt very much like a hamster in a glass aquarium that hadn't been filled with any decorative rocks or fake plants.

"I'll direct your questions elsewhere, please, because I really don't know." He was the quintessential snarky nerd, defensive, and clearly not used to being in a position of ignorance. Thick glasses, a white lab coat, thinning hair, the only thing he really lacked was a pocket protector. "They pulled me off of something that was, frankly, kind of important, and brought me here, to the one part of this project that is actually *working* and doesn't require my attention. They told me to operate it and if you woke up I should call a number. They told me to warn you not to 'accelerate.' What is that supposed to mean, anyway? Accelerate?"

"Who did you call?" I asked.

Another figure stepped into the control room.

From that far away all I could see was an olive uniform and good posture. I squinted and things suddenly became painfully clear.

"Huh… You still do that squint thing." The voice was

familiar... The military uniform was certainly Army, decorated. The man was late thirties, more or less, ashen blond hair, and thick brow... "Ever thought of getting glasses?"

"Alan!" I cried out with joy.

He leaned over the console and took a good look at me. "I wouldn't have believed it if I couldn't see it with my own two eyes," he said, slowly. "God, you look twenty years younger than you should. This is so amazing. So amazing."

"What are you doing here?" I asked. "Can you get me out? Quick, we probably don't have much time!"

"No!" he sounded surprised and amused that I had asked. He kept staring at me and I felt more than ever like a hamster behind the glass. "No, no, don't you see... I helped catch you. By luring you here."

His betrayal rang in my ears as I sat in silence until finally squeaking quietly in reply, "But, why?"

"Oh," he sighed, his voice dripping with sarcasm, "gosh, I don't know. Patriotism, maybe? Fear? Whatever. Apparently I was on a hotlist just for having been your friend for a couple years in High School. You contacted me and they knew, but they didn't confront me, they just listened, gathering evidence. I started asking some questions about Lab Majorana on your behalf, which must have triggered all kinds of alarms. I also asked some questions about you! It was only a matter of time before connections were made. Department of Energy answers to the President and so do I, so I kind of had to cooperate. Didn't have much choice, did I? In case you couldn't tell by the uniform, I'm a patriot, not a traitor."

His voice sounded accusatory and I couldn't understand why he'd done this to me. "Yes you are," I spat. "You're a traitor. You have no idea who these people are and what they did to me."

He paused a moment then continued slowly, a hint of disgust in his voice, "When they told me what you did to your family and how you spent all that time in Vegas as a criminal, stealing from tourists, molesting people… It wasn't that hard to go along with it. I think I know who the *criminal* in this story is."

"You son of a bitch," I screamed. "I reached out to you for help! I didn't do anything to my family. They lied to you. They are the ones that did something to my family. And to me! These are the bad guys, not me!"

"Woah!" the nerdy technician raised his hands. "Uhh… studying at MIT and getting a good job doesn't make me a bad guy. Sheesh."

Alan raised his voice, "You don't know what I've been through because of you. I have a kid. My wife is pregnant. I have a family. I have a career. And I've had Tactical and Technical Response in my house every damn day tracing my calls and investigating everyone I've every known. I don't deserve that!"

"Ok Alan," I said, defeated. "So you're just gonna hand me over to Majorana?"

"Exactly. They're here already. They wanted me to steer you to Stonyhaven because this Van de Graaf generator is online already and the one at the Tevatron isn't. They're going to conduct an experiment here before transferring you back to Illinois. That is, if any of your electrons are left to transport." The hate in his voice was unmistakable.

It still wasn't sinking in. "Alan, where is all this coming from? You were my friend…"

"Shut up," he spat, his voice betraying genuine fury. "We

were never friends. I was just someone to make you feel better about yourself. If you were my friend then none of this would've come as a surprise to me, but apparently you had a lot of secrets, didn't you? The entire time that we were *friends*, you were never once honest with me. That's not a friend."

I thought for a moment about the value of closure, and how Alan was finally getting some at my expense. There was some truth to what he said, but I was too wrapped up in fear at the moment to leave any room for guilt. He turned to go and I called out and asked, "So all that crap about a group trying to infiltrate and shut down Isabelle and the Tevatron, that's all bull?"

Alan shrugged and nodded. "Afraid so."

"Actually," the technician chimed in, "that's not bull at all." He raised a metal chair with both hands over his head and slammed it down on Alan's back. The chair bounced out of his hand as Alan slumped to the floor.

CHAPTER 33

"VIOLENCE! VIOLENCE, OH boy, that was bad, sorry…" He knelt down to check Alan's head. "Sorry!" he whispered again to Alan's crumpled form. "I'm so sorry. This is really not who I am as a person."

I had no clue what was happening. "What the…?"

"Uh, yeah," the technician said, stroking his moustache nervously. "Questions later. I have some for you, too. You can answer mine and I'll answer yours. Since there are bad men on their way up here to get you. Umm…" He seemed genuinely pained by the process of figuring out a plan. Clearly I was in good hands. "Oh God," he continued, "planning is not my thing, planning is *not* my thing…" He buzzed about, flipping levers. "Umm… Okay, tomorrow, 10PM, someone will meet you at… Umm… Mind blanking! Buh…. Buh… Ice cream."

"What?" I asked.

"Ice cream! Ok, the Carvel on Middle Country Road in Selden. Remember that. 10PM. Tomorrow."

I nodded and he continued. "The generator has been powered down, so you can do whatever it is they don't want you to do and escape but first…" he cried, cringing as he formulated his next idea. "First… Oh God help me…" he cried. "Well, do your thing, and then hit me on the head with the chair, butnottoohard! I don't quite feel like going on the lamb right now, thankyouverymuch. Not too hard, but hard enough, but, not too hard. Just make a show of it."

"Thank you," I said, and in the brief moment before I accelerated I was consumed with fear that my electrons would be sucked out of my body. True to his word, everything worked out fine. My new technician friend had left an exit for me, which I followed around to the control room. He was squinting, clenching his fists and bracing himself for the blow. I picked up the chair and bonked him on the head in as civilized a manner as I could. He fell down and a little bit of blood trickled from his head. That should do the trick.

Something occurred to me, moments after. Wouldn't Alan know that the technician attacked him from behind? He certainly would, and so I'd have to do my best to make sure Alan stayed unconscious a lot longer. With unmasked joy, I gave Alan a swift and rewarding kick in the head, sending his prostrate body down a half flight of stairs.

I stepped out of the control room and headed down the stairs, hopping over Alan in the process. At the base of the stairs were four soldiers in black carrying automatic weapons. They had just begun climbing up to the control booth. I passed them by and headed out.

Then I returned to them and took one soldier's hand and put it inside another's back pocket. I tied the third soldier's shoelaces together (classics are the best). And with the fourth one, who looked a little like Alan and therefore I hated him the most, I stripped off all his clothes and tossed them in a utility closet. I also, out of habit, took all the money from their wallets.

Once outside I saw quite an array of dark vehicles flanking the main entrance, some with flashing lights, others were utility vans and trucks that held God knows what. They were probably there because of me. I should've felt honored.

Afraid to head back to the comfort of my rental, and having no belongings to be concerned about, I hoofed it down Country Route 46 until I reached the Suffolk Meadow Race Track. I picked my way through the crowd to the densest part, where anxious gamblers held tickets in their hands and were caught mid-shout as the horses emerged from the gates. It wasn't until safely in that crowd that I released control and let the horses take off full bent down the track. The deafening roar of the impassioned crowd replaced the silence immediately. Too focused on the horses, nobody noticed me appear in their midst.

I stayed at that track all night, feasting on hotdogs and sodas, learning the horses' names, reading a paper, and keeping my eyes peeled for anyone carrying a syringe. After they closed early the next morning before sunup, I caught a bus to Cathedral Pines County Park, open dawn to dusk. I crept in, sticking to the shadows, avoiding the light of the moon, and settled in for a freezing cold, miserable night on the pine needles.

I woke early and picked my way through the protective blanket of the forest until I was in sight of Middle Country Road. Ice cream, he'd said. Carvel. 10PM. I had no convincing reason to trust that technician. For all I knew he'd rescued me from Alan's goons because he wanted me for his own evil purposes, but I didn't have much choice. Unwilling to go out in public when there was no doubt a diligent search in progress and yet unable to stay in hiding unless I filled my stomach, I started hunting for food. Once I spied a classic Long Island bagelry from the bushes, I accelerated again, slipped into the store, and had my fill of everything bagels slathered with cream cheese and washed down with coffee. It was delicious and nearly perfect. A toasted bagel would have been flawless, but these were still warm and almost melted in my mouth. Once I was full and warm, I left a few dollars on the counter then retreated again into the woods where I let time continue to pass. It felt as though 10PM would never come, and I certainly wasn't helping by accelerating when I emerged from hiding for breakfast, lunch, and then dinner. It only served to make the day that much longer.

A dark blue Chrysler LeBaron pulled into the unlit parking lot outside the shuttered carvel. The flickering fluorescent sign cast an eerie glow on the dusky sedan. The rear door opened slightly and the car just sat there idling. In the darkness I couldn't see in, but who else could it be but this mystery group? Somehow, I imagined they'd be driving something more interesting than a boxy K-car, but I wasn't in a position to be picky. After much hemming and hawing, I began to fear they'd drive off without me, so I emerged from the shadows and walked up to the car, ready to accelerate the moment things seemed fishy.

I opened the back door and took a long silent look at the man sitting in the back seat and his chauffeur. They looked as menacing as any of the other thugs I'd come across in recent days, but were these ones out to help me or harm me?

"Hi," I said to the silent chauffeur and the man sitting in the backseat next to me.

Silence in reply. "So, you guys are with the technician at Stonyhaven?"

Silence. "Okay, that's cool," I said. Apparently these people either didn't speak English or had nothing to say. "So…" I was starting to feel a bit like a streetwalker picking up some Johns. "Where are you going?"

The man in the back patted the seat next to him and continued to look forward. I shrugged. At least the car was heated. With few other choices, I hopped in. In the dim light of the Carvel parking lot I could see the driver's reflection in the rear view mirror. He seemed to be a younger man than his passenger. He had dark hair and soulful eyes. He wore a black tie, white shirt, and a dark jacket with wide lapels. The moment the door closed, he accelerated out of the parking lot. After two straight days wandering aimlessly in the cold, it should have been nice to be driven about, heading somewhere with purpose, but I had too many unanswered questions. I'd been blown about like a leaf on the wind ever since I resurfaced in 1979. Although my destination was a mystery, at least I was on my way somewhere other than the dark recesses of a forest and I assumed I'd be warm and maybe even fed a nice meal before the next awful thing happened.

Before long we pulled into a service road at RC Murphy Peconic River County Park. The LeBaron crunched on gravel as trees swallowed it up on both sides. The driver shut off the headlights and we were driving blind along a narrow dirt road. I could barely see anything and I clenched the door's handlebar in anticipation of whatever we might hit. He took a sudden sharp turn off the road and made his way through dense brush. I was petrified as the thick ancient trunks whizzed by me, looming large in the shadow of the moon. Though I was tempted to shout, to question, or to wisecrack, I felt it was probably best to let him focus on navigating. He seemed to know where he was going, because soon we pulled up in front of a small, dark cabin.

Neither man made a move to exit the car. Instead, the driver looked back over his shoulder and examined me from head to toe. I felt like a specimen under a microscope as he inspected me. "Biologically eighteen or so? Problematic. Not insurmountable. I expected younger." This only made me feel even more like a streetwalker than before. Although I had missed its debut in 1972, I had seen Francis Coppola's film *The Godfather* on Duffy's recommendation when it aired at a second-run theatre in Vegas. That education was what allowed me to identify the driver's accent and his dark features as distinctly Italian.

"Who are you?" I had a sneaking suspicion I would not like the answer.

He fixed me in his gaze and said, "Ettore Majorana."

CHAPTER 34

ETTORE MAJORANA. MY hand flew to the door handle but the large brute next to me leaned over casually and grasped my wrist in one meaty hand, pulling it away from the door.

"Relax," said the goon, a New York accent making him sound all the more tough.

"Relax?" I cried. "I spent years locked up in your lab in Chicago."

The driver chuckled. "Lab Majorana," he said. "Yes, an amusing trick. They named it after me, knowing this would make me angry, hoping to draw me out. It nearly worked. This is infuriating to me, seeing my name on something I abhor."

I paused. What had Alan told me? Ettore Majorana had disappeared in 1938 when he was twenty-seven years old. I certainly couldn't do the math, but by my calculations, this guy should have been over eighty and yet he looked just like Michael Corleone in the first *Godfather* movie.

"Where is your sister?" he asked.

"I was hoping you would know," I replied.

"I see," he said, not masking his disappointment. "She is like you?"

"Yes," I admitted. "We're the only two."

He chuckled again then said, "Of course you are not." He stepped out of the car and I had no choice but to follow. "There should be only one," he continued. "Your existence is a terrible mistake. So terrible."

I had been feeling the same way. I followed him inside the small cabin. The goon remained out in the cold, keeping watch.

"When I... vanished," Majorana said as my eyes adjusted to the candlelight, "I left behind enough of my notes and research for them to recreate my experiments. It took them years.

I was the beta, of course, by my own choice. I thought I might be gone minutes. Nanoseconds, perhaps. Smart of them to use fetal subjects. Brother and sister might provide good data, but I, personally, would have used twins."

To my dismay, I found it was practically as cold inside as it was outside. The only source of heat and light was a single kerosene lamp. There was another figure inside, sitting at a table, drawing furiously with a pencil.

Majorana settled into a cracked brown leather chair. "There are things I don't know yet," he said. "The whole equation still eludes me."

The man at the table put down his pencil. "We'll get there, Ettore. Hello, I'm Ted," he said, genially, extending a hand to me. He wore a flannel shirt, had long hair and a graying beard. "Won't you sit down?

He gestured to one of the empty wooden chairs at the table, but I didn't take his hand and I remained standing, rubbing my hands together for warmth. I could have hoped for a better-stocked hideout. Clearly my new companions didn't have the resources of my old enemies.

"Dick," Ted continued, "the technician you met in the generator, wanted me to convey to you that he's never been in so much pain in his entire life."

"He asked me to hit him!" I protested.

Majorana said, "He's just being a big baby."

Ted continued, "He's just not used to that sort of thing."

"Tell him thanks for getting me out," I said, unsure what else to do.

"I will. Now," he began, "I can believe something exists without ever seeing it, assuming I have empirical evidence and good reason. I am a mathematician, you see. I believe in the Higgs Boson. I believe in Santa Clause. I have seen neither. Even though Dick told me what you did, and I know it is possible, I'm going to need to see that for myself."

Happy to oblige, I accelerated then hopped into a seat on the other end of the table. I released my hold on time and, from his perspective, I simply disappeared and reappeared in a different place.

"How's that?" I asked.

"Wonderful!" he said, calmly.

"Abominable," Majorana said, without a hint of emotion. "The most imminent threat to humanity's existence."

Ted interrupted, "If you believe that then why didn't you slay the boy?"

I swallowed hard. Majorana replied, "I believe it. I can't prove it. I will not act on hypotheses when the opposite might be true. I am not an impulsive child."

"Anymore," Ted supplied, laughing.

"There is, of course," Ettore continued, "the slight chance

that this boy may have a greater part to play in things to come. There are too many variables."

I'm glad they were having a gay old time of it, but I interjected, "How about sharing your ideas with me cause I don't have too many of my own to go on."

"Frankly," Ted said, "I wouldn't know where to begin and I doubt you'd understand me. I am only a PhD of Mathematics but while I was at Harvard and Berkeley I became involved with a group… a group where a working knowledge of physics was necessary to participate in any conversation. So I'm fairly well versed. You, however…"

"Okay," I interrupted. I could have mentioned that I studied at Case Western Reserve University, but that was only technically true. "So, who are you people? A group trying to keep accelerator collider thingies from coming online?"

Majorana remained silent. Ted took the lead in this conversation. "In this case, yes. I'm not out to halt the march of progress but when there's a distinct mathematical possibility that an irresponsible government funded project could result in the annihilation of the entire solar system, one feels a civic duty to step up. There are many ways we've managed to delay these projects, political, economic, and, in some cases, violent."

"Ted has a particular skill, or a hobby, perhaps," Majorana supplied dryly.

"In the past," Ted supplied, "when traditional means have proven unproductive, I've been able to deter certain projects simply by mailing a very small explosive to just the right address. They are intentionally identifiable; indeed nobody alert could ever be harmed by one of my little gifts. There have been a few cuts and bruises here and there, but I assure you the result far outweighs the small price paid."

"Ok," I said, "So you're trying to get Isabelle shut down before they turn her on. What are you going to do in order to stop the accelerator?"

"We've already done quite a lot," Ted answered. "I think we've almost succeeded here. First, we've had some well-placed technicians." He smiled devilishly. "Their magnet prototype just keeps on failing, I can't imagine why. The magnetic field simply will not reach the level necessary to begin full scale testing. We have Dick to thank for that, of course. The result has been a dramatic rise in costs as they try to meet their deadlines in getting this thing online. In the meantime, and this has been one of my more devious moves I must admit, an ally in the Department of Energy put forth a plan for a bigger, more effective collider, with innovations supplied by our friend Ettore Majorana, which essentially makes Isabelle redundant and obsolete before she's even been activated."

I gasped. "Why would you want another, bigger collider?"

"We don't!" Ted said. "That would be terrible. However, these things take decades to build. Once they scrap Isabelle because they are certain they can do better with a newer, more powerful design, they'll be signing off on fifteen years of construction before a single proton or anti-proton collide. That will give us plenty of time to make our case to the public or, if necessary, sabotage the new one. Or put forth plans for something bigger! And, of course, we'll need the time to deal with other problems."

"Majorana," I said.

"What?" Ettore replied.

"No," I corrected, "I didn't mean you. I meant that we have to stop Lab Majorana. And then there's my sister."

Majorana continued, "Yes, we certainly have to stop you

and your sister, I'm glad you understand, but the more pressing concern is Lab Majorana's Tevatron."

"What do you mean?" I cried. "No, I don't understand!"

Ted seemed surprised. "The Tevatron is next on our list. It could be operational shortly. You're familiar with Lab Majorana?"

"They were the first ones to abduct me, and they were behind me getting caught at Stonyhaven. I think they may have taken my sister, too. They kept me locked up in their Chicago lab and ran tests on me for years before I escaped."

"That's immoral," Ted clucked, "but you're special, aren't you? I suppose they couldn't resist."

"If they have my sister I have to find her. They might know what happened to my parents, too."

"I'm sorry for all your loss," Ted said. He seemed sincere, although that didn't provoke him to clarify the dizzying comments that Majorana had just made. It was interesting to be the subject of another human being's pity. I'd been on my own for quite a while. I wasn't used to sympathy. He continued, "First things first. We need to get you out of here. This project is well in hand and I think it will come to a close soon. Once we set our sights on the Tevatron, I may be in a position to help you with Lab Majorana. For now, the best thing I can do is keep you out of their hands. This is a hazardous location for you right now."

I wasn't in a position to argue. I'd been running for so long, fleeing powerful unseen enemies with no assistance, that I was happy to let someone else make a decision for once. I slept on a blanket on the floor of the chilly cabin that night. Early in the morning the goon in the Chrysler LeBaron took me to a ferry on the north shore. He deposited me at the terminal, handed me a ticket, and told me I'd be met on the other side.

It was a beautiful trip. An honor guard of seagulls accompanied me across the channel. I spotted fishing boats and cargo ships on the clear horizon. I pigged out at the snack bar on bagged pretzels, chips and soda. Finally, we pulled into New London, Connecticut, where another Chrysler LeBaron was waiting for me. Perhaps it was the choice automobile for physicists and mathematician anarchists.

An equally untalkative female driver took me to the Groton New London Airport, handed me a ticket, and walked me across the tarmac to a propeller plane boarding by stairs. I stepped on board, handed the stewardess my ticket, and continued towards my seat. As an afterthought, I turned back and asked the stewardess, "Where's this plane going?"

She looked at me oddly. I guess it is kind of uncommon to board a plane not knowing where it's going. "Cleveland, Ohio," she said.

"Whoa! Wait a minute!" I pushed past her to the door of the plane where my host was walking back towards her LeBaron. I called after her. "Hey! Stop! Why am I going to Cleveland?"

"It's the last place anyone would think to look for you. Who would ever want to live in Cleveland?"

"Yeah, that's true." I moped back to my seat, hoping this second-rate prop plane at least came equipped with a bar cart, because I needed a stiff one.

CHAPTER 35

I SETTLED IN FOR a long and bumpy ride. My eardrums nearly burst on several occasions, both from the loud noise and the sudden changes of altitude. This wasn't the most luxurious plane in creation, but I suppose it was a fitting chariot to return me to my Cleveland exile. How long would it be? I didn't know if I could handle it.

At the Cleveland-Hopkins Airport I was met by, you guessed it, a Chrysler LeBaron. I didn't even bother trying to strike up a conversation. Apparently Ted and Ettore recruited their men based on their affinity for Chryslers and their inability to speak. He ferried me from the sprawling west side of Cleveland, through the downtown area, past the desolate mid-town section where I'd seen a play at the Cleveland Play House, and into University Circle which housed the Cleveland Orchestra and Case Western Reserve University in a more bucolic part of the city. He pulled up in front of an apartment complex just off campus and handed me a key.

"Apartment 305," he said. "Stay there. Answer the phone. Blend in with the students but don't stand out and don't make any friends."

"Fine. For how long?"

He shrugged and drove away. I reached my apartment, inserted the key, shut the door behind me and almost immediately there was a knock at the door. Once again, I found myself wishing I carried a gun. Who could it be? Had Lab Majorana found me so quickly? I found the window, tugged it open and glanced at the fire escape. That'd be my way out if syringe-wielding goons came looking for me. I went to the door, unlocked it, stepped back towards the window and then called out, "It's unlocked!"

A plump and sweaty bald man in a bright bowtie entered carrying a wide leather-bound briefcase. "Hello!" he said, stepping in and placing the briefcase on a counter. He flipped it open and pulled out some kind of complex mechanical device covered in dials and digital displays. He pointed the thing at me and as I prepared to scramble down the fire escape he said, "Beep beep beep! We have a live one here! Boop, beep!" He spoke in an eccentric, almost falsetto voice.

"What? Who are you?"

"Come in? Don't mind if I do." He pushed further into the room and closed the door. He immediately began pacing around the small room, inspecting everything.

"Eww, it's filled with dorm furniture. Probably crawling with cooties. Good thing you won't have to stay here."

"Again," I said, impatiently and still maintaining my position near the fire escape, "who are you?"

He leaned in confidentially, "I'm Professor Raines. I have wonderful news. Izzy's dead!" He giggled gleefully. "The Department of Energy decided that two hundred million dollars was quite enough to piss away and they finally pulled the plug. Ah, that's funnish. Department of Energy. Pulled the plug. Hah, hah. Now hold still."

Again he pointed that device at me and adjusted a knob.

"What is that?" I asked. "What are you doing?"

"Testing a theory. This is a miniature particle detector. I built it myself. I also designed one of the detectors currently being installed at Lab Majorana. Beep? Beep? Nope," he said, sadly. "Oh well, just a theory. I'd probably need more sensitive equipment anyway."

"So... what's the plan then?"

"Well I am here to collect you. With Izzy shot in the head we're going to do our best with Lab Majorana. Since my theories were the basis for their detector, which is, by the way, some five thousand tons and three stories in height, I am going to oversee its activation. Sadly, if I see an opportunity to sabotage it, I'm supposed to take that chance. Rather like stabbing Mona Lisa right in the smile. Sigh. All for the good of the universe, right? Shall we?"

Seven hours in the car with this man on the way to Chicago made me want to drill a hole in my head, insert a straw and suck out my own brains. He never once stopped talking, except for when he was singing, "clang, clang, clang went the trolley!" and yet I learned almost nothing. At least he didn't drive a LeBaron. His was an old Cadillac that rode smoothly and comfortably, absorbing every bump in the road so it felt like we were gliding on air the whole way. I'd have fallen asleep if he had shut up for a minute or two.

Back in Chicago, I was once again sequestered inside a hotel room. This one was significantly more posh than my Cleveland digs or the cabin in the woods. Raines was keeping me under cover, stashed in his room, which was really quite opulent. Considering I couldn't leave or speak to anyone, it soon felt like a prison. All I had was the TV to keep me company. On the seventh day, Raines returned home with Ted, Ettore, and Dick in tow.

Dick, the mustached technician from Brookhaven, insisted on showing me the bump on his head. There was hardly anything there. "I've never been in so much pain in my entire life!" he declared.

"I'm sorry," I said. "Thanks for helping me escape."

Ted began, "Dick has a theory."

"I have a theory."

"Would you like to explain it," Ted asked.

"Well, it is *my* theory."

Raines chimed in, "Touchy!"

Ted said, "Go ahead then."

"Well, the way I see it, we can spend a few years of our lives here trying to throw golems in the gears to get this project shut down, or, we could possibly do it all in one fell swoop. With your help."

"How?" I asked.

"This little talent of yours. I suspect that if you were to try and use it in the presence of a large-scale particle accelerator that was active or had recently been active, you would be thrown backwards in time—"

"Or forwards," Majorana interrupted.

"—Or forwards," Dick continued. "Thank you. You'd be thrown forwards or backwards in time—"

"Or he would—," Raines tried to jump in.

"I'm getting to that. Shut your donut hole! You'd be thrown forwards or backwards in time or you would disintegrate."

The idea stuck in my mind. "Backwards…" I was nearly twenty and my life was in shambles because of being thrown forward in time. Could everything be righted by going back? There was a lot of appeal in that.

"Or forwards," Dick corrected, "or disintegrated." As if I could have forgotten. "Either way," he continued, "that's not a risk we'd care to take. However, I believe that if you were to accelerate yourself here, far away from any active accelerator matrix, that you could safely enter the facility. Once there we can give you instructions that would shut down the experiment for good. Then sneak back out and poof! You've saved us all years of work and possibly the universe as well. Yippee."

My math isn't all that good but by my best estimate I was about nineteen years old by then, plenty old enough to act like a man and do something heroic. I don't think it was heroism that motivated me to accept Dick's challenge and invade a highly guarded facility filled with people who had been hunting me for my entire adult life. It was something of a death wish. It was practically suicidal. I felt that I had no justifiable reason to live and if I could go out doing something for mankind, then so be it. Or perhaps it was the minute chance that I could somehow find a window backwards in time. Dick armed me with schematics of the plant, told me exactly where to hit and what to do, and he even gave me a set of wire clippers and some gloves to keep my prints off the site. Ted gave me a package that he wanted me to leave on a particular desk. North Tower, fourth floor, room 216A. Ettore took my pulse and gazed deep into my eyes using some kind of handheld device with an attached light. I don't know if he found what he was looking for, but I didn't ask.

We had a meal that felt suspiciously somber, like the last supper, then I said goodbye and set off, leaving them frozen at the table. Raines was in the middle of taking an inhumanly large bite out of his napoleon, Dick was wrinkling his nose at Raines's display, Ted had his pencil out and was scribbling something incomprehensible, and Ettore had his eyes fixed on me. If all went well, then for them I'd be gone only a fraction of a second and we could all sit back and watch the news reports about how all funding for the Tevatron suddenly dried up due to a series of expensive mishaps.

From my perspective, I had one hell of a long walk ahead of me. Every train and taxi in the city, in the world perhaps, had ground to a halt. It felt like hours before I was standing in front of the facility. It was well guarded but I walked on in, sidestepping the metal detectors and brushing past the brawny guards.

"Sorry lads," I said to the frozen security desk at the front, "must've left my badge at home." I continued deeper into the complex, having to use the stairs because the elevators were just as frozen as the people. I hit the first site Dick had told me about. I had to use my screwdriver to remove a panel and pull out a circuit board, clip one small wire, then replace the board and the panel.

"That'll piss them off!" he'd said. "And they'll never find what's wrong. They'll have to replace the whole unit!"

My next stop was the North Tower, fourth floor, room 216A, to deliver Ted's package. The office was empty, but the placard on the desk read, "Bertram Llewellyn."

My uncle! This was my uncle's desk! At this point, you must realize I didn't know that my uncle was involved. I hadn't made the connection between him and the plots to kidnap me. I hadn't yet been to the red building in NYC or met Black Esmerta. I knew I wanted to talk to him about what happened that day in the desert. I wanted to ask him if he knew where my parents were or if he knew what had happened to Joan. I had no suspicion that he was anything more than a cog in this machine. He might not have known anything. I recalled that he used to work for BERN, the Bureau Européen pour la Recherche Nucléaire. In my mind, my Uncle Bert was someone important, because he had answers, and because he was family.

The package in my hand was wrapped in brown paper and twine. My instructions were to set it on the desk in this office. What could the package be? I contemplated opening it up. Then I thought back to what Ettore had said about Ted's "special skill" when I first met him, well-placed explosives aimed to interrupt research.

I held the package up to my ear, which, in retrospect, was kind of silly, since even if it was the "ticking" kind of bomb, it certainly wouldn't be ticking while I was in my accelerated state. I looked over the package again. It read, "ATTN: B. LLEWELLYN," and that was all.

There was no doubt in my mind. In my hand I held a bomb that was designed to kill or hurt my uncle. Having to choose between my loyalty to a shadowy group of misfits I had just met and a family member that might be the key to finding my missing parents, it was an easy decision. I wouldn't leave that bomb there for him to find. I wouldn't be responsible for killing my uncle, the only family I had left.

In that moment I began to question Ted's motives. Were people with evil intentions using me as a blunt instrument? How far could I really trust Ted, Ettore, Dick, Raines, and the rest? Saving the universe by killing scientists? What sort of people had I gotten mixed up with? Maybe I should let time return to normal right then and there and simply wait in

Uncle Bert's office for him to come back. I'd finally have my chance to ask him questions that had been burning inside me since 1979.

I decided that after I was finished with my work I would return to meet and question my uncle. In the meantime, Lab Majorana was still my enemy, and I would do what I could to shut them down. In the hallway I lifted the lid of a heavy metal garbage can and tossed the package inside. If it actually was a small explosive, then the can would contain it. I pulled out my clippers and progressed further into the belly of the beast. I stopped once to crack a small vacuum tube then again to adjust the levels on a magnetic field detector.

At last, I sidestepped another thick layer of security and found the heart of the facility, the room that Dick said would house the Tevatron's proton accelerator. He'd never seen the device and hadn't seen specs on how it operates, but he'd examined the engineering of the entire building and said that there was no other place the accelerator could be. I kicked the door open, but there was no machinery inside.

There was a bed. There was a woman. It was the older version of my sister.

I ran to her. Her eyes were slightly open. Electrodes dotted her frail chest, tubes penetrated her nose and mouth, needles and tubes perforated her arms, and an intricate metal frame streaming with wires was affixed to her head. I shook her. I hugged her. I screamed out loud. And I cried. I tried to remove the frame but it really did seem to be actually screwed into her skull. I realized I couldn't talk to her because I was still in fast mode. So without much forethought I let things return to normal.

"Joan!" I cried out. "Can you hear me?" Her eyes were

fluttering between half open and closed, but there didn't seem to be any sign of consciousness. I pulled again at the frame. I ripped the electrodes off her temples and chest. Machines monitoring her whirred and buzzed in protest. "Come on, wake up! Wake up!" I pleaded.

I heard voices shouting and an alarm was raised. Sirens blared and red-flashing lights filled the hallway. Heavy boots came running. Somewhere far away there was an explosion. I heard screams. The heavy door swung open and there stood my uncle. Three large bleeding gashes lined his face and four fingers from his right hand were missing. He held up the bloody stump, grasping his wrist to stop the flow of blood. Three guards appeared behind him with their weapons fixed on me.

"Uncle Bert?" I said.

He lifted his good arm and pointed a small shiny revolver directly at me before ordering, "Fire!"

I hugged Joan as tightly as I could, hoping I could take her with me, wherever I was going. According to Dick, there were only three possibilities: forward, backward or disintegration. I couldn't tell you which one I was hoping for. Whatever it was, I didn't want to do it alone. I felt a familiar lurching sensation and I knew what would happen. How many years would it be this time?

CHAPTER 36

I N 1983, AFTER an outlay of $200 million, Stony-haven National Laboratory's Isabelle project was cancelled. That figure began to look wistfully small in the early nineties after the first $2 billion out of a projected $12 billion was spent on the Superconducting Super Collider. It took an act of Congress to obliterate that money-pit. It was 1993 and only fifteen out of fifty-four miles of tunnels had been bored deep under Waxahachie, Texas. Upon cancellation of the project, a fifteen-mile string of dynamite obliterated the tunnel. Talk about a bridge to nowhere! Had the United States gone through with plans to build that collider, it would've cost more than NASA's contribution to the International Space Station. As it turned out, our country couldn't afford both. On the upside, the Waxahachie site, surrounded by the poverty its cancellation caused, would prove to be an excellent post-apocalyptic back-drop for Jean-Claude Van Damme's 1999 movie *Universal Soldier: The Return*.

The Texas project would have been four times as powerful as BERN's Large Hadron Collider set to begin operation in Switzerland in early 2009. Its cancellation was a tragedy for that Texas town and for the scientific community, but it might also have saved the universe. Maybe. There's no way to know. I assume that Ted and Ettore must have had something to do with it, but again I can't be certain. I'd ask him but I think he'd be a hard man to reach. I hadn't any idea what happened to him until the other day when I was watching *A Cultural Look Back at the Nineties* on VH1. I always enjoy watching shows like that. It helps me fill in the gaps, to see what I missed. Usually it seems like a lot of garbage, but I did learn that I'm significantly more upset about having missed seven years of the eighties than I am about missing all of the nineties. Eighties music, style and culture was a little bit more interesting than the nineties. I digress.

On the VH1 *Cultural Look Back*, there was Ted, in a montage of iconic photographs from the nineties, wearing an orange jumpsuit and posing for his mug shot. I hopped on Google and after a little rummaging I found out quite a few interesting things about him. I found it particularly amusing that the cabin where we first met is on display at a D.C. museum.

That answers the first question you may have had. Although I suppose it goes without saying that my stunt at Lab Majorana didn't result in my disintegration, since you're reading this story. I reappeared in the summer of 2001, eighteen years after my aborted attempt to sabotage the Tevatron and rescue my sister. She'd been in my arms when Uncle Bert's goons opened fire and I tried to accelerate us both to safety. From my perspective, she vanished, along with Pac-Man cereal, stick-up bangs, slap bracelets and legwarmers, in short, everything else that was good about 1983.

Lab Majorana in Chicago had been deserted. The trail to my sister, to my family, and to my uncle was once again cold, though I had no doubt they were still out there, and they were still looking for me. Wearing my dated Calvin Klein jeans, which, thanks to the cyclical nature of fashion, were once again extremely cool, I stowed away on an Amtrak train to New York City. Remembering my earlier observations, it seemed like as good a place as any to get lost in the crowd. Although I'd learned Ted's fate, I'd lost contact with Ettore, Raines and Dick. Alan had turned out to be a filthy traitor. My uncle was evil. David and Julia were probably the only people I could trust, but they were most likely being watched, and I had no desire to curse their existence as I had apparently done to Alan. After my Chicago adventure I wanted no more intrigue. I wanted to hide again.

My timing, as always, was the worst.

I found a studio to sublet in Harlem. It took all of my remaining cash just to get that. Since I wasn't about to submit to a credit check, I had to be persuasive when it came to how much money I put on the table. For those of you who have never lived in New York, you won't appreciate the exorbitant amount of money one can piss away for so little. The neighborhood wasn't particularly frightening. Harlem had undergone gentrification and become another expensive hot spot. The apartment itself was a fourth-floor walk-up that faced a loud and busy street. The building was festering with all manner of creepy-crawlies, and the hallways were a constant noisome battle between scents of curry and garlic.

In an effort to reduce my thieving and feel like a normal member of society, I actually took a job. It needed to be something cash-based since I was strictly off the radar and didn't have any of the documents I'd need to book a real job. I started doing gigs for a few different catering companies. I'd usually pull in about $20 an hour, with tips, and it was all cash. I found that nobody really looks closely at a cater-waiter so I toiled on in obscurity.

September 11th was the climactic end to many stories, but not to mine. I was scheduled to cater a business luncheon at a law firm on Broad Street, so I had to get an early start that day. I was heading downtown on the 2 train when the first plane struck the North Tower, though none of us knew it at the time. The conductor announced there was a fire ahead and so we'd be delayed. With the train packed full of commuting New Yorkers, there was immediate tension and anger as people realized they might be late for work. We were kept down there in the intermittent and ineffectual air-conditioning for at least thirty sweltering minutes before they backed the train up to the Fulton station and announced that the entire subway system was being shut down. Shut down! All of it? There was a mad rush up the stairs as people tried to be the first to hail cabs so they could make it to work on time.

This was at about 10AM. I looked over to the southwest where I ought to have seen two shining towers. Instead, I saw a gigantic column of smoke, as grand in scale as the mushroom cloud I saw in the desert, only much closer. Indeed, ash was blossoming up into the sky, blotting out the sun. The first tower had just fallen.

Nobody knew what was happening. A crowd had gathered outside the window of a cigar shop where CNN news graphics flashed captions about attacks at the Pentagon and evacuations at Sears Tower and the White House. It was just at that moment that a wall of smoke and liquefied cement came boiling down the street. The crowd ran and I joined them. We ran east towards the water. Shouts, the rumbling ground, and the smoke overtook us. I covered my mouth with my shirt, unsure of what it was I'd be inhaling, and I continued along with the mob. I reached the water and the crowd was splitting. Some were heading towards the Brooklyn Bridge, anxious to get off the island, and some were heading north out of the smoke. I continued north, stopping to brush the rubble off my clothes. A shopkeeper was handing out plastic cups of water to the crowd and I grabbed one as I passed, thanking him as I continued on. There was plenty of compassion, warmth, and charity, but precious few answers. The sky was still stained and when we heard the screaming sound of jets overhead our collective hearts pounded with fear. In the middle of the street I saw a man pushing a shopping cart that wore a boom box around his neck. He shouted at us, "Don't go north, you dumb assholes! They're gonna hit the Empire State Building next!"

I like to think that if I had had any clue what was really happening I could've helped in some small way. Someone with my abilities could've saved a lot of lives that day, if I had gotten an earlier start. Unfortunately, I was trapped in the subway, unaware, and by the time I realized what had happened, it was too late. Luckily, New Yorkers are pretty good at taking care of their own. There was no shortage of heroes that day. I'm not a hero. I'm a caterer with a secret.

Business was slow in the weeks that followed. Once the clean up was underway and lower Manhattan was reopened for business, things began to pick up. A number of businesses were hard hit and the stock market took a dive, but people still needed to eat, so I continued to dish it out as cater waiter.

I met a lot of actors in that profession. They are a desperate, penurious, transient people and I fit right in. Most of the caterers I met professed to really be actors so I learned a bit about the trade. Since I was a poor waiter, most people just naturally assumed I wanted to be an actor, so I let that illusion alone. I'd let them believe I was an actor if simply being a caterer was so hard to swallow. This wasn't a problem until just a few weeks ago. One of my catering cohort, a monstrously tall and stick-thin blond named Jerrold, cornered me as I filled ramekins with butter.

"Jay!" he cried. He was addressing me by my pseudonym du jour. "I'm directing a showcase and one of my actors just dropped out because he got an audition for a commercial. An audition! Dropped out of a play just for an audition. Insane, right? Anyway, it opens in less than two weeks and you look perfect for it and I know you're an actor so will you do it?"

"Uhh…"

"It's at The Kraine Theatre which is a great downtown space, the cast is wonderful, great script that I wrote myself, really sexy, it's an Equity showcase so there's no money in it but you could get great exposure."

The last thing I needed: exposure. "Sorry Jerrold, I really don't think I'd have time."

"I'll work around your schedule," he insisted. "If you need to pull shifts here, we'll work around that. You have to do this, please. Come on, you're an actor, right?"

"I mean… not really," I admitted.

"Come on Jay, you've got to *believe* in yourself."

"Yeah…"

"Awesome! Thank you so much! I'll get you a script. You're the best, man."

Funny, I had no recollection of saying yes, and yet that's how it seemed to Jerrold. However, once I saw the script I realized there was no danger of anybody coming to see this play. It was utter garbage. Not only that, but there was one scene that took place entirely on a bed where a topless woman would be straddling me. Well, maybe acting wouldn't be so bad after all!

Having settled into this odd routine, I had begun to think that I was enjoying the dénouement of my story. I'd been in NYC since 2001. I'd been through a catastrophe that made me feel like part of the city. I hadn't had any hint that Uncle Bert was on my heels. I had a job and an apartment that I paid for without committing felonies. I hadn't had any run-ins with nefarious outlaw scientists from the past.

It still wasn't quite ideal. Mine was a lonely existence. I was dismally short on friends and family. I was meant merely to survive in solitude, observing the world around me but studiously avoiding participation. I had started to accept my lot in life.

It was 2008. I was on my way to a rehearsal at The Kraine Theatre. In the distance, out of the corner of my eye, I saw a red building.

CHAPTER 37

YES, DEAR READER, you may breathe a hard earned sigh of relief. The pieces have come together at last! No more jumping back and forth. We have returned, finally, to the room behind Black Esmerta's fortune-telling parlor. The end of this tale is nigh.

"So," she said, lighting a cigar, "what are you going to do?"

"You're missing the rest of your *Simpsons* episode, you know." The fact remained that I didn't know what I was going to do. The thick stench of incense and the questions from the greedy psychic were keeping me from thinking straight.

"Black Esmerta has TiVo. This might be more interesting."

"Well, what would you do in my situation?"

"Consulting fee, is twenty—"

"Yeah, yeah, whatever," I said, emptying every last dollar from my wallet onto her couch. It's a good thing I get paid in cash. "Here's everything I have left, you crook. Just sit there and listen while I talk this crap out."

She puffed a thick black cloud of smoke into my face. "Be nice," she said, rifling through the bills. Seemingly satisfied, she clasped her hands behind her head and leaned back on her sofa. "So, talk."

I needed to organize my thoughts, and though I'm loath to admit it, I also needed to confide in someone. Esmerta was perhaps the worst candidate, but there she was, rapt with attention. I gave her the Cliff's Notes version of how I spent my last thirty or so years. She looked incredulous, at first, and even interjected at one point to say, "Baloney," but gradually that was replaced with a sense of wonder as she became rapt with the story and quietly chomped on her thick brown cigar. She was so absorbed that she didn't even interject to request more money.

I explained how they experimented on me in Chicago then I executed a daring escape, fleeing to exile in frigid Cleveland until Alan's advice sent me to Long Island where I was captured at Brookhaven in Alan's snare. The sting of that betrayal still hurt. Esmerta was particularly amused by how Ted and his Freedom Club (the "FC" that Alan had mentioned) sprang me and returned me to Cleveland before mounting an assault on Lab Majorana in Illinois. I still couldn't make sense of Ettore Majorana's role in this drama and I suspected he knew a lot more than he had shared. Then I told her how I found my sister integrated into the Tevatron, literally drilled to the equipment. My uncle tried to have me killed. I skipped eighteen years, yadda yadda yadda, moved to NYC, catered, rehearsed a poorly written but delightfully erotic play, and today stumbled upon a large red building, which as it turns out, belongs to my evil uncle.

"I can't go back to the Bell building. I think it's built from those bricks, the red stone, that material they tested on me back in 1979."

"Is like your kryptonite," Esmerta said, enthralled.

"It won't kill me, but if I try to accelerate near that building I'll get sick. Puking twice in one day is enough for me. Also, there are no exits or entrances except for that one gate that opens from the inside. I couldn't get in if I tried."

Esmerta considered. The silence in her back room was interrupted only by the occasional distant horn blare of New York City traffic.

"You have two choices," she said, gesturing with her soggy cigar. "No, three. Choice one: do nothing. You are good at that."

I couldn't argue. I had become quite good at inaction. By choosing to actually do something I'd bear all the responsibility when things inevitably came crashing down.

"Second, you have another address for your uncle. It's still up on my Mac screen. I could print it for you, very cheap. Maybe that's something you're not supposed to know about. Maybe it's not protected in same way and you could get in and find answers. Go there. See what other secrets you can find out."

"That's an incredible idea!" I stood and began pacing. "He won't expect me there. I'll do that right now!"

"Sit!" she commanded, then paused for a pensive puff. "Third option. You do your acceleration baloney here, far from red building, then go to red building, rescue sister. If that worked at Lab Majorana in Chicago, it can work here, too."

Suddenly the money I'd lost here seemed well spent. Why hadn't I thought of that? If they wanted to keep me out so badly that they constructed an entire building of that material, then it must be where they were keeping my sister. I assumed it was impenetrable, but if I approached it having already accelerated, perhaps I could sneak in while that limping guard takes his next smoke break.

"Wait," I said. "In Chicago, they were using her as a particle accelerator in their Hadron Collider, but there couldn't be a collider in Manhattan. Maybe she's not here. Unless... the subways?" I asked.

"No," Esmerta snapped. "That's stupid. This story is sci-fi enough as it is. Particle accelerator in the subways," she scoffed. "Stupid. There couldn't be one. They use her for something else here."

"So what should I do?" I asked.

"Come," she said, standing and heading through the curtains to her front parlor. "We consult cards."

"No, seriously, I just wanted advice. I have no more money."

"Is freebie." She sat down in the chair that I had occupied earlier to throw off my pursuers. She pulled out her cards from the cabinet where I'd gotten the crystal bowl and I grudgingly took a seat across from her. Spread before her were cards from a well-worn tarot deck. "For you I pull hanged man, upside-down devil. Give in to will of fate. Don't fight fate. Also, you will have wealth today."

"Fat chance lady," I said, rising to leave, "you took every penny I have. I'm going to start with that other address. Things are too hot at the red building right now."

"Luck! Let me know how it goes!" she said as I departed.

The other Llewellyn property I'd found was on West 86th and Riverside Drive, a wealthy and exclusive residential area. I took the 1 train to 86th Street, looped around to 84th and walked down to Riverside Park. From the modest anonymity afforded by the trees and benches I scoped out the building, which was visible from the park. On the plus side, it wasn't made out of red brick, which was encouraging. It looked more like a mansion or townhouse than a scientific institution. It was five stories tall, faced with white stone, and gated. The main entrance was an opulent heavy wooden door painted a brilliant blue and there was a smaller servant entrance off to the side. Each floor boasted three expansive curved windows and a narrow balcony with stone balustrades. I ventured to leave the protection of the park and walked down 86th. There was plenty of foot traffic so I didn't stand out all that much. A closer inspection revealed nothing out of the ordinary, except perhaps for the sheer cost of everything. I had at least expected to see some of those bulky old style video cameras covering the exterior, or perhaps a guard or two. There was nothing. Could it be that nobody was home? I pulled the brim of my Mets cap down low and opened the gate, climbed three stairs then rang the doorbell.

A screen flickered to life just above the ringer and a plump dark-faced woman with an island accent spoke, "Who is it?"

"Delivery," I said, clutching my backpack and looking downward.

"Just a minute."

Finally the door clanked as a bolt slid aside and the woman answered.

"Who's it for?"

"343 West 86th."

"Dis is 345 ya dolt," she said, exasperated.

"Sorry," I said, trying to look sheepish.

"Open your eyes, man," she snapped. She turned to go, letting the door shut behind her. Whatever amenities this mansion may have had, protection against accelerators clearly was not included. Before it could lock me out, I accelerated and stepped past the grumpy housekeeper into the city equivalent of a palace. A giant circular staircase that stretched five floors dominated the building. Not wanting to miss anything, I first headed downstairs to the basement. There was a glass-enclosed wine cellar. I was no connoisseur but I'd be willing to bet they were worth a pretty penny. There was a bar in a den-like room with arched ceilings and more pillows than in *The Arabian Nights*. The television was on and a vacuum stood in the middle of the room. This must be where the housekeeper was headed. Down another hall there were bathrooms and an empty office, all fairly desolate.

On the first floor there was a parlor with lovely Victorian furniture. The second floor boasted a kitchen that would make any chef drool. The third had a dining room with a 360-degree mural, so when sitting at the heavy oak table it gave one the impression of eating in a peaceful forest. I could see the appeal, but it actually looked kind of tacky. There was another sitting room and bar on that level, with a giant flat panel television and a view of the park. On the fourth floor was a library stocked with books, more booze, and artwork. In the rear there was a door leading to a roof terrace that wrapped around half the building. There was an opulent garden with a fountain in the middle. Finally, on the fifth floor, I found what I had been looking for.

The colossal master bedroom with its king sized bed made my uncle looked diminutive by comparison. It was a shock to see him looking like that. He must have been well past ninety. He was hooked to all sorts of machines whose purpose I could only assume was to prolong his malevolent life so he could continue to inflict misery upon the world. I took a fair amount of satisfaction at seeing him hooked to machines, as I had been for so long.

His gray hair had disappeared, revealing wrinkled and splotchy skin. His sallow face hung on his bones like wet tissue paper. His eyes were open, watching the widescreen, though the sagging skin from his eyelids must have obscured half of everything he saw. He looked helpless, but I knew better. I locked the door to his bedroom. I took the belt from a robe hanging off the bathroom door and tied his hands together, trying not to look at the missing fingers, his swollen arthritic knuckles, and his teary eye. I took a quick look around for any weapons he might have stashed, any silent alarm buttons he might be able to push, and any possible booby traps he might have set for me.

I let time return to normal. The first word I spoke was: "electroencephalography."

He looked at me through eyes that narrowed, sharper and more clear than one might expect from a man his age. "They told me you'd made your way to New York." His speech was overloud and spit-laden. His smile revealed a mouth devoid of teeth.

"Electroencephalography," I said again.

"Beg pardon? You're not making any sense."

"Electroencephalography," I repeated, louder this time. "It's a word I learned at Lab Majorana. Was it you that taught it to me? Were you the one speaking to me in that room?"

He thought for a moment. "Guilty. Yes. It was I that spoke to you all those years ago in Chicago. I wanted to personally oversee your examination. We are family, after all."

"I figured. I don't have an E.C.T. device to shock you, but my guess is that you'd be pretty damn uncomfortable if I pulled this plug right here." To prove my point, I yanked out the power cord that connected his respirator to the wall. He began wheezing and clawing for air. It looked quite painful. I plugged it in and as the machine did its job he relaxed back into his pillows.

"Did that hurt?" I asked. "That looked like it hurt. Now, where is my sister?"

"Not the wisest question," he coughed. "You've never been particularly bright but even you must know she's in my facility downtown. That information will do you no good."

"Why not?" I asked.

"Two reasons. First, I designed the facility specifically to negate threats like you. The second... Many years ago, during your ill-conceived attempt to infiltrate my Chicago complex, after your explosive mangled my hands..." he waggled his wrinkled fingers-the six that remained. "I chased you through my Chicago facility. I admit I was livid and perhaps not thinking clearly. My intention was to shoot you somewhere nonessential. Legs perhaps. What happened next is a tragedy, and it was entirely your fault."

"What happened?" I asked.

"Bloody stumps for fingers and a wounded eye would take its toll on any marksman. A disappearing target... Well, who could blame me? Your sister took two bullets."

I gasped. "She's dead?"

He continued to taunt me. "No. Not exactly. It's a matter for interpretation. Whatever was left of your sister's mind has vanished. She still serves an invaluable function, but the soul, if you believe in such things, has most certainly departed."

I reached down and yanked the plug from the wall again. Bertram's suffering didn't allay much pain. I plugged him back in and fell to my knees. I'd been searching for her for so long, and she'd been essentially dead for years.

After Bertram regained his composure, he pleaded, "It's time to think about the future. Your future. The future of mankind. There is a grand equation of which you are an integral element. With your help, we can move forward with this grand experiment, finally. These particle accelerator experiments have already changed the world. The worldwide web. Cloud computing. We would have none of these things were it not for this work. There is still so much to learn about the universe, how it came to be, how it will inevitably end."

"What are you suggesting? Do you honestly think there's a chance I'd let you strap me to a chair again? Lock me away in Chicago or New York?

"You would be more useful in Geneva, at this point, but that is a detail we can discuss. If you go willingly, we can conduct our experiments, you can perform certain tasks, and you can lead an otherwise normal life." The thought was so ridiculous that I might have laughed, had I not already been drowning in grief.

"There is one other consideration…" he said. "I am not blessed with a large family. You are my sole heir. Consider this, when I pass, if you allow me to reintegrate you into society, and if you do my bidding with respect to the particle accelerator, then you will inherit considerable wealth. This home, for instance, would be yours. I have others, too. A home in London. In Rio de Janeiro. In Switzerland. A Penthouse in Chicago. Real estate holding to make Donald Trump jealous. All of this can be yours with a few strokes of my pen. My dear nephew, you will be as rich as a king."

Black Esmerta certainly had been right on the money when her Tarot cards predicted wealth for me today.

I had no attractive options, but I knew that I would never sell out like that. "You can go to hell."

I reached again to the plug but he cried out, "There are some other compelling reasons you should cooperate. Your sister is no longer effective leverage. Consider your friend Alan."

"Are you kidding?" I laughed. "Fry him, what do I care?"

"Poor choice, I suppose," he said. "Let's go down the line then. Julia. Julia is far too old for you, but I think you still have affection for her."

"What have you done to Julia?" I gasped.

"Simply collected her, as a bargaining chip. I did the same to your old high school friend David. And to that colorful fellow from Vegas, Duffy. Also, that infuriating lab technician, Dick. We don't have your colleague Ted, but he's within our reach in a federal penitentiary."

I hesitated. He could be lying. I knew I had been under surveillance. He might know about those people, but he certainly wouldn't have captured them all. Would he?

"You seem unconvinced," he said. "I saved the piece de resistance for last. How would you like to see your mother and your father again?"

CHAPTER 38

I WAS STILL LOW to the ground or the force of his words might have knocked me off my feet. Mom and dad? Alive? I had given up hope of ever seeing them again. Yet there I was, standing in a room with the only man that could possibly tell me what happened after I disappeared in Nevada all those years ago. He knew what happened to my parents. I moved toward the plug again, determined to force the information out of him by any means necessary, when I saw something move out of the corner of my eye. The room was expansive, and my eyesight has never been particularly good, but there was definitely a shape in the corner that hadn't been there a moment ago.

I squinted until the image sharpened. For the first time, I knew something that the smug old man didn't. "You've kidnapped everyone I've ever known," I said. "There's someone you forgot to mention."

Bertram replied, "There's only one person that has ever eluded me, besides you. In your case, it was sheer luck or stupidity. I cannot say the same of him."

"I am almost flattered, Bertram," Ettore Majorana said as he stepped around the bed to stand beside me. He still wore a dark wide lapelled suit and didn't look a day older than when I had last seen him.

For the first time since I'd stepped in that room, the arrogance melted from my uncle's face. There was for the first time a genuine emotion piercing the cool façade and causing his wrinkled face to twist: fear.

"Ettore," Bertram said.

"Che piacere vederti," he replied dryly.

"Come stai?"

"Sto bene, grazie, e tu?"

"Non mi posso lamentare."

"If you two are done with the Italian lesson, let's question him some more," I interjected.

"No need," Majorana replied. "We've heard everything we need. Further words will only poison us. I know what we must do next."

He turned and walked toward the door. I followed, leaving my uncle coughing, struggling against his bonds. "He knows where my parents are," I insisted, after we stepped out into the hall.

"As do I. We do not need him."

From the hall I heard Bertram calling out after us. His feeble old voice didn't carry, and I couldn't make out what he was saying. As we climbed down the wide staircase and reached the main level, I said, "Won't he just alert the troops in his fortress downtown? His housekeeper-"

"Is locked in the wine cellar, for the time being." Ettore was silent and I continued to follow. We soon stood at another service entrance in the rear of the mansion.

"Were you looking for me? How did you find me here?"

"You strayed from our plan at Lab Majorana. You decelerated while in that facility." He didn't sound accusatory. He was just stating a fact. "After I learned you disappeared, I jumped ahead after you, and eventually picked up your scent."

"Why didn't you come talk to me?" I asked.

"In the years we skipped, Ted failed and was imprisoned, and the rest of our organization fell into disarray. I became convinced that the only way to make progress again was to kill you. Therefore, talking was not the wisest course of action."

I swallowed hard. His soft features and big brown eyes seemed incongruous when he spoke so casually of murdering me. He continued, "Do not worry. I changed my mind. Today has been a very interesting day. In fact, if I had killed you, we would all be doomed. Sometimes inaction is the best action."

I could hardly argue there.

"In his prime, Llewellyn was a fabulous engineer," Ettore said. "He never would have designed something like this, for instance." He gestured toward a control box inside the back door of the mansion. "This entire house has a battery back-up system. Very wise. His medical equipment would continue to work even in a citywide blackout. This switch here, turns off access to the grid, and this one shuts down the battery backup."

A lever in each hand, he yanked both down. The lights in the mansion flickered out. I could still see Ettore's face by the half-light spilling in through the window on the exit door.

Four stories away, I was grateful that I couldn't hear what must have been a painful end to Bertram Llewellyn's miserable life.

*

Ettore and I walked south along a winding path in Riverside Park. The sun had just dipped below the squat buildings that made up the skyline on the Jersey side of the Hudson. A burning yellow roiled above the roofs, capped with clouds that had turned an angry red and purple. The water was smooth as glass, reflecting the sun's waning light and the city's rising luminescence.

"Let me tell you why you exist," he said after a long but somehow comfortable silence. The death of an enemy has a calming effect. "This was never meant to be a project to cost billions, to gut cities, to cause pain. My dream was for two particles to collide at near infinite speed, unlocking the key to creation. We can do this, perhaps, with tunnels and machines, and billions, and governments. My vision was instead to create two particles that could move at unfathomable speeds. These two particles would be guided by conscious thought. Free will. You are one of those particles."

"The other one is my sister," I finished.

"Forgive me, it's been a long time since I've taught. Please feel free to ask questions. When a proton and antiproton collide, two things may happen. They may annihilate. This is messy. Quarks, antiquarks, gluons, all scattered, with a release of energy. Or, they interact and create a photon, a particle of pure energy. This, I believe, is your destiny."

"What am I supposed to do?" I didn't understand all he said and I felt helpless in the face of all these forces that had been put in motion long before I was even born.

"Llewellyn, he spoke truth about your sister, but there is still a way to save her. It is time to do what you were born to do. It is necessary, to save our little planet."

Again, I thought about Esmerta's cards. What had they said? Don't fight fate.

"What about Duffy?" I asked. "And Julia, Dick, David, Alan."

"Lies," he said. "Exaggerations. No doubt all those people are in his grasp, but he had no reason to hold them hostage. He could have grabbed them any time."

"My parents?" I asked.

"I suspect I know where they might be. They are in no immediate danger. First, your sister."

We took a cab down to the red building. I objected when the cab stopped right by the front entrance, but Ettore told me not to worry and I took him at his word. We walked up the concealed drive to the sole door of the massive edifice, which was wide open. "I followed you here before the mansion. While you were in with your psychic, I may have left things a little messy."

Lining the interior hallway were ten guards, all face down with their hands and legs zip tied. "It took forever," he said. "It was very exhausting."

He led me to a service elevator, pushed the button for sub-basement six, inserted a key he'd taken from a guard, and we began our quick descent. The door opened to a sterile lab, white and steel everywhere, with familiar red brick accents. Three zip-tied technicians lay on the floor. A stainless steel tube stood conspicuously in the center of the room, surrounded by control panels, access grating, and various instruments. Thick braided wires emerged from the tube.

"What is this?" I asked, dreading the answer.

"It is a super-cooled chamber. -272 degrees Celsius. Only slightly above absolute zero. The coldest place in the universe. She was frozen only moments after Bertram's unfortunate misfire. They thought the cold would stop the reaction, but they were wrong."

"What reaction?"

"A runaway fusion process. The cold slowed it, no doubt, but it is only a matter of hours or days before she reaches a critical point."

"What happens then?" I asked, afraid to hear the answer.

"Something like a micro black hole. The entire planet will become an inert hyperdense sphere about one hundred meters across, with what used to be your sister at its center. Other planets in our solar system will likely be pulled from their orbits."

"Is she..." I didn't even know what to ask.

"She is in a constant state of acceleration. Just as you and I have so often experienced, if she were awake, we would look still to her. But she is frozen, so every second that passes by for us is an eternity for her."

"Is she aware?"

"I hope not. It would be maddening."

I remembered Llewellyn's defensive red brick, "Will the..."

Ettore interrupted, "The effect of the subsidence rock is too weak to inhibit your acceleration here, at the center of the building, where the reaction is about to go critical. The forces involved are too powerful."

I knew what to do. It felt instinctual. I was compelled to do it and once I made the decision to go with my impulse, to not fight fate, a tremendous peaceful wave passed through me. Joan was already in her acceleration state. It was time for the collision we were destined for.

I accelerated and fought only a momentary and subtle bout of nausea. Ettore stood frozen beside me.

I climbed the metal scaffolding that surrounded the stainless steel tube. I twisted the seal and then the top popped open with a hiss, white gas billowing out. I peered into the canister but could only see a vague dark shape in the distortion of the super-cooled fumes. Without seeing, I knew what was in there. I had seen it in my vision in Esmerta's bowl.

I stepped over the edge of the scaffolding and plunged into the smoke. Expecting the icy embrace of super-cooled gas, I instead felt an enormous blast of heat. Then nothing.

*

I awoke and found myself lying on the ground, having rolled away from the canister, which had split open like a giant metal banana peel. The smoke had dissipated. There was no sign of my sister.

I apparently had released my hold on time, since Ettore had come up to me and was peering into my eyes using the same instrument he'd used before. A satisfied smile on his face was my clue that things had worked out to his satisfaction.

"Squint," I thought.

Or did I?

"Squint," it felt like thinking, but it wasn't coming from me.

"Joan?" I thought, in response.

A moment of silence, and then I heard, or felt, "Thank you."

EPILOGUE

I CAN'T ACCELERATE ANYMORE.
In the moments that followed my collision at the red building, I gave it a try, at Ettore's behest. I willed the world to pause and it no longer obeyed. Ettore had a theory that I, of course, didn't understand.

"No matter," he said, "a photon is the purest kind of power. You will have new abilities, greater than what you have lost."

He told me where to look for my parents, which is an entirely different adventure, far too much to include in an epilogue. I may tell it, if you wish, but you'll have to let me know if you want to hear it. Suffice it to say, I thought this was an "origin" story, and yet I truly didn't understand my origins until I delved deeper into my past and discovered how my parents were involved in this whole mess.

The Large Hadron Collider, a twenty-seven kilometer underground tunnel near Geneva in Switzerland, was designed to be almost eight times as powerful as the Tevatron. It was scheduled to go online in 2008, but a devastating and costly malfunction delayed the project by over fourteen months. Particles began colliding, and BERN collected data. They first discovered a Higgs boson on July 4, 2012, although it took another year of tests to confirm that it was indeed what they'd hoped. The inevitable march toward particle accelerators may have been delayed, but it was not stopped.

My dearly departed uncle wasn't kidding. I was his sole surviving heir. His estate was willed to a charitable trust, but the trust was to be controlled by a corporate entity only in the absence of a legal heir. I sold that Upper West Side mansion for $28 million, less than it was worth but hey, the economy. Whatever new abilities the collision had gifted me were still to be discovered at that point. The power of vast sums of money, however, was immediately at my disposal. It's quite astonishing what someone can accomplish when they are disgustingly wealthy. With financial resources, I began the search for my parents. As I encountered resistance to make Lab Majorana seem benign, I began to discover the spectacular nature of my new powers.

Money! Super powers. Batman, you got nothing on PARTICLE MAN!

THE END

Photo credit: Kellyn Uhl

ABOUT THE AUTHOR

DR. DERIC MCNISH is an Assistant Professor at Michigan State University. He's an actor, director, dialect coach, and professional audiobook narrator. This is Deric's debut novel. Look for his second novel, coming soon.

dericmcnish.com
Twitter: @dericmcnish